Brides Unveiled

Designer. Dresses. Drama.

YVETTE
KLOBUCHAR

Dear Jayne,
I hope you enjoy reading Brides
Unveiled. It was a pleasure
writing it. Best wishes,
Yvette Klobuchar

PAPERGIRL
PUBLISHING

Category: Contemporary Women's Fiction/Chic Lit
ISBN-13: 978-0-9967501-0-3

Editing: Written Dreams/Brittiany Koren
Cover art design/Layout: ENC Graphic Services/Ed Vincent
Cover illustration © Kninwong/Shutterstock.com
Map layout: ENC Graphic Services/Ed Vincent
Map illustrations © Darii-s/Shutterstock.com

First Print Edition November 2015.
Printed in the United States of America.
0 1 2 3 4 5 6 7 8 9 0

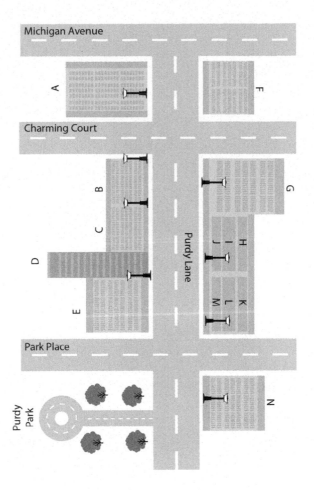

Map Key

A - Magnificent Mile Hotel
B - Fancy Fine Art Gallery
C - Confettti Cupcakes
D - Ritzy Residences
E - Central Synagogue
F - Fashionista Shopping Plaza
G - Purdy Residential Towers

H - Princess Pilates
I - Purr Salon
J - Mio Amore Ristorante
K - Belle's Bridal Workroom
L - Belle's Bridal Shop
M - Sparkle Jewels
N - Contempo Arts Center

This book is dedicated to my amazing son, Alec, who has provided me with the inspiration to write this book. I love him dearly and feel blessed to have him for a son.

Dear Reader,

The first item on every bride's wedding checklist is finding the perfect dress. Forget about the three-tier lemon mousse cake decorated with spun sugar ribbon and the arch adorned with gilded branches. Choosing the wedding gown takes every ounce of the bride's attention and is far more important than anything else on her to-do list.

Following the marriage proposal, the overjoyed bride immediately begins the search for the perfect dress. Over the next few months, she pours through stacks of bridal magazines and tries on countless gowns, hoping to find the most important dress she'll ever wear.

How can I be so sure? I've designed thousands of bridal dresses: A-line, empire, sheath, trumpet, and mermaid silhouettes. You name it. I've made it.

And I've fitted, tucked, buttoned, and hemmed dozens of dresses for blushing brides who, well, let's say let their nerves get the better of them.

I've learned over the years that nothing makes a bride happier than when she finds her dream dress (or crazier when the tiniest detail isn't in place—yet). After breathing a sigh of relief, she can finally focus her attention on planning the wedding.

The bride can choose the cake. And select the imported table linens from France. Oh, and order the bridesmaids dresses. As long as everything from the flowers to the headpiece revolves around the dress, the bride is happy.

After the wedding, the dress becomes the focal point of the newlywed's living room. There, above the crackling fire on top of the antique limestone mantel, sits an oversized, gleaming silver picture frame featuring the artistically posed bride dressed in a romantic silk-satin gown dripping in pearls.

Who knows? Perhaps I designed the dress in the photo.

Yvette Klobuchar
2015

CHAPTER 1

Monday, February 15, 1999

Who in the world could be pounding on my shop door at 4:45 in the morning? A combination of fear and irritation made me freeze, willing the intruder to leave.

"Juliana Belle!" I heard my mom's commanding voice inside my head. "You march yourself strait up to the front door right now and tell that lunatic to go away!"

Unfortunately, I was not my fashionista mother, Bianca Belleski, who would have no problem getting rid of the trespasser. Unlike me, always trying to avoid confrontation at all costs. Why did Mom have to retire and leave me here to deal with this maniac on my own? All I wanted to do was change the window display without any distractions.

I'd come in early to prepare for another hectic day—the second time this week. Everything began so peacefully, just me and the snow plow and salt truck drivers out on the road at this ungodly hour. Ominous black ice covered the streets at the gray dawn of a bitter cold, February morning in Chicago. Light lake-effect snow continued to fall throughout the night while the wind-chill factor reached a frigid twenty degrees below zero. I watched the keepers of our streets work undaunted by the dangerous arctic cold conditions, bulldozing their way through the narrow pathways and clearing the slick roads for the morning rush hour.

I appreciated their efforts, even as a fresh blanket of powdered snow covered the tree-lined street they'd just plowed. Looking through the frost-covered window, I saw how serene the town looked before the first light. The normally busy sidewalks were practically empty, except for a few early morning walkers holding hands, trying not to slip on the unshoveled walkways. I imagined they were going home after their long night out on the town celebrating Valentine's Day.

Yes, that would be nice, I thought, coming home from a romantic dinner with a man I loved, barely able to carry the bouquet of roses wrapped in crinkly cellophane, a soft teddy bear, and a cardboard candy box.

I tried that once.

I designed the dress, married the man, and gave birth to his beautiful son. But never again was I going to be left alone with a dancing teddy bear while he went off to celebrate with another conquest. Besides, I had a fine dinner last night with Jack. Okay, so he's only four years old, but he's the best thing to come out of my sorry marriage. We spent our night at a hole-in-the-wall place on the south side of town. But there was no place I'd rather be than with my sweet boy at The Chicken 'n Biscuit for an early-bird supper.

Louder knocking broke through my daydreaming. *Just go away, already.*

I returned my attention to taking down the window display. As I removed a heart-shaped prop, there were three more knocks. The exterior hallway was dark, and I could barely see through the glass. The sinister shape on the other side made my heart skip a beat. A tall figure loomed there through the glass. *Geez! What do you want from me?*

As a business owner, I prided myself as someone who never stopped moving—a productive powerhouse, a type-A woman of action. Fanatical about tidiness, I wanted the store to look perfect before any client walked through the front doors of Belle's Bridal. I needed all satin bows tied without knots, so they could slip off with one simple pull. I always double-checked to ensure the sales staff fastened every button running down the back of all gowns on display in the showroom. Afterward, I scoured the clothing racks to make sure that the dresses were hung straight and faced in the same direction. And I never understood why none of my employees wanted the job of inspecting the chandeliers for burnt-out light bulbs or dusting the jewelry cases. Usually, I received a great deal of personal satisfaction from wiping away the old fingerprints and making the glass sparkle again.

"Oh, brother," I said under my breath.

The intruder was hopelessly trying to pull open the locked door. But I was nowhere near ready to unlock the bridal shop. I glanced at the door again and saw a face pressed up against the glass, but the visage was too distorted to make out. I eased my way past the drapes and positioned myself behind a mannequin. Keeping one knee slightly bent, I popped my hip to one side and placed my hands on my hips, trying hard to blend into the window display. While I waited impatiently for the person to leave, I squinted my eyes and began counting to one hundred. If the intruder were still there when I finished counting, I'd call the doorman to escort him or her out.

I used to think that having my store located on the mezzanine level of a prestigious building, staffed with a 24-hour doorman, was a perfectly safe place to work. Being a petite-sized gal with no upper-arm strength, I felt comfortable working all hours of the day or night with the security staff provided by the building management. When I had opened the Gold Coast location, I never let the fear of a potential burglary get in my way. My father armed me with a pink keychain that included a small canister filled with mace, and that was all I needed to feel secure.

My false sense of security changed rather quickly when a fur-coat wearing bandit the size of a grizzly bear held me up at gunpoint last year. I remember how I arrived at work early, my arms aching from carrying an oversized garment bag full of wedding gowns and a tote bag packed with customers' files. I had unlocked the door and rushed over to the worktable to set everything down. Seconds later, I returned to lock the door when this massive woman kicked open the glass doors, shattering glass everywhere. When she shoved me out of the way, her wig flew off, and I realized that *she* was a man dressed in women's vintage clothing.

Not only had he stolen two weeks' worth of sales, but the Fur Coat Bandit demanded that I give him my favorite necklace. When I refused, he yanked the pendant, cutting into my neck. On his way out, he scooped up a bunch of bridal purses and a handful of strapless bras and shoved them into garbage bags.

"Not on my watch," I shouted as I charged after him down the back stairwell and out the building. But outside, he pointed a gun at me, causing my kitten heels to sink into the snowy sidewalk. Now that he had my attention, he waved the gun in my face.

I stood frozen, trembling, and unable to move. He traced the gun across my lips and flashed a menacing smile before he ran away.

I realized that I wasn't so tough after all. The robbery had shaken my confidence and made me face my vulnerability. Soon, surveillance cameras were discreetly hidden in every corner of the shop and clients were buzzed in through the front door.

The door banging grew louder and faster. I continued counting. "Ninety-eight, ninety-nine, one hundred." Grabbing a thick yardstick from the table, I walked slowly towards the entrance of the shop.

When I got to the door, I could make out a suspicious-looking woman wearing a black mink coat with a matching hat. I pointed to my watch and mouthed, "Sorry. The store's closed," mustering a half-smile. I went over to the reception desk and picked up the phone to call the doorman.

As I dialed his number, she held down the door buzzer. The incessant, piercing sound gave me an instant headache. I slammed down the receiver and marched back to the door.

She finally released the buzzer.

I kept an eye on her while I bent down and pushed open the mail slot. "The shop opens at ten o'clock," I stated in the firmest voice I could manage. "Please, come back later." I released the brass plate, the sound of metal on metal reverberating in the air as it clanged shut.

She all but knocked out the brass plate when she wedged her pointy-toed leather boot in the mail slot. "Wait," she said, bending over. "Let me in. It's an emergency."

"What kind of emergency?" I asked.

"A wedding dress emergency."

I shook my head. "I wish I could, but…"

"I'm begging you." She did sound desperate. "I promise it won't take long. I know what I want."

"Why don't I check the appointment book and see if I have any openings for this afternoon?"

I could see her head in silhouette form shaking an unmistakable no.

"Then I'm terribly sorry, but I can't help you." I tried to shut the mail door, but her boot was wedged in tight.

As I waved goodbye, she slid her hand into her pocket. I ducked and ran to the side, pressing up against the wall. A few seconds later, I realized I was overreacting, thanks to my grizzly bear intruder. She wasn't holding a gun, but rather a large roll of cash that looked big enough to pay for an entire semester of private pre-school tuition.

I stared at the wad of money and thought to myself that I could certainly use the extra cash these days.

When I had relocated the shop, I began paying sky-high rent for premium square footage and found I needed more staff. I hired a talented male Vietnamese pattern maker, Phu Tôn, and lured two seamstresses away from a competitor to add to my fashion family of twenty-two temperamental Eastern European women. Once I filled the store with fine antiques and artwork, purchased more sewing machines, and paid taxes, I was back to square one financially.

I had to admit, the offer was tempting, but it wasn't yet five o'clock. I hadn't had any coffee or a chance to change into my work clothes or fix my long and tangled curly blond hair. My creative juices just weren't flowing.

Her sobbing loosened my resolve. As her cries grew louder (they reminded me of the noises my Persian cat, Needles, made when she'd get stuck in the clothes dryer), I straightened my black slacks and threw the matching jacket over my white t-shirt. It would have to do for now. I grabbed my keys from the countertop and unlocked the door.

"Come on in," I said. No smiles of welcome. Not at this hour.

The woman made her way into the store and stood in the middle of the showroom, dripping tears onto the freshly polished marble floor.

"Let's get you some tissues." I took a tissue box from the center table and brought it over to her. "I'm Juliana Belle," I said, handing her the box, "but most people call me Jules."

"Scarlett Smith."

"Nice to meet you, Scarlett."

"It's a pleasure meeting you," she said, pulling out a bunch of tissues and blowing her nose with a loud honk.

Scarlett was an attractive woman; I'm guessing, in her late thirties. She wore her raven hair styled in a severe, shorter version of a pageboy cut. I wondered why, at this time of the morning, she would be wearing a pristine navy crepe dress (that suited her hourglass shape) and discreet jewelry (that complemented her oval face). She looked more like a flight attendant returning home from some exotic location overseas than a crazed bride-to-be. But even in the soft, early-morning lighting of the shop, I could see hard features beneath the tawny foundation and reflecting powder that made her look as though she'd recently been through some tough times.

"I don't know what's wrong with me," Scarlett continued through her tears. "I never get this emotional. I think I'm just feeling discouraged." She pulled out more tissues from the box. "For the last few months, I've gone to every bridal store in town searching for my dream dress and always came out empty-handed. The gowns were cheaply made, the fabrics scraped my skin like sandpaper, and the stitches felt scratchy." She handed me the ball of sullied Kleenex and continued. "I hear the quality of your workmanship is exquisite, and one can practically wear the gown inside out."

Hmmm, a reversible dress? Might not be such a bad idea, I thought as I threw the Kleenex into the trashcan next to the receptionist's desk.

"I've officially run out of time. Can you *please* help me?"

I placed my hand on Scarlett's back and began walking her into the shop. "Let's see what we can do."

The tears stopped, replaced by a big smile. Scarlett looked around the store, and walking to a rack of bridal gowns, touched an elegant Alençon lace dress. After wandering through the remaining aisles of gowns, she joined me at the worktable.

"Have a seat," I said, motioning toward a tufted chair.

Scarlett placed her coat and hat on an empty chair and sat down across from me at the carved wood table. She set down a huge organizer, along with a stack of Polaroid pictures and bridal magazines marked with post-it notes. "So, how long have you been designing wedding gowns?" she asked.

"I've never had an official start date. My mom says that I was born with a silver drafting pencil in my hand and have been designing ever since."

We both laughed.

"In all seriousness, about nine years," I said. "Ever since we moved the business from the suburbs to Lincoln Park."

"When did you move here to Purdy Lane?"

"In October of 1998, when I took over for my mom."

"You couldn't have picked a better location," Scarlett said.

"I agree."

"I live only a few blocks away. So, when I saw the light on in your shop, I ran home to get this monstrosity," said Scarlett, slapping the large binder with her hand.

Her hands looked remarkably youthful. Not a hint of dry cuticles or a hangnail in sight; just beautiful, long, French-manicured fingernails. The kind of manicure a woman regularly gets, just after receiving a marriage proposal and a gleaming ring. Strangely enough, I noticed that her ring finger was bare.

Being a perceptive salesperson, I always liked to get a good look at the engagement ring. It was a reliable indicator of whether the bride would choose shantung or duchess silk. Naturally, there were certain circumstances when a bride may choose to go ringless: during a kickboxing lesson or traveling by public transportation late at night. Otherwise, most brides wanted her sparkling ring to shine brightly to attract attention.

I tried not to stare and refocused my attention back to Scarlett and her heavy binder. "It looks like someone's done her homework," I said, smiling. Since she wasn't wearing an engagement ring, I decided to skip my usual, "So, when were you engaged?" line of questioning. Instead, I asked, "When you close your eyes, can you envision yourself in a wedding gown?"

"Absolutely!" she said brightly. "I've dreamt of my wedding dress since I was a teenager."

"That seems to be the time when a lot of girls begin to dream of their wedding day."

"Not this girl," Scarlett traced her finger over a gown on the cover of her overstuffed scrapbook and smiled. "My dreams were all about the dress. Ever since college, I've been obsessed with finding the perfect dress. Some people go antique shopping on the weekends; I go dress shopping."

After a moment, she picked up the photographs. "Here, take a look at these," she said, handing me the Polaroid pictures. "Over the years, I've collected more than one hundred pictures of dresses that I've tried on."

I took the stack of photos and examined each one with great interest. It finally occurred to me that she wasn't exaggerating. She had, indeed, tried them all: halter, strapless, and A-line. She was a bridal junkie.

"I know what my dress will look like," she said, opening the binder with a thud. Scarlett had the book divided into ten sections: bodice, sleeve, skirt, train, and so on. Certain areas of the dress were circled, with specific notations describing what she liked about each photograph.

"May I?" I asked, reaching across for Scarlett's binder.

She slid her Bridal Bible toward me. "I've done all of the legwork. All you need to do is combine all the parts of the puzzle."

I smiled. "Great presentation." I flipped through the pages and stopped at section four, studying the third bullet point discussing the fabric. "Are you sure you want organza? It's more of a summer fabric." I asked, scratching my head.

"Yes, I believe I made that very clear in section one, second paragraph."

"Well, there's nothing more beautiful than a summer bride," I said. "When's the wedding?"

"Oh, I don't have a date."

"How about the season?"

"Nope."

"Okay." I cocked my head to the side and asked, "Have you decided on a location for the ceremony?"

"Not yet. But I'm good with any venue that has an aisle long enough for an endless train."

"Should I bother asking about flowers?"

She bobbed her head. "Miniature white zinnias."

My stomach began to churn as I started gnawing away on my thumbnail. I was struggling to keep the conversation flowing. Usually, brides made an appointment to meet with me the day after the proposal. The "wedding talk" would officially begin, and the newly engaged women couldn't wait to share the mind-numbing details of their wedding plans.

What had been so important for her to meet with me at 5 AM? "You're in an incredible hurry to get a dress for your wedding, and yet you haven't selected a date, location, or season?"

"And here I thought I was meeting with the designer, not the event planner." She sounded irritated and jabbed her finger at the scrapbook pages. "Everything you need to know is right here."

"The design elements are relevant. But I also want to make sure that the dress complements you, and not the other way around," I said, forcing a smile.

"That's fine. But I'm the one used to asking all the questions."

"Really? What do you do for a living?"

"I'm a divorce attorney."

"That must make your fiancé a little nervous," I said, joking.

"I never said that I had a fiancé," she said with a straight face.

I scratched my forehead. "What do you mean you *don't* have a fiancé?"

"As of last night, I don't even have a boyfriend and, believe me, I'm in no rush to get one."

"So, you've designed a dress for your wedding to a man you've never met?" I asked.

"Please don't take this personally, but I don't have to explain myself to you."

I realized I was going about this situation all wrong. I cleared my throat and tried to start again. "You're right.

Maybe I'm not the right person to make your gown, after all."

She seemed deep in thought for a while before she said, "My boyfriend of seven years broke up with me last night over Valentine's Day dinner."

I bit the corner of my lip. "Oh, gosh. I'm terribly sorry."

"Last night, we enjoyed a delicious dinner at The Pump Room. An hour later, we were waiting for our Chocolate Lovers' flambé when all of a sudden, he sprang to his feet and blurted out, 'I can't do this anymore!' The next thing I knew, he was hightailing it out the door, yelling, 'The flambé's on me!' I sat at the table, completely blindsided. I was certain he was going to propose last night. Instead, I left the restaurant in tears, feeling rejected. I walked the streets for hours, wondering what I did wrong?

"When I reached Purdy Lane, I looked up at your beautifully decorated Valentine's Day windows. The gowns sparkled like diamonds in the moonlight. Never have I seen such a magnificent collection of wedding dresses. And then it hit me: I wasn't crying over the breakup. I was crying over the idea that I was never going to see my dream wedding gown. I realized then that for all these years, I've wanted my dress more than I wanted my boyfriend."

Hmmm. This was a new one, even for me. I continued to listen to her story.

"While I was standing outside the shop admiring your beautiful window display, I saw a shadow moving past the windows. I ran home to get my binder and prayed that someone would still be here when I returned."

"I'm sorry to interrupt, but I'm surprised that the doorman allowed you to come upstairs."

"He tried calling. But all he got was your answering machine. He said that I seemed like a nice person and buzzed me inside."

"Well, it's reassuring to know that my doorman, Lloyd, is such a good judge of character," I said. Note to self: Time to have a heart-to-heart with Lloyd.

"Like I was saying," Scarlett said, ignoring my quip, "I've had enough relationship drama for a lifetime. So, I figured that if I owned the wedding gown, the dress would never cloud my judgment again."

"I've never thought about it that way before, but it certainly is an interesting approach," I said, trying to make sense of her strange logic. Then again, who was I to judge? My track record wasn't great, and I've been known to act impetuously at times.

Scarlett nodded and began flipping through the pages of a *Modern Bride* magazine in her binder, stopping when she found a picture she liked. The photo featured a bride without a groom. The bride's structured organza dress, with hints of mermaid running throughout the design, flowed in the wind as the model looked off into the distance. "I like this one, the independent bride," she said, pushing the magazine towards me. "I'm sick of waiting around for some guy to get down on one knee. I want the wedding fantasy without the reality of marriage."

I searched for an understanding tone. "You have to do what's right for you. Unfortunately, many women do not come to these types of realizations until it's too late."

"Admittedly, I've become jaded over the years. But I just don't understand women who conform to their spouse's bad behavior."

"Well to be fair, every situation's different," I replied, as I picked up a paperclip and began playing with it. "What if the wife doesn't know that her husband's behaving badly?" As I spoke, I never took my eyes off the clip that I had unfolded into a straight piece of metal.

"Oh, they know, but they're in denial."

"Or, maybe they're trying to fix the relationship."

"Some problems you can't fix," she said, quite adamant about it. "I can't begin to describe the unspeakable acts of intentional cruelty I see on a daily basis. One minute, everyone's blissfully in love. The next minute, they're getting kicked out of the house. Or, they're kicking me out, for not preparing a prenuptial agreement.

"Sometimes, when I finish a case, I feel my spirit has been permanently damaged by the revolting behavior I've witnessed. I hate to say it, but I should give you a stack of my business cards because half your brides will need a good divorce attorney within the first three years of their marriage."

I surprised myself by what came out of my mouth next. "I'm sorry that we didn't meet sooner."

"You're divorced?"

I nodded.

"Sorry, I just assumed that you were married being in the bridal business."

Funny how most brides did assume marriage was a prerequisite if you owned a bridal salon. I learned the hard way not to share the news of my divorce with potential brides. I couldn't believe the look of terror I got the one time I did talk about my misfortune. The bride actually scooted her chair away from me, as if I had smallpox. I had to soothe her and promise her that divorce was not contagious, adding that I was certain she would have better luck than I did. I had just been unlucky; I told her. But unlucky wasn't the word to describe my marriage; sheer misery was more like it.

It was such a cliché: fool me once, shame on you; fool me twice...well, we all know how the rest of that saying goes. Scarlett had me pegged—I was an expert at hiding my husband's dirty little secrets. Unfortunately, I was so good at plastering a smile on my face that I had fooled myself into believing his lies. Until I was killing time in my dentist's waiting room and happened upon an article in *Vanity Fair* listing the top ten reasons why people divorce. I took the short quiz and though it was a silly exercise, I couldn't forget the results: I'd checked off eight out of ten boxes. I felt terrible sadness, but it woke me up enough to search for more professional answers. I couldn't hide in fool's paradise any longer.

I'm not sure why I had decided to share my private life with Scarlett, but it felt good not to hide my secret for once.

"I'm sorry," Scarlett said.

"I'm not. I have an amazing four-year-old son."

"You look too young to have a child. Do you mind my asking how old you are?"

"Thirty-one."

"Wow, I would have never guessed," Scarlett said and seemed shocked. "You look young for your age."

"I get that a lot. My mom tells me I am lucky to have her superior genes," I told her, recalling all the crazy things Mom has done to keep herself looking younger.

"Lucky girl."

"I'm more grateful that my son got my dad's deep blue eyes and my wavy blond hair. And a great set of teeth—not his father's camel-tooth smile."

"Aww. Your son sounds adorable. What's his name?"

"Jack."

"I love the name, Jack. It's a strong name. He's a rebel. In Latin, it means to overthrow and defeat."

"How do you know that?" I asked.

"It's a hobby of mine. I look up defendants' names when I begin a case. I like to know who I'm dealing with."

"Well, Jack is nothing if not resilient. He likes to tackle life, just like his mother."

"He must have endless energy."

"Oh, yes. He keeps me busy."

"So, that must not leave much time for dating?" She paused to see if I was going to respond to her question. I didn't. "Ah, you haven't dipped your toe in the dating pool," she continued.

"Not even a toenail. I'm afraid to jump into the deep end."

"Your hubby must have done a number on you," Scarlett said.

"The next time you're researching names, try looking up William Spencer III?"

"Don't need to. The name says it all."

William came from family money. Being a trust-fund baby, he lived under his father's direction and control. Not surprisingly, after our engagement on, what else, April Fool's Day, his parents insisted on an extravagant wedding, which included countless social events. Even though I felt uncomfortable with the idea of a large wedding, William caved to his parents without a complaint.

A month before our wedding, we met with his parents' estate lawyer to go over various legal documents his parents had prepared for us to sign. William was furious to find out he would not be receiving his entire fortune after all, but that it would be spread out over twenty-five years. I still recall his exact words, "Fuck the wedding. We're eloping!"

And we did, with a quick ceremony and honeymoon in Vegas. That was the only success that marriage ever had. The rest of my bridal tale was an epic failure. By the time I filed for a divorce, Jack and I had just a month to move out of our luxury condo and into a modest two-bedroom apartment, about a ten-minute cab ride from our old shop in Lincoln Park. As I had packed up our belongings, I came across our wedding album. Seeing the book evoked a reaction not unlike coming across vomit splashed across the ground at an amusement park.

It didn't come as much of a surprise that William proved to be an unreliable father after the divorce was final. My first year as a divorcee was a life-changer. The people who seemed delighted for my good fortune were now talking behind my back. I never wanted to feel that kind of humiliation and disappointment again. I just wanted to live a more private life with my son. Even though my heart ached for a family, the truth was, Jack and I *were* family.

"Well, maybe someday," Scarlett said, probably more to fill an uncomfortable silence than to be encouraging. "If you do decide to try a second marriage—and I know this sounds cynical—but stay on your toes."

"What do you mean by that?"

"Because you're a passionate bridal gown designer. That means you hear all about the happy couples' lovely plans for their wedding day. It's bound to rub off. On the other hand, I'm a cynical attorney. I hear the shocking, unimaginable client stories of why they want a divorce. Like the control-freak husband who closes his wife's bank accounts while ordering new credit cards for his mistress. Or the client who declares bankruptcy, then takes the company jet to the Cayman Islands for the weekend and parties on a yacht full of bikini-clad girls half his age. Oh, and here's the icing on the cake; during his trip to Hedonism, he replenishes his briefcase with a load of crisp hundred dollar bills that his estranged wife will never know exists."

I watched as Scarlett picked up the straightened paperclip and pierced it through the face of an unsuspecting happy groom on the cover of the magazine. She looked on the verge of tears.

"I've gone with clients for paternity testing so they could avoid paying child support," she said. "For crying out loud, during a follow-up appointment, my client asked me to begin drafting his next prenup. And as an attorney, I feel as if it's my responsibility to tell you that before you ever say 'I do' again—be sure to get a prenup."

"I appreciate your candor."

"There is so so much pressure on women these days to get married and throw the perfect wedding. They don't have time to think about what happens after. You should consider adding group therapy for brides to your roster of store services." She laughed but didn't sound as though she were kidding.

"Only if you promise to be the Counselor, *Counselor*."

"I just might take you up on your offer," she said, smiling again.

We both laughed.

"But we digress," I said. "Enough with the sad stories. We need to finalize your design. Shall we get to work?" I asked, grabbing a pen and sketchpad.

"Absolutely." Scarlett tore a page out of her scrapbook and handed me the picture of her dress.

I carefully studied the design.

"It's perfect, isn't it?" she asked, almost begging for my approval.

"Yes, it's lovely."

"Sold!" yelled Scarlett as she slammed her binder shut and stuck out her chin defiantly. "I want to *have* my wedding gown and not *hold* you up any longer.

CHAPTER 2

Scarlett was just leaving (a lot happier than when she arrived, I might add) when my staff started trickling in at 7:30 AM. Thank heavens I'd dealt with Scarlett *before* they arrived. They liked to share stories of our Bridezillas, and I was fast growing fond of Scarlett. Protective even. Girls like us, who weren't wild about marriage, needed to stick together.

Nathaniel, my personal assistant, knocked on my office door and entered with a small tray of tea, sugar, and a croissant. I hadn't realized it until then, but I was starving. I grabbed a teacup and spoon from the cupboard where I kept my emergency stash of snacks and poured myself some tea.

"Thanks, Nathaniel," I garbled through a big bite. "You're always there for me," I said, pouring too much sugar in the cup.

Hiring him was one of the best decisions I'd ever made. After a year of being miserably unhappy, Nathaniel dropped out of engineering school to follow his dream in fashion design. Overnight, he went from being a metrosexual male carrying around a pocket protector to a full-blown homosexual wearing second-hand Prada shirts and pants.

Since applied creativity factors into the success of both an engineer and a fashion designer, Nathaniel effortlessly transitioned into his new role as my right-hand man. He turned his skills of designing complex pieces of equipment for a healthy ecosystem into designing complex pieces of clothing for women with unhealthy spending habits. He was indispensable—and I wouldn't know what to do without him.

"What do our appointments look like today?" I asked.

"We have Rebecca Burns coming in to shorten her gown so she can wear it as a cocktail dress." He sat down in the client's chair and kept talking. "Did I tell you about the crazy bride that came in last week to try on wedding dresses? She brought a food coach with her. He goes everywhere with her. She picked up a Madeleine from the cookie plate, and he grabbed it from her hand and crushed it in his fist, allowing the cookie sawdust to pour out through his clenched knuckles while staring into her eyes with sheer disgust. At first, she looked like she was about to cry. Then, all of the sudden she smiled and asked his opinion about the color the bridesmaids dresses! Crazy, right?"

"Not as crazy as the bride I had yesterday. I think you greeted her. She was the one who chewed her food and spat it out into a napkin."

"How about the one who went on a diet of strawberries?" Nathaniel asked, getting wound up by the recollections of the crazy things we'd experienced together.

"I almost forgot about her. Do you remember the one who injected vitamins into her thighs?" I added, not to be outdone.

We meant no harm by the silly shoptalk. Sometimes we needed to let off steam. It seemed easier than acknowledging the truth of how some women became overly obsessed with their wedding planning. They spend all their energy thinking about their wedding day, looking to create the perfect happy ending, instead of focusing on their relationship with their groom, and the days and years following the wedding.

"So what's the deal with the woman with the mascara marks under her eyes?" Nathaniel asked.

I knew he was dying to know all about Scarlett. I trusted him not to make fun of her vulnerability, so I told him her story. When I got to the dress-but-no-groom part, he interrupted. "Oh, I hope you didn't burst her bridal bubble, did you?"

"You know me better than that," I said. "And no, I didn't tell her that her wedding dress would cost a lot less than her divorce attorney!"

"That's good," he said, sighing with relief.

"I didn't tell her that because she *is* a divorce attorney. She'll save a lot of money that way!"

"Do you think it's a good idea to make a wedding gown for someone who just went through a break-up?"

"Honestly, Nat, I'm not really sure. She's determined to have it made. So, I'm going to honor my client's wishes." I was about to head over to the workroom and begin instructing the staff on the day's schedule, when Zoë, my spiky-haired receptionist, interrupted us.

"Wow, I totally forgot why I came in here right now," she said, looking around the office.

If Nathaniel was my right-hand, then Zoë was my left foot. She was a sweet, good-intentioned nineteen-year-old girl who not only talked slowly but walked slowly—and ate even slower. Naturally, she was painfully slow to get a joke or take a hint. But I loved her for her optimism.

"Think for a change, Zoë," Nathaniel said.

"Stop it, Nathaniel, or you're going to make me..." Zoë paused. "...cry!" She turned away from him and actually ran (I didn't even know she could move that fast—she was a sensitive soul who cried in private) to the weeping closet, the place we hung abandoned wedding gowns that were never picked up due to canceled weddings or runaway brides. "The closet is getting full again," she called out, seemingly trying to shift the attention away from her.

"Well, I hope Miss Scarlett's dress doesn't end up in there," Nathaniel said.

"It wouldn't be the first one," I added. "I think we can safely remove some of the dresses. I can bring a couple home with me."

I was notorious for hoarding my wedding gowns; it was possible that some have remained in the shop since the business opened in 1969. I had more gowns hanging on folding racks in my apartment and even a few packed away in my storage locker. I was afraid to toss even one of them because I thought that, like an adorable puppy in a pet shop, my gowns were waiting patiently for their new owners. How would I ever know which dresses to give away? (Okay, maybe the Glinda Good Witch '80s styles needed to go.)

Zoë pulled out a dress and asked, "Do you want yours?"

I nearly choked on my croissant. I hadn't even looked at that simple satin ruched gown in five years. "You have my permission to burn it," I told her.

"You can't burn it! It's a gorgeous dress," Zoë said.

"Then donate it." I shrugged. "I never want to see it again."

"What if you decided to wear it again someday?" she prodded.

I shook my head. "That won't happen because one, I'd never jinx a marriage by wearing *that* dress again, and two, I'm never getting married again."

"You don't know that for a fact."

"Yes, I do. I may not love the idea of being single forever, but it's better than being under some man's thumb—or worse, believing his lies."

Nathaniel sighed, frustrated with my attitude and finally walked away from us. Being a divorced bridal shop owner was like being a diabetic working in a chocolate factory. I needed to keep the candy away before I got sick.

CHAPTER 3

"Jack, where are my keys?" I asked my son.

He'd done it again. Hidden my keys. It didn't take Sigmund Freud to appreciate that the kid missed me and didn't want me to go to work. I missed him, too. But this game of his was getting old.

We'd had a good evening together last night. After that crazy early morning yesterday, I left the shop at a respectable time, and easily gave up on the possibility of having dinner with this guy, Rocco Delgado, I recently met, who'd been calling me for a couple of weeks now. But I'd rather be home early enough to make Jack's favorite supper of mac and cheese and dinosaur chicken nuggets. (I ate a salad though I did munch on some of his mac and cheese.) We watched a little TV (well, Jack watched a Barney video while I answered emails sitting next to him). And then he won the battleship fight while he soaked and splashed in the tub. So why the acting out this morning?

"He had a good time." That would be Tatiana, his babysitter. Her smug look, baiting me for a reaction. Tatiana had come over from Minsk last year, fresh from her victory as first runner-up in the 1998 Miss Belarus pageant. She used her winnings to get here, and now she was an aspiring model and a full-time prima donna.

"What?" I asked her.

"I know what you were thinking; why's he doing this now? Like it takes a genius to know that he enjoyed having you home last night instead of working late. He doesn't want the fun to stop."

I felt peeved, embarrassed really, and upstaged by a twenty-one-year-old. I'd lived hostage to Jack's live-in babysitter/nanny/beauty queen/know-it-all from the moment my mom gifted me the shop. But running the shop without help was never an option. Like it or not, I needed Tatiana to keep a semblance of normalcy in my home life.

"Jack?" I said again. "Come on, I've got to leave. I promise I'll be home this evening at a reasonable time."

"That's right, Jack," Tatiana added. "I have a big date tonight, so your mom *has* to come home at a reasonable time."

"That was not helpful, Tatiana," I hissed under my breath. "Now he thinks we're both leaving him out."

Tatiana just shrugged.

It took another ten minutes of searching before I found the keys hanging from the dinosaur mobile over his bed. I grabbed them and headed for the front door, where Jack stood like a sentry, arms out, blocking my way. What a little heartbreaker, his eyes shining with a mix of mischief and sadness.

I bent down to give him a big hug and whispered in his ear, "Stop with the keys, already. You know Mommy needs to work to keep you in broccoli and spinach."

"Yuck," he spat out, as though he could actually taste his least favorite foods. But he had a good sense of humor developing and chuckled at my joke. Then he hugged me back.

"See you tonight," I said. A look from Tatiana made me add, "well before six o'clock."

I loved Jack, and I loved my work, at least the designing part. All the chitchat about true love was lost on me, at least since I went through what Scarlett described as the "inevitable divorce." Was I getting as cynical as she was? Well, it sure didn't help that I was reminded daily of my wedding and marriage by working in the bridal industry.

Brides were spending excessively on the "once in a lifetime" event. I knew I benefited from this trend, but when we started the shop, it had been for the love of designing beautiful clothes to wear. Now, this $32 billion industry was growing at such a rapid pace I bet that by the time Jack got married, it would be close to $50 billion. And that also meant this burgeoning industry could easily gobble up my privately-owned small bridal business in a flash. I knew I couldn't afford any mistakes or mishaps. I had to service brides constantly, day or night. Weekdays and weekends.

The walk to the shop was uneventful, and the workday went remarkably smooth. Mercifully, that happened from time to time. Not often enough, though. And how could it? The powder keg of brides, fashion, emotions, and romance, was an accident waiting to happen. But today, I stopped all the work and worries for a moment so I could sit in my office, alone, with the phone off the hook. I realized how much I loved this place—the rustle and colors of the fine fabrics, their soft drape as pretty as a beautiful sculpture. The clickety-clack of the busy machines like music; the chatter, laughter, and inevitable arguments of my wild but devoted staff the chorus. I put my feet on the desk and drank it all in.

I must have drifted off because I came to with a start, and the early winter darkness had already crept in. Oh, that had felt good.

The staff was still working, and it seemed they'd gotten along fine without me. I stretched and stood up, eager to leave without anyone noticing. I needed time to think, and I knew I couldn't do that at home with Barney in the background. I checked my watch. Just enough time for a walk along the lake without incurring the wrath of Tatiana.

I never took the lakefront for granted. It was my private

getaway. I loved walking along Oak Street beach any time of year. And I hoped the freezing temperatures tonight might lift my spirits.

Giant frozen waves in Lake Michigan spanned the city's shoreline and winds carved exquisite formations in the sand along the beach. After nightfall, the blowing snow blurred the glimmering skyline, but enough light shone through to brighten the sky. As I walked, I thought about all of the conversations I had overheard today.

"Arthur is so generous with me."

"Do you think I need liposuction before my wedding?"

"David surprised me with a puppy!"

"Please hurry. I need to get a facial in thirty minutes."

"Jason wants me to join him in the Bahamas during his convention."

I just wanted to feel comfortable with a guy the way I felt when I came home from work and changed out of my suit and heels into my comfy pink velour tracksuit and favorite rock band t-shirt from Journey's Don't Stop Believing 1981 tour. That's when I'll know he's *the one*. I wasn't sure if I could ever feel that comfortable again with a man. I had been so oblivious to the lies, why would I know the difference the second time around? Even with my newfound vigilance, I wasn't sure love wouldn't play its sleight of hand tricks again. My self-worth felt as buffeted as I did after my bracing walk along the beach. Time to go home to my little guy.

I loved the ease of my four-block commute, which included a nail salon, a coffee shop, and a palm reader. And for the time being, I thought of my doorman, Terrance, as a surrogate husband. He opened the door for me and greeted me with his warm smile every time I saw him. He always seemed happy to see me. He'd ask me how my day was and helped carry up any groceries or bags. Honestly, that was all I wanted in a man these days.

I liked coming home to my cozy, kid-friendly apartment.

I didn't have to worry about the expensive Turkish carpet or fine crystals I'd left behind. I just slipped off my shoes and into my track suit before jumping into the mesh ball pit with Jack for some fun make-believe wars.

When I opened the front door, I could see Jack sitting alone coloring at the kitchen counter. When he saw me, he jumped out of his seat and rushed over to give me a hug.

"Hi, honey," I said. "Where's Tatiana?"

"Talking on the phone in her bedroom. I think it's her sister again, but she's talking in Russian so I don't know."

In the ritzy Chicago Gold Coast neighborhood, it was nearly impossible to hire a budget-friendly nanny. I was embarrassed to admit that I paid for most of Tatiana's discretionary spending habits—including her sizeable phone bill and beauty treatments. She thought she was a drop-dead gorgeous beauty queen, but in reality, beauty queens in America look much different from Eastern European beauty queens. She'd adopted a harsh look of hennaed hair and matte burgundy lipstick; she over plucked her brows and penciled in a thin black brow line. I'll admit, though, that she did have a great body that she loved to flaunt. So, the pressure was on to hit the daily sales quota I needed to cover Tatiana's expensive tastes and time off for her modeling casting calls. If not, I'd probably lose another sitter to a stay-at-home mom waiting to pounce on my nanny at the park across from Water Tower Place.

"I wasn't talking on the phone, Jack." Tatiana stood in the kitchen entrance. "I was folding your laundry. And now I need to get ready for my date," she added with a vixen's smile.

"And hello to you, Tatiana," I said.

"Oh, and I need Saturday off," she said, in her heavy accent.

"You know I can't do that. I've told you before; the weekdays are a typical horserace at the shop, but Saturdays are the Kentucky Derby."

"I don't understand this 'Derby'? Why you work with horses when you're designing wedding gowns?"

"I'm trying to make a comparison about… Oh, never mind."

"And this is Illinois, not Kentucky."

"Tatiana, I told you when I hired you that I needed you to work all Saturdays."

Things went back and forth like this for a while until we created a reasonable compromise: I agreed to give Tatiana the afternoon off and get Mom to watch Jack until I got home from work. I caved more often than she did out of fear of losing her—and tonight because I could smell the delicious goulash she had made for dinner. I was an easy mark anytime I didn't have to worry about dinner. Tatiana was a great cook when the mood hit her, and in all fairness, cooking wasn't in her job description.

Jack and I were just finishing up dinner when the phone rang.

"Hello," I said.

"Uh, yes. May I speak to Juliana?"

"Stop with the phone etiquette, William. You know it's me."

"Okay, we can play it that way. Good evening, Juliana. Excuse the late hour, but I need to discuss something with you."

I waited, but he didn't continue. "Okay, and…"

"Well, as you know I've remarried."

I rolled my eyes. "Yes, to Vanessa, not Candy, or all those others in between. So?"

"Knock it off, Juliana. I'm serious. It's time Jack had a father."

"Jack has always had a father. In name, anyway."

"Well, we're moving back to Chicago, and I can be there for him now. I thought you'd be happy."

"Happy? Happy about what? That you're declaring your fatherhood?"

William sighed into the phone. "I don't know if you're being obtuse on purpose or what, but I want to share custody."

I was speechless. Sure, I wanted Jack to know his father better, but he barely knew William. William moved to London not long after our divorce, and he'd been only a brief presence at the occasional birthday or holiday these past three years. But now, he deigned to reenter our lives because he was moving back to Chicago? William was absent for most of Jack's life. He had no idea how to raise a son. But that didn't stop him from turning our lives upside down.

"Hello, Juliana? Are you still there?"

"Yes, of course. But you can't just call out of the blue and expect an answer? I'll have to think about this."

"There's nothing to think over. I've got my lawyer working on it as we speak."

"You've never shown much interest in Jack. And I don't know the first thing about your new wife. I can't just send Jack off to someone's home I've never met." I was grasping at anything, trying to stall the worst news I'd ever received.

"You'll hear from my lawyer," William said and hung up.

I stared at the phone a moment, too stunned to move.

CHAPTER 4

Swirling snow, bone-chilling winds, and frigid temperatures didn't stop Chicagoans from shopping. With collars turned up and eyes peeking over thick knitted scarves, they filled the sidewalks of Michigan Avenue, shuffling their way into the department stores.

The clock in the showroom read 7:45 PM, roughly two hours past closing time. My insides were tied in curly-ribbon knots as I continued playing the selling game with Dianne Cassidy. The trouble was, not for all the pearls on Princess Diana's bridal gown could I seem to come up with an ideal neckline or silhouette for her mother-of-the-bride suit.

My stomach rumbled as I discreetly popped another almond in my mouth. Unfortunately, munching on gritty nuts didn't reduce the hunger pangs. I wished I was back home, sitting at the cramped kitchen counter and eating a warm meal with Jack.

Four blocks away, Jack probably munched on dinosaur-shaped chicken nuggets while Tatiana happily hammered away at a lobster shell she'd had delivered from Shaw's Crab House. Even though I was dead tired, I wasn't going home until I designed a drop-dead gorgeous mother-of-the-bride outfit that would pay for at least a portion of Tatiana's expensive tastes.

Dianne Cassidy, the widow of the legendary plastic

surgeon, Stuart Cassidy, was an attractive, plump woman in her late sixties sporting over-arched eyebrows, light brown eyes, and upper lip injections. Her silver hair was pulled back in an elegant French twist. Mrs. Cassidy's standing joke was that her deceased husband had left her with three beautiful children, a great set of knockers, and a bank account in Switzerland that allowed her to continue living her lavish lifestyle.

Since money was no object, Mrs. Cassidy was in no hurry to return home to her empty penthouse overlooking the Mag Mile. She was delighted to spend hours (make that *weeks*), discussing the fabulous, head-turning jacket she planned to wear to her daughter's wedding ceremony in Tuscany. She was looking for an awe-inspiring design that would put every other mother-of-the-bride's ceremonial suit to shame.

My frustrating designer's block seemed to have gone on for weeks. Every time I pulled out my sketchpad, I found myself in the throes of the pressures I faced from William, Tatiana, and mothers and brides of all stripes. I stared at my drawings, gripping my pencil tightly and grinding my teeth, with no idea what this quintessential mother-of-the-bride would be wearing on her daughter's wedding day.

Tonight, I was a woman on the verge of a nervous breakdown, giving myself pep talks. *Jules, you can do this*, I repeated to myself over and over. Still, I was hopeless. My mind went blank every time I tried designing her dress. I stared bleary-eyed at the thick blanket of pink eraser shavings that covered my sketchpad, the worktable, and my black crepe dress. With a quick flick of the wrist, I ripped the top page from the sketchpad and shook the piece of paper. The flecks floated like confetti onto the marble floor.

I looked carefully at my sketch of a three-quarter-sleeve jacket with notched lapels and an ankle-length skirt. Using my mechanical pencil, I pointed to the empty area of the drawing covered in pink eraser smudges, asking in the most energetic way possible, "Have you made a decision about the waistline?"

"What are my choices again?" Mrs. Cassidy asked.

"Single or double-breasted?"

"Double. Nope. Single. Wait. Scratch that."

I wanted to yell, "Single!" but I didn't dare interrupt her thought process. I'd be here all night.

When she didn't respond, I looked up from the jacket I had redesigned four times and saw she was holding a swatch of silver brocade fabric like it was a dirty hanky. After a few moments, she threw it down on the oversized maple table stacked with dozens of swatches and bolts of fabrics. I could see the tension building in her, and all the Botox on the North Shore could not stop the deep crevice from forming between her eyebrows.

"I know!" she blurted out.

"Tell me," I said, anxiously.

"Well, let's be a little creative."

"Sure."

"Maybe we should forget the whole jacket-skirt concept."

"Okay, you mean, like the suit?" I said, feeling deflated. "Then, how about a dress inspired by British royalty?"

"No, that's been so overdone. I'm thinking something avant-garde. You know something like neoprene, only edgier. Hmm, I know. I could honor my husband's memory with a dress made from his favorite sculpting material: silicone!"

"Silicone?" I could feel my jaw drop. "What if the skirt gets stuck to the church pew like a suction cup?" I was trying for a little levity.

She rolled her eyes. "Don't be cute, Jules," she said with more heat than the situation warranted. "It's a marvelous idea."

"Seriously, I appreciate your enthusiasm, but I can't make a dress out of silicone."

"Are you kidding me? It's the perfect statement piece. I thought you could make anything at your atelier." She frowned even more and added, "Am I wrong?"

I remembered one of Mom's famous sayings: "Sweetheart, the customer is always right—even if she is nutty as a fruitcake." I felt queasy. "I'll make you anything you want," I said. "Except this. You need to trust my opinion on this one."

"I don't know. I wish your mother were here to give me her thoughts. I'm pretty certain she would agree with me. In my eyes, she was more the risk-taker in the family."

As I listened to Mom's client reminisce about the good old days, I felt empty inside. "I miss working with my mom, too," I said, trying to sound agreeable rather than upset, which I was. At times like these, I wanted to run home to my old childhood house in the suburbs and beg my mom to come back to work. I felt as though she were the only person in the world who understood the unique nature of our business.

Thirty years ago, my mom first placed me in my baby carriage and pushed me into the family business. It's felt like home ever since. When I was five years old, I tried to keep busy while she worked with a client. One day, not long after the appointment began, I came up with a new game. I searched her desk and found a spiral ring journal and went off to hide in a tiny corner of the old boutique. At the same time Mom designed a gown for her client, I sat quietly observing their interactions and listening carefully to the client's comments. Then I began sketching a dress of my own for the client. It took me a while to come up with the design, but I was pleased with the finished product.

After the appointment, I proudly presented Mom with my detailed drawing. She studied the sketch carefully, smiled, and said, "What a lovely gown. It's your best work yet!"

I strove to impress her with my enthusiasm and couldn't wait to receive the next assignment.

"Juliana, pass out the paychecks before the girls get impatient and sew your pant legs together."

That's all I needed to hear. Before long, I was off in the same corner, busily sketching designs for Mom's clients while she created the real ones at her worktable. My early drawings were more like stick figures with triangles for dresses, but with her encouragement, my designs began to evolve as I matured.

But it was during those last nine years, when we worked closely together, that we began to complement each other's unique, creative talents while connecting in other ways. Besides having a traditional mother-daughter relationship, we became business partners, confidantes, and even best friends.

I was twenty-one years old when I graduated from design school. After years of working on improving my design skills, I finally was ready to join Mom at the worktable. All these years later, whenever I showed her my latest creation, she still said, "Jules, what a lovely gown. It's your best work yet!"

Mom had a way of saying something so utterly funny and nonsensical that I'd laugh until I couldn't breathe. I sure needed that today. Sure, I was thrilled to be the new proprietor of Belle's Bridal, but the store still felt so vacant without her.

"Don't worry, Jules, you're doing fine," Mrs. Cassidy assured me, as though she could read my thoughts. "How's my sweet friend, Bianca, doing these days?"

"Mom's great. She still has her condo in the city. But she and Dad spend most of their time at Lake Geneva. They bought a beautiful home there last year and enjoy spending a lot of time on the water."

"Good for her. I remember when I met your mother," Mrs. Cassidy said with a wistful smile. "Stewart and I were out and about window shopping when we came across the store. We decided to walk in and look around. If I remember correctly, you greeted us at the door."

"Yes, I offered you a beverage and asked if you required

any further assistance."

"That's right. You were just six or seven years old at the time and cute as a button. And having so much fun playing fashion designer."

"Was I only seven?" I asked in disbelief. During my childhood years, I spent a lot of time around grown-ups, so I felt like a little adult for my young age.

"Yes, you were a tiny little thing, busy scribbling away in your journal."

Mrs. Cassidy didn't understand that I wasn't *playing* a fashion designer. In my mind, I *was* a fashion designer carefully observing clients' interactions and taking meticulous notes. Because I learned how to sketch, sewing, and make patterns in my early teens, I was more advanced in design than fashion school graduates. After graduating design school, I realized that there was no such class that taught the type of intricate sewing and embroidery work the shop workers performed.

I was about speak up and inform Mrs. Cassidy that I stopped scribbling in kindergarten when Mrs. Cassidy said, "Even though we'd just met, Bianca and I immediately clicked," Mrs. Cassidy said, still reminiscing. "It felt like we had known each other for years. I couldn't believe how much we had in common, and I knew we'd become close friends. I admired your mother's openness and positivity; I found her bluntness and ability to give her honest opinion refreshing. Rare in this industry."

I chose to keep quiet and nodded in agreement. "I agree. I would rather hear the terrible truth than a happy lie."

"Boy, was she direct. 'Dianne,' Bianca would say, 'that style looks atrocious on you. Not only does peplum make you look hippy, but it looks as though you're wearing an old-fashioned swim skirt over a dress.'" Mrs. Cassidy laughed. "God, I just loved that about your mother."

I can't say that I loved having my flaws pointed out by my mom, but eventually I did appreciate her honesty. Every morning before driving me to school, she eyed me like Karl Lagerfeld eyed his models before sending them down the runway. Unlike Karl, she insisted on a permanent smiley face, not a pouty puss.

I had been an ugly duckling right up until my freshman year in high school. With her help, I began my transformation from a pimply-faced, eyeglass-wearing teenager with bad fashion sense into a sophisticated and fashionable designer. By the end of college, I looked like one of Oprah's head-to-toe makeover contest winners.

Mom wanted me to find my look first as a young adult, but when she realized that her daughter was drowning she jumped in to save me. Mom spent a considerable amount of money on a dermatologist to clear up my complexion and an orthodontist to close the huge gap between my teeth for braces, rubber bands, and a painful night-guard. Once I was old enough to wear contact lenses, she got rid of my over-sized glasses and bought me soft lenses. Next, she replaced my color-coordinated culottes with Bianca Couture fashions and asked her hairdresser to highlight and style my dark blonde hair. Finally, she bought me a package of tanning sessions and accompanied me to my monthly manicures and pedicures. I was a work-in-progress and didn't mind the beautification process. But if I were to change one thing, I would have preferred she didn't pinch me every time I slouched.

But all of her efforts had finally paid off. My posture rapidly improved, my skin glowed from all the exfoliation, and my braces came off to reveal straight pearly white teeth. Best of all, I received a college scholarship that balanced out the high cost (emotionally and financially) of my mother's beauty regimens. By the time I graduated, I no longer tucked my sweaters into my pants, bit my nails or rocked a unibrow. I was tweezed, waxed, buffed, and ready to enter the big and exciting bridal world.

"Mrs. Cassidy," I said, "I am my mother's daughter, and I

promise you that I will always give you my honest opinion."

"You know, Juliana, you can call me by my first name."

"That I can't promise."

We both laughed.

"I miss the good old days, but it sounds like Bianca's enjoying her retirement. Please send her my regards the next time you talk to her."

"I will." Little did Mrs. Cassidy know I had my mother on permanent speed-dial and was already planning on calling her to vent after this long appointment finally ended.

"So, um, do you think we can put aside the idea of silicone?" I asked, trying to be gentle with my words.

"Well, I guess since you are my designer these days, I'm going to trust your opinion," she said, sounding defeated. "I just wanted to feel beautiful and have people notice me. You know, Jules, not all of us are lucky enough to be a size zero. You could wear a burlap sack, and you would still look phenomenal."

Phenomenal? I didn't feel phenomenal; I felt utterly rung out. Rings of mascara encircled my blue eyes. No hint of lipstick remained on my lips, and I had a run in my stocking. The only thing I had going for me these days was my sculptured cheekbones, and that wasn't from doing an excellent job of contouring my makeup. It was from always being hungry because I never had time to eat. I wondered what happened to that bouncy, easy-going gal, who once had the perfect manicure to show off her sparkling engagement ring and wedding band?

Oh, that's right. How could I forget? I no longer had those rings—just the ones under my eyes. And I was paying for Tatiana's manicures while my nails looked as though I'd put them through a paper shredder. I didn't want Mrs. Cassidy to see my atrocious nails and slid my hands underneath the worktable. For once, I was grateful my mother wasn't there. She would have never approved of having a disheveled appearance at the shop.

Trying to divert Mrs. Cassidy's attention away from me, I decided to go with a bad joke. "For your information, burlap makes me look hippy," I responded.

Mrs. Cassidy's expression softened. "Amusing," she said, then laughed out loud.

"Speaking of hippy, what is dear Abby wearing?" she asked, pursing her lips. "Jules darling, you know that I don't want my outfit to look like the mother-of-the-groom's."

"Abby is wearing a lavender chiffon dress," I replied calmly, carefully sidestepping the question. "It's an entirely different look from your suit."

"Really?" she said, giving me a knowing look that told me I had to keep her away from the workroom at all cost. I wouldn't put it past Mrs. Cassidy to storm in there and tear the place apart in search of the dress that her best friend and mother-of-the-groom was wearing to the wedding of the year. I also couldn't take the chance of having Abby Tucker berate me for revealing her design.

Several years ago, a good client of mine asked to see her future family member's gown. I naively thought nothing of it and proudly showed her the dress. Immediately after her appointment, she called her future in-law and told her that her dress looked like something a retired drag queen would wear. Needless to say, my other client was so enraged she demanded that I design her a new gown. All I could do was apologize profusely, absorb the cost of the first dress, and start over from scratch. From that day forward, my policy had always been never to show a client's dress without her consent.

Knowing Mrs. Cassidy, I was certain that even if she completely hated her friend's design, she would cancel her order and demand to have a lilac dress made just to stick it to her. It's the unwritten mother-of-the-bride advantage.

Finally, Mrs. Cassidy asked the all-important question. "If you had to choose, whose would you say was prettier?"

Even though they were both my designs and were

beautiful in their unique way, my answer was obvious. "No contest. Her dress can't hold a candle to your suit."

Mrs. Cassidy looked content with my response. She stood, picked up the fabric swatch once again and walked to the antique gold full-length mirror by the window that overlooked Purdy Lane. As she held up the cloth to her tightly stretched face, she turned slowly side-to-side, checking out both profiles. Considering that she recently had another surgical procedure in celebration of the upcoming nuptials, I didn't think her neck could turn without ricocheting back to center.

After a while, my gaze turned from Mrs. Cassidy's red sleeveless, St. John knit silhouette to the horse-drawn carriage passing by an oil-burning street lamp decorated with a red velvet bow. I sighed. To think, I was only two short blocks away from the million lights along Michigan Avenue, and yet I couldn't manage to get out of my store to shop in anyone else's magnificent store. My subconscious screamed to charge exorbitant amounts of money, choose my hours, and refuse to work with difficult clients, but I knew that wasn't going to happen anytime soon.

By 8:45 PM, my fingers were stiff, and I had a monstrous callus on my middle finger. My blood pressure rose at the thought of redesigning the same suit that I had designed for Mrs. Cassidy during her last three-hour appointment. And my stomach growled so loudly I was afraid she could hear it. But I wasn't just craving dinner, I was hungry for the sale.

My cell phone rang.

It was Rocco—his persistence finally paid off, and we just started dating. He seemed nice—and he acted as though he found me charming, something that felt good after my husband's philandering. Besides, I'd decided if I was scared of jumping into the dating pool again, well, that was exactly what I needed to do.

Rocco owned Delgado's Fruit and Vegetable Market on Randolph Street, the best place in town to buy exotic fruits and vegetables from around the world. I ran into him in the kumquat section. Literally. I was buying dragon fruit when some kid knocked over the entire kumquat display, and tiny little oranges rolled everywhere. I helped him clean up the mess. It may have the elements of a romantic comedy, but honestly, it wasn't the least bit romantic. And I liked that about the relationship. Working in fashion, I've come across my share of self-absorbed men. Rocco was different. What you saw was what you got. He was a hard-working guy with simple tastes, and that was just what I wanted—a simple relationship, nothing serious. I stepped away from Mrs. Cassidy and answered the phone.

"Hey, Kumquat, what's going on?"

"Rocco, please don't call me that," I whispered.

"What's the big deal, Jules? It's just a little pet name. Usually, the babes love that sort of thing."

"And please don't call me babe," I added. I didn't mean to sound grouchy, but I was tired, and I hated pet names. "Listen, I can't talk now. I'm with a client."

Rocco didn't seem to hear me and rambled on about the price of rhubarb. Or was he refereeing a rhubarb among his workers? Whatever, I stared a hole through the back of Mrs. Cassidy's head in hopes of eliciting a response—something to help me get off the phone. Besides, it was about time she made up her mind and handed over her credit card. I *needed* this sale to make it through March.

Finally, I gave up on both of them and whispered into the phone. "I'm about to make a sale. Gotta go." I hung up on Rocco before he could object.

Mrs. Cassidy turned away from the mirror and walked back to the table, where she took a seat. "Be honest, Jules. Is the suit too flashy? The last thing I want to do is take away my daughter's spotlight."

Her comment came as no surprise to me because it was the most commonly asked mother-of-the-bride question. Mrs. Cassidy, like other mothers, needed reassurance that she looked as beautiful today as on her wedding day.

"Cross my heart," I said. Unless her daughter had a severe case of premature aging, I wasn't worried about that in the least.

"Are you sure?"

"Of course I'm sure," I said with deep conviction. I had spent four long hours with her and didn't want to say anything to sway her in a new direction.

She sat in silence.

"So, what do you think?" I said, trying to remain impassive. "Single-breasted?"

"Oh, what the heck!" Mrs. Cassidy finally said as she slammed her hand with the gigantic diamond ring down on the table. "Let's make it a swinging single, just like me."

My heart skipped a beat. "That's wonderful!" I said, flashing a huge—and genuine—smile. Maybe this day really was about to be over. I quickly finished drawing the missing part of the jacket and sprang out of my chair. After refilling Mrs. Cassidy's champagne glass, I began filling out the paperwork. First, I figured out the sales tax using my ten fingers and a few toes. Then, I pulled out a beautiful Crane and Co. gold-stamped cream envelope and stapled a fabric swatch to a note reading, "Designed especially for you." I slid a copy of the sketch and swatch into the left inner pocket, placed the invoice in the envelope and handed it to her. Voila! Good night and goodbye!

"Thank you, Mrs. Cassidy. It's been a pleasure designing for you. I'll let you know when it's time for your fitting."

The next morning I was so drained I had trouble walking the few short blocks from home to work. Once I arrived at the front door of my shop, I fumbled with the keys as I unlocked the door and almost forgot the code to disengage the alarm system. I flipped on the long row of light switches, illuminating the showroom section by section. I dragged my tired body past the display cases, wiping away a few noticeable fingerprint marks with my scarf. I stood at the reception desk, took a deep breath, and pushed the voicemail button.

"You have twelve new messages," my machine announced politely.

I pressed the pound sign and began listening to the endless string of demands. I made it a rule never to answer the phone when I was with a client, unless, of course, it had something to do with Jack. Then I dropped everything. (Last night with Rocco was an exception—after all, Mrs. Cassidy had stolen our evening.)

The voice messages started at 7:00 PM and I had to scribble like crazy to get them down on the notepad. The first three calls were from my mother asking random questions: What size clothing was Jack wearing these days? Had I placed the order for her favorite seamless bra? Did I remember her Amazon password?

The machine finally announced the last message. "Jules, darling. Dianne Cassidy here. You'll never believe the message I just received when I got home. My personal shopper from Saks called to tell me that the store received another of the limited-edition Armani suit that I had been obsessing over. Saks sold out of their entire stock weeks ago, but my amazing salesperson got one in my size! Can you believe it? I am over the moon! Soooo, needless to say, I'm canceling my order. But don't worry, if need be, you can do the alterations. Okay, let's do lunch soon. Ciao!"

I stared at the telephone for a long time, letting the message sink in as waves of disappointment washed over me. Well, that $60 alteration fee would certainly go a long way towards paying for a single Lego erector set. As things stood now, I'd need to figure out new ways of cutting corners. But for the time being, I had to find the willpower to have an eye-opening conversation with my nanny about her dining budget. I sure hoped Tatiana liked Red Lobster!

CHAPTER 5

The next morning, I walked into the workroom ready to begin production on Scarlett Smith's wedding gown. She'd approved the design, and we were ready to cut, sew, embellish, and fit.

"Good morning, ladies."

All the seamstresses let out a collective, "Hi Boss." It still struck me funny to be called Boss; that's what they used to call Mom.

I made my way through the tight quarters. Not only was my clothing line made in America, but it was produced smack dab in the middle of Chicago's Gold Coast. I could buy a small factory in China for the amount of money I spent on rent, production, materials, and staff. Every inch of space counted, so everything required to make an exquisite gown was tucked away in every nook and cranny of the room.

The workroom and showroom were on two separate floors, with a private staircase for staff to go between to mezzanine and the second floor. Shelves stocked with every kind and color of fabric lined the perimeter of the workroom, and three load-bearing columns separated the cutting tables and the rows upon rows of sewing machines. Custom-pattern forms hung from the ceiling on pulleys. The ironing and steaming stations set near the lunchroom came in handy both for ironing dresses and making paninis.

As I walked past the lines of sewing machines to the cutting table, I did my usual line of questioning. "Olga, did you get my notes on the latest changes to the Gillespie dress?"

"I did," Olga said.

"Good." Moving on. "Elizabeth, did you see that Patricia now wants a *pink* wedding gown made from the same taffeta?"

"Pink? No. Why didn't anyone tell me?" Her look of surprise made me glad I asked. "I've been looking for that dress everywhere."

I listened to the various questions and complaints before I finally stood in front of my fifty-year-old expert pattern-maker, Phu Tôn.

"There you go," I said, handing him the sketch I'd drawn of Scarlett's dream dress. Phu let out a small grunt and stopped what he was working on, put on his coke-bottle glasses and looked over the sketch, clearly trying to figure out how he was going to create the template for the gown. We took a few minutes to discuss everything at great length. Even the smallest detail mattered in constructing a wedding gown. Once he understood my vision, he picked up his pencil and climbed his sturdy step stool.

Before he began to draw, he tapped the gold medal sharply with his pencil several times where it hung on the wall as if it was the opening bell of the stock market.

And to me it was. The sound the medal made when it hit a metal plate on the wall notified the staff that we had sold another dress. Even though it was a silly tradition, the ladies always made it a point to clap. Phu liked the attention; it made him feel respected, like the old days when he performed on stage.

What Phu lacked in height, he made up in strength. In Hanoi, he had been a famous Vietnamese body builder. Everywhere he went, he proudly carried the gold medal that he had won for his bodybuilding team at the Asian Bodybuilding and Physique Sports Championships in Macau. His town celebrated for a month after his team snatched three gold medals on the first day of the competition.

On his first day in the shop, Phu hung his beloved medal in a prominent spot on the wall behind the cutting table and said he was ready to begin a new chapter of his life. I added the metal plate to start a new tradition at Belle's.

The senior staff had a way of trying to intimidate new employees, their way of initiating the newbies and showing them who's boss. *Funny, I thought that was me, but I was beginning to wonder if they were just patronizing me.*

But Phu took no part in their scare tactics. He'd flip back his reverse half-mullet haircut (long in front and short in back) and puff up like a peacock. They would back down immediately.

After he'd finished drawing the design onto dotted-pattern paper, Phu sharpened his cutting scissors, like they were a Dao saber, and carefully cut out the fabric pieces for the dress. Next, he passed out sections of the dress to the team of seamstresses, waiting to put together the latest, greatest, bridal masterpiece.

Nathaniel walked into the workroom hardly able to contain his excitement. "Juliana, you'll never guess who just called?"

"My mom?"

"Well, that's a given," Nathaniel said, rolling his eyes. "But I'm talking an even bigger personality."

"Bigger than Bianca Belleski? Now I'm curious to find out."

"Max Marshal, from the Style Network!"

"Really? What did he want?"

"He's producing a new show about over-the-top celebrity weddings and is considering you for the role of the fashion expert."

"Nat, that's great news."

"I know. Apparently, he saw you on last week's news segment where you were discussing bridal blunders and loved your style. He's going to stop by the shop sometime within the next few weeks to shadow you for a day."

"Did he happen to mention a specific date?"

"No, he's showing up unannounced. He wants to observe your normal, everyday interactions with clients and staff."

"You know how much I hate surprises. Can't you call him back and ask him to give you some notice?"

"I tried. But he refused to give me any clues as to when he was going to show up. His specific words were, "I want business as usual, and nothing staged.""

"Well, our showroom is our stage. Let's pray that he picks a slow day with very little drama."

"Speaking of drama, your mother called and said she was running late for Jack's gymnastics class. She's going to meet you there."

"Gymnastics class! Oh my God, I almost forgot. Tatiana has the day off for one of her modeling tryouts, and I have to get Jack. Olga, do you understand what you need to do?"

Olga looked up from her work. "Yes, Juliana."

"If you don't, ask Phu. Or better yet, call me. I can talk you through it."

"I can help her," said Phu. "Go. Enjoy your time with Jack and your mom. We'll be fine here."

I smiled at Phu, grateful for his support and understanding. "Okay. Nat, when's my next appointment again?"

"Ramona Black. Two o'clock."

"See you then," I said, then grabbed my coat and hurried out the door.

For once, traffic cooperated, and I arrived almost on time. Jack was running around playing with some of the kids in his class; he waved at me and kept playing. I loved the resilience of that little guy. Mom wasn't so relaxed.

"Where have you been? I've been waiting for you?" She had her hand firmly on the bench, saving me a seat.

My mother, Bianca, was a stunning woman with glowing skin and camera-ready hair and makeup. (She colored her hair a different shade of blonde every two months.) I can't remember all the diets she'd been on though she rarely followed them. She managed to take such good care of herself by hiring the best people in the industry to give her the cutting-edge beauty treatments of the stars.

"Come on, Mom, you know what that shop can be like."

"Yeah, so how's work going without me?"

"Okay."

"Just Okay?" She nudged my shoulder. "Do you miss your mother?"

"You know I do. Wanna come back?"

"And miss spending time with my grandson. Never. Any good gossip?"

I shook my head. She never tired of hearing the gossip from the shop. "One of my pregnant bride's water broke during the ceremony if that's what you mean."

"I hope you remembered to line the dress with a plastic petticoat," Bianca said, laughing.

I shrugged my shoulders.

"Or told her to strap a mop to her leg." She slapped her knee, laughing.

Oh, please. I didn't have the energy to laugh at that one.

"Sveetheart, you always laugh at my jokes. What *is* going on with you?"

I thought for a moment. "Why did you have to take on William's mother for a client?"

"Ahh… So, now it's my fault you married that ne'er-do-well?" she asked.

"Technically, it's William's mother's fault. If she hadn't insisted on setting us up on a blind date, my life would be completely different today."

"True, but then you wouldn't have Jack."

"Oh, you know how much I love Jack. Obviously, I wouldn't take anything for him."

"Then what's really troubling you? Tell me." She patted my hand.

"Some days, all the fuss about weddings and happily ever after just gets to me. And now I might have an opportunity to have a reoccurring role on a new television show about dream weddings for the Style Network. What do I know about a happy marriage? I didn't have one, and who knows if I ever will. I feel like such a phony."

"William was the phony, not you, Jules. I don't know how you managed to deal with that pathological liar for so long."

I shrugged and looked at Jack, not wanting to meet her eyes. "I suppose it was the eternal optimist in me."

"Still, what William did to you was unforgivable," Mom said. "How in the world he got away with keeping that horrible Candy on the side throughout your whole marriage, is simply mindboggling."

"I don't blame her anymore. William's trust fund meant more to him than both of us put together. And his parents were very clear from the beginning that he'd lose his inheritance if he ever married Candy." I thought about what I'd just said, amazed that I could share that bizarre logic as though it made sense. And yet, in its own strange way, it did. At least from William's perspective.

"So you're saying that William wanted to have his candy and eat it, too." Mom chuckled.

I began to laugh and cry at the same time.

"There, I knew I could make you laugh," she said.

I nodded and wiped the corners of my eyes.

"Sveetheart, remember, your divorce has nothing to do with your talent for designing the best wedding gowns in the city. Of course, that used to be me, before I retired. But please know that you're now the fabulous fashion darling when it comes to bridal gowns. And the Style network will be lucky to have you."

"Don't get me wrong—I still love designing. It's the brides chatting in my ear on a daily basis that's killing me. I'm tired of listening to all the gory details of their weddings."

"'Gory'?"

"Did I say 'gory'? I *meant* glorious. But I don't know how much longer I can feign excitement over fine linens imported from France. Or, listen to all the ingredients that go into a five-tier lemon mousse cake. I'm just going to call up Max Marshal and tell him that I'm not interested in hosting his wedding show. Frankly, I don't know if I can manage to work in the bridal industry any longer."

"Of course, you can. Be positive."

"Okay, I'm positive I can't do it anymore."

Mom looked at me steadily for a few moments, and said, "Hey, wait a minute. Isn't today Tuesday?"

"Yes, why?" I shrugged my shoulders.

"Well, isn't it Positivity Day at the shop?"

Positivity Day was a silly team-building idea I came up with years ago to encourage the women to try to be more upbeat and less gossipy. Following the adage: if you don't have something nice to say, don't say anything at all. It didn't do much to lift the rapport, but it did help lower the noise levels—at least for a little while.

"Technically, I'm not at the shop."

Mom sat up straighter and stared at me. "I don't recognize my daughter anymore. Who are you?"

I gave her my best put-upon, teenager look and kept quiet.

"Oh, come on, Juliana. You were the one who came up with that fabulous idea when you were in high school."

As I thought back to those days, a warm feeling began to replace some of the day's stress and anxiety.

"Back then, all you wanted was to be a fashion designer. Remember?" She nudged me again.

"Kind of…"

"You can't let anyone take away your dreams." She started to rummage in her purse. "I have something for you; maybe it will help."

"What is it?" I asked, excited now. I loved surprises.

She pulled the item out and handed it to me. "I was doing some spring cleaning and came across this yesterday. Do you remember this?"

"I haven't seen that in forever!" She'd found one of my old journals. I began flipping through the pages filled with my sketches and observations dating back to 1984. "I must have been five when I started this thing," I said, seeing my younger self busy at work.

"Mommy, did you see my somersault?" Jack called out, bringing me out of my reverie.

I waved and blew him a kiss. I always tried to focus as much attention as possible on Jack when we were together, but there were times when my mind wandered. Sometimes, I unintentionally zoned out during some of our conversations about Matchbox cars and geckos. Lately, we'd spent a lot of time together, and honestly, I didn't think he would mind if I missed seeing one of his many forward rolls. Besides, this journal meant the world to me.

I turned to the last page, and my heart began to race as I stared in disbelief at a sketch I drew as a teenager. Just holding the journal in my hands again allowed me to feel the magic of that day deep inside. I traced my finger over the drawing of the dress and the memory of that day almost twenty years ago came rushing back to me in a flash of emotionally-tinged longing.

I'd walked into the showroom like any day, but then I saw the most beautiful bride I'd ever seen: gold-hued, shoulder-length hair, long legs, and deep green, penetrating eyes. She radiated self-confidence and carried herself with such poise. An accomplished ballerina about to marry her dance partner, she displayed perfect posture as she admired herself in the mirror. I could practically see her performing on stage as she twirled around the store in her regal gown. I thought Mom had outdone herself with this design, and I wanted to capture the memorable moment.

I had grabbed my journal and began to sketch furiously, aware I had only a few minutes to finish the drawing before she changed out of her gown. Fortunately, I was able to complete the sketch, and now, seeing it in its permanent place in my journal, it gave me the uplift to my day I needed. I gave Mom a quick hug.

"Juliana, never forget the excitement you felt that day. You need to have confidence in yourself and *your designs* if you are going to survive this business."

I nodded and hugged her again, holding on for a long moment. We sat in companionable silence for a while, letting the shouts and laughter of the kids wash over us. The warm-ups finished, and the young gymnasts were working on more advanced equipment now.

"Hey," Mom said, elbowing me, "look at the way Jack ran to help that little girl get up after she fell from the balance beam. He's chivalrous at such a young age. I believe he's going to be a heart breaker. Who does he remind you of?"

"Dad, of course." I saw a lot of my father, Stephen, in Jack. These days, I described my gray-haired, blue-eyed, seventy-year-old father as a distinguished gentleman. He held chivalry and politeness in high regard, in part due to his traditional upbringing in Warsaw, where he and Mom met. Some might consider his act of kissing a woman's hand old-fashioned, but I disagreed. I adored the way my father treated me, and the special attention he always gave me made me feel loved.

As though she could read my mind, Mom tapped my shoulder and said, "Hey, don't worry, you'll find a new husband soon."

I gave her a look. "And what makes you think I'm looking for a husband?"

"Because you want to get married again."

"No, I do not. *You* want me to get married again."

Good Ol' Jack stopped an argument before it could get heated up. "Mommy, Glammy, look what I can do." He managed an impressive flip on the trampoline. We both applauded as he ran off to the rings.

"Obviously your first marriage has soured you," Mom continued, never one to let the controversy die. "But you have to look at the future. Jack needs a father—and siblings. You need to forget about William, and all that hurt he dumped on you."

The whistle blew. Class over. The kids were allowed some free time without instruction so they could play and just have fun before heading home. Jack ran over to us and threw his sweaty arms around me. "Mommy, is Daddy visiting today?"

I swear my son was telepathic. He asked about his father all the time, but I was puzzled as to why he was asking about him now. "No, not today, honey."

"Okay, Mommy. Maybe tomorrow." He sounded more hopeful than sad, and once again I couldn't help but admire him. I had a lot to learn from that little guy. I'd made the mistake of telling Jack that William was back in town and would start visiting him more. I'd hoped William might show up today, and even though he was a no-show, I felt terrible for getting Jack's hopes up.

Bianca shook her head in displeasure as Jack ran off to play. "When is William supposed to visit Jack?"

"It's been practically two weeks since we talked, and I told him about today, but…" I shook my head. "I just don't know what he's thinking…"

"I know what he's thinking. That selfish bastard is thinking about himself, as usual!"

"Your probably right."

"Your momma's always right. Just remember that."

I shook my head and gave her a half smile. "I wish I could give William a good poke in the ass like I did to that bride."

"Are you talking about the bride whose zipper broke right before the wedding?"

"Yes, that's the one. We had to sew the gown on the

bride's body in the taxi on the way to the church."

"I remember," I said. "Boy, did she freak out when you accidentally poked her in her tush with that thick needle."

"Oh, she was mad alright. I had to calm her down by telling her it was an old Polish tradition. Being poked with a needle before the wedding meant that she would have a baby by the end of her first year of marriage."

I giggled. "You acted so believable. Didn't she insist that you poke her a second time?"

"Because she wanted twins," we said in unison and broke out laughing.

"I made you laugh for a second time today," Mom said with pride. "It's a good start. But I know something else that will help get you back in designing form again."

"What?"

"You'll see."

I looked at her skeptically.

"Don't worry, Sveetheart. It's just what the doctor ordered."

CHAPTER 6

"Oh, no! Tell me this isn't happening again." I'd opened the fitting room door to see my mom holding court inside.

"Hush!" Mom held up her finger, signaling me to wait while Dr. Darren finished injecting Botox between her eyebrows.

"You promised you wouldn't do this at the shop anymore."

"Yes, but I did this for you."

"I never asked for you to get collagen injunctions for me."

"No, you're too nice to point out your mother's flaws. I meant that I know that you would never take time off from work to go to a spa."

"That's true."

"So, I decided to bring the spa to you. I called Dr. Darren to come here to give us both a little mother-daughter lift. Now, don't be rude, Juliana. Say hello."

I forced a smile and acknowledged Mom's dermatologist. I closed the door behind me and tucked my hair behind my ears. "Hi, Dr. D. How's the family?"

"Doing well." She smiled at me. "How's Jack?"

"Oh, growing up fast. Thanks for asking."

Dr. Darren handed Mom a small ice pack. "Apply some light pressure to the middle of your forehead for about a minute."

Mom winced as she pressed the ice pack between her brows. "Dr. Darren was kind enough to make a house call."

"Then why aren't you at your house?" I asked.

"Come on, Jules. You know very well that your father is squeamish about anything that has to do with doctors and hospitals. If I had this done at home, he would faint at the sight of blood."

I shook my head in disbelief and looked around the room. Bloody cotton balls, used ice packs, and empty injectable syringes covered the floor. I'd put a lot of time and thought into decorating this room when I chose golden sconces, peach moiré wallpaper, and dainty antique furniture. My objective was to create an inviting space with a warm boudoir effect for my brides, not a pop-up MediSpa.

I focused my attention back on the scene that was unfolding. "Please, ladies. You have to go somewhere else."

Mom removed the ice pack and handed it to me. "Where would you like us to go? Starbucks?"

"As long as the Barista supplies you with enough ice for the bruising, I'm fine with that." I dropped the thawed ice pack into the garbage can.

"Bruising?" Mom looked up at Dr. Darren with a worried expression on her red face. "How would I explain that to my husband?"

"Relax Bianca," Dr. Darren shot me a look. "When have I ever caused you to bruise?"

I decided to interrupt the conversation before it unraveled. "Here's a thought," I said. "How about going to Dr. Darren's office like a normal client?"

"Well, most of my clients aren't all that normal," Dr. Darren interjected.

I could relate to working with quirky clients. Fortunately, my clients flew here to work with me while Dr. D traveled the country to work with her clients.

Dr. Dina Darren was a famous dermatologist with a huge celebrity following flocking to her offices in Chicago, New

York, and LA. Naturally, she had the most perfect, luminous skin; a freckle wouldn't dare show its ugly, little mark anywhere on her body. Even if it tried, Beyond Spotless, her line of miracle organic skin-care creams, would annihilate it.

You couldn't open a fashion magazine without finding Dr. Darren sharing the newest procedures available on the market. All across the county, gently and not so gently aging women waited months for an appointment to see the talented doctor.

After Dr. Darren carefully studied mom's features, she removed her surgical gloves with a snap. "Finished!"

"Perfect timing," Mom said. "Now, Jules, let's get to work on you because Olivia should be here any minute to perform our cellulite treatment."

Before my jaw could hit the floor, Mom said, "Just relax, Sveetheart. It will take only fifteen minutes, at the most."

A loud knock on the door made me jump. "Juliana," said Zoë. "Paige's mother is getting impatient."

Massaging my temples, I told Mom, "Let's get something straight. No way am I having any treatments performed here today. Nothing personal, Doc."

"None taken," Dr. Darren said.

"Mom, you have fifteen minutes to finish up in here."

"Impossible. Can't rush perfection."

"Nor can it be achieved," I said, grabbing the door handle.

Before I left the room, I turned to mom's dermatologist, trying to remember my manners. "Dr. D, always great to see you."

As I popped back into the second fitting room, I noticed my walk-in bride, Paige, quickly crinkle up a small piece of paper, closing it tightly in her fist. Turning her back towards me, she said, "I need help buttoning the gown."

I looked to Wing, Paige's petite Asian mother, who turned her torso away from me to look at a dress that was hanging on the hook on the side wall. The two women didn't seem related. Paige was a tall, plump, alabaster-skinned, all-American-looking golden blonde with almond shaped eyes. Wing, on the other hand, was short and thin with a turned down mouth and a short bob haircut. Maybe Paige was adopted?

Earlier, when Paige introduced Wing as her mother, I never gave it a second thought. Nothing surprised me anymore; I worked with unconventional families all the time. But as I stood in the fitting room, something about Wing was familiar. I had the feeling I'd met her before, but I couldn't put my finger on when or where.

As I frantically fastened the bridal buttons, my fingers turned numb. I wanted to say, *Am I the only person in this room that knows how to fasten a button?* But Wing was much too busy asking never-ending questions to be bothered with buttoning her own daughter's gown.

"What size are those buttons?" asked Wing.

"I don't recall," I said. "Covered buttons come in a variety of sizes, and I don't know the answer off the top of my head."

"Hmmm, interesting." She sounded suspicious as if I were purposefully trying to keep the information from her.

Wing picked up the bottom of the dress and stretched it out full length. "Would you say that would be about nine yards?"

I gently took the fabric from her small, wrinkly hands and let the skirt fall to the floor. "Yes," I answered her.

Like a spastic pterodactyl, Wing made screeching sounds while she critiqued every dress that Paige tried on.

"No good. Bring more dresses," ordered Wing.

At this rate, Paige would have tried on the entire spring collection by the end of her visit. So I said, "Ladies if you're feeling overwhelmed by all of the choices, why not go home and give it some more thought?" I looked at Paige hopefully. "You can always schedule a follow-up appointment."

"No. No," Wing barked.

"Mom, please," Paige said. "Let me handle this. What my mother is trying to say is, we would like to make a decision on a dress today."

The back of my neck started to burn. "Sure. I'll have Zoë show you more gowns."

I noticed the corset Paige wore was loose because she didn't have it zipped up all the way. I flipped back my hair, grabbed hold of the zipper, and managed to yank it closed. Her back fat rose over the corset like a fleshy donut. "There, much better," I said, feeling pleased with myself.

Paige groaned and tried to catch her breath.

Zoë knocked on the door. "The photographer is asking for you."

"I'm sorry, but I have to leave," I told them. "A former bride is having a photo shoot here today, and I promised to attend. Don't worry. You'll be in great hands with Zoë."

"I guess that's fine," Paige managed to say, trying to breathe shallowly.

"Tell her to bring more strapless gowns," Wing added.

"Of course, I'll let her know. Excuse me," I said and stepped out of the fitting room.

As soon as the door shut behind me, I noticed flashing lights escaping through the cracks of the doorframe. I was about to walk back inside to see what was going on when I heard sounds similar to a vacuum cleaner coming from Mom's fitting room. The cleaning crew always came in to tidy up after closing, so I dashed into the adjacent fitting room to see what was going on.

Mom was standing in the middle of the room wearing only a bra and a pair of ridiculous-looking high-waisted tights. She pulled me into the room, causing the door to shut on my skirt.

"Jules, I'm glad you're back. I have a question for you." Mom sounded emotional even though she showed no expression lines on her newly paralyzed face.

I smiled uneasily at the woman who was squatting

between Mom's legs, holding a vacuum hose with rollers that connected to a freestanding machine.

"Jules, Olivia. Olivia, Jules," Mom added, remembering her manners in spite of the loud suctioning.

As I tried to release myself from the clutches of both my Mom and the door, I acknowledged the latest member of Mom's glam squad. Her aesthetician, dressed in a tight cream turtleneck, stretchy black jeans, and tall, black studded ankle boots, looked like a thirty-eight-year-old woman with a twenty-year-old body. I was fascinated as I watched Olivia roll the contraption up and down Mom's right thigh. I had to admit that for sixty-four, Mom also looked ten years younger than her true age. Even in the silly nude pantyhose.

I tugged at the hem of my skirt still jammed in the door. After giving it one final yank, the fabric dislodged, and I fell into Mom's loving arms. Who, of course, pushed me away.

"Jules, what's wrong with you?" she cried, "Can't you see that Olivia is working? It takes a very steady hand, and I can't afford any bruising. Remember?"

"No worries, Bianca. Everything is coming along great," Olivia said, with a smile.

I smoothed out my skirt as if nothing had happened. Before I could say anything, Mom added, "Tatiana told me that you've been dating someone. Someone named Loco?"

"His name is Rocco," I said, correcting her.

"His name doesn't sound very Polish to me.

"Because he's Argentinian. His name is Roque Ricardo Delgado. But he goes by Rocco in that he hated his childhood nickname, Babalu.

"Oh my God! That was my favorite episode of "I Love Lucy". Olivia, have you seen that show?"

Olivia removed the hose from mother's thigh, and said, "I don't know what you're talking about."

"Oh, never mind," Mom said. "You're probably too young to remember. You can go back now to making my thighs cellulite free."

Olivia shook her head and got back to work.

"Whatever, Desi Arnaz looked hot in that tuxedo when he played the bongos."

"Hot?" I asked. "Really, Mom? I thought you preferred Polish men."

"Of course, I do. Your father is a very good-looking man. But, I tell you, there's something about those Latino men that gets my heart racing. Rocco must be gorgeous."

"Well, I wouldn't say 'hot'. Tepid, maybe."

"So, you're not going to date anyone handsome now because William's looks attracted too many women?" Mom asked.

"Maybe, if, and I mean *if* I ever decide to date again, I'm going to find a man that's the polar opposite of William. So far Rocco's off to a good start, but at this point it's nothing serious."

She gave me a look that said she didn't believe me. "It must be a little serious; I hear that he's invited you and Jack out for dinner."

"We're just friends, and I haven't agreed to his dinner invitation yet."

"Has Jack met him?" she prodded.

"No. I don't want Jack to feel confused or worried. It's too soon."

"Was Rocco born in Argentina?"

"No, his parents are originally from San Juan. In their early twenties, they moved to Chicago and opened a small market on Randolf Street. Rocco was born and raised on the Southside of Chicago."

"What's his Astrological sign?"

"I have no idea."

"Have you met his parents?"

"No."

"Does he want kids?"

"I'm not sure."

"I thought you wanted more children. Wouldn't you want to know if he feels the same way, sweetheart?"

"I have an idea. If you promise to stop grilling the babysitter, I'll consider bringing Rocco up to the lake house so you and dad can meet him. How about that?" I smiled my prettiest smile.

"I don't know if that will be possible," Mom continued. "I'm afraid that your father has caught something awful."

I gritted my teeth at Mom's expert passive-aggressiveness. "Are you still talking about the hypothetical lead poisoning? No, that was two weeks ago. Last week you thought Dad had narcolepsy."

"Okay, so I might have overreacted the last few times. You have to admit his skin tone looked unusually gray, and he falls asleep in the most random places. But this is serious. Have you heard of Tourette's? I hear it's very contagious."

"Tourette's is a disorder of the nervous system, not the flu," I said calmly.

"Jules, does your father swear?"

I thought for a moment, and then said, "No, I can't recall that he ever has."

"Well, listen to this. Last weekend, we drove to your Great Aunt Audrey's house. You remember dear Aunt Audrey, don't you? The only living relative we have left. Who, by the way, you need to call because she doesn't have much time."

I swear that was one sentence in one breath, no punctuation, and no pauses, just oozing guilt.

"Yes, Mom. I remember Aunt Audrey. She squeezes too hard on purpose every time I give her a hug. You and I both know that she hates me, so please, let's not go there."

"Don't take it personally, dear, she hates everyone."

"I don't want to discuss Aunt Audrey. You were talking about Dad's cursing."

"That's right," Mom said. "As I was saying, we were on the highway when a grungy looking teenager was driving a beat-up van with all of these bumper stickers saying the dirtiest, disgusting, filthiest..."

"Mom! Get to the point."

"Fine. Stop being so impatient. Now, what was I saying again? Oh yes, Daddy was driving forty-five in the left lane of the highway—a little fast for my liking, but you know how your father always did have a lead foot."

I rolled my eyes.

"This hooligan comes flying out of nowhere, pulls up in front of our car, and steps on the brakes. Daddy practically screeches to a halt. The guy turns around, gives Daddy a nasty look and takes off." She shudders at the memory. "Then, Daddy turns beet red and floors the gas pedal. He pulls up next to the kid and shows him his index finger while yelling ungentlemanly swear words." She paused and shook her head. "I thought we were dead, and that I would never see my daughter and grandson again." Mom took a deep, theatrical breath before adding, "You have to talk to your father."

"I cannot have this conversation today," I said. "I've got brides waiting, and you know what that's like."

"My goodness, Juliana. It doesn't have to be this second. Just sometime today."

"Fine," I said, conceding.

"Good! You tell him that's not how a grown man behaves."

"Absolutely. If he's going to give the finger, he needs to know he's using the wrong one." Both Olivia and I laughed.

Mom shrugged. "I'm being serious."

I squared my shoulders. "You know what? I change my mind. I'm not going to talk to Dad after all."

Mom looked shocked. "Wait. Why not?"

"Because I don't think there's anything wrong with him. Dad was just mad and standing up for himself. You have a problem with his behavior? You talk to him. Now, I've got to get to the photo shoot." As I turned to leave, she had to have the last word.

"Wait. What should I say?"

"Don't say anything. Just show him." I clenched my fist and raised my middle finger.

"Juliana, stop that!" Mom scolded.

I didn't know if I should laugh or cry as I stepped out of the fitting room. I made my way over to Marcel, the photographer with a black goatee and a creepy lightning-bolt tattoo on his bald scalp.

"Marcel, how's everything going upstairs?" I asked, forcing a smile.

"The hair and makeup people are almost finished working on Rachel. So, we need you on set in five," he said with a pronounced French accent. "I'm heading up there now."

"Great. I'll be right up."

"Bien," he said, waving as he walked out the door.

I turned to Nathaniel, who was sitting at the reception desk most likely talking on the phone to his boyfriend. "Nat, could you print tomorrow's schedule for the workroom?"

"Oh, sure thing," he answered, quickly hanging up the phone.

"And hand me the mirror that's lying by the printer."

He gave me the compact mirror, and I went racing for the elevator.

On the short ride up, I allowed my excitement to show as I thought about attending the photoshoot for *Rock the Frock Magazine*. After sharing the news with me last week, my former bridal client, Rachel Lake, approached my building manager to get permission to shoot the editorial using the rooftop of the building. Since free publicity and photo credits go a long way in commercial real estate, he happily agreed.

As the elevator doors opened, I checked my face in the mirror and wiped away pink lipstick smudged across my teeth and headed towards the door leading outside. After I had pushed open the heavy metal door, I was blinded by the bright sunlight. A burst of cold air caused me to wrap my arms tightly around myself.

I'd never been on the rooftop before and had to squint my eyes to adjust to the sunny day. The light reflecting off of the other buildings caused me to sneeze several times. When I stepped onto the roof, I couldn't help but think what a strange place this was for a wedding photo shoot.

Typically, bridal photo shoots are shot in exotic warm-weather locations with romantic backdrops like castles, gardens, and sprawling mansions with ornate interiors. But besides a fantastic west-facing view that revealed a panoramic vista of heavy stone and glass skyscrapers as far as the eye could see, there was nothing unusual about the low-sloped roof—just the standard tar and machinery, concrete walls stained from air pollution, and a sticky resin floor that emitted an unpleasant odor.

I wasn't going to let the crisp air and a few piles of filthy snow bother me. Even with an odd location choice, photo shoots were always fun. You could feel the excitement building while watching the crew busily running around, trying to frame the scene the way the photographer had envisioned it. I looked towards the middle of the roof, where Marcel and his team were testing lights and setting up multiple cameras. The tall, silver light reflectors on wheels surrounded the area selected for the photograph. A seamless white backdrop paper roll secured with large painter's buckets covered the ground.

Behind the set, I spotted Rachel chatting away with the makeup artist seemingly paying no attention to the commotion around them. Not that the artist had a tough task. Rachel had that girl-next-door beauty: adorable dimples, a great figure, and brown, wavy, shoulder-length hair she'd combed into a half updo. Rachel sat upright on a folding chair, with a blanket over her shoulders to keep her warm, looking very relaxed. As with many of my brides, I had great memories of my time with Rachel. Seeing my old client again reminded me of our year working together and the many laughs we shared.

A woman's life becomes chaotic when punctuated by the incredible experience of getting married. Often, after the reality hits, and the bride realizes the enormous amount of work involved in planning a wedding, she begins to panic and lose her composure. A meltdown might happen at any given moment. Along the way, her family members begin to wonder what was happening to the sweet, little girl who has now morphed into the dreaded Bridezilla!

I'd seen it happen so many times and knew just what that nice girl needed: a retreat where she could decompress and safely release some of that stress and frustration. She needed someone to talk to who understood the challenges she was experiencing. My store was that place, and I was the retreat leader.

A made-to-order wedding gown took about eight weeks to produce, and the bride-to-be could have up to five appointments, depending on how complicated the style. During the hour appointment, she would fill me in on the joys and miseries of wedding planning. On a bad day, when a severely stressed bride walked into the shop, she felt at home and let down her defenses. She could vent, laugh, and cry during her lengthy fittings. The bride treated me like a confidante, and I treated her like a dear friend. Once I finished listening to her problems, I always seemed to be able to give her some good advice that helped calm her nerves. Miraculously, by the end of the appointment, she walked out of the shop feeling rejuvenated and ready to face the world again.

Naturally, once the wedding was over, my client moved on to a new chapter in her life and my job was officially over. However, I always considered her a friend and looked forward to the occasional phone call or a Christmas card featuring a photograph of her growing family.

I regarded today's photo shoot an excellent opportunity to reconnect with Rachel and reminisce about the fun time we shared designing that glorious gown for her Paris wedding. I took another moment to admire the dress. The pristine white satin ball gown was still in excellent condition. I could tell that the dress was dry-cleaned and meticulously ironed. The delicate lace bodice looked fantastic against her S-curved back.

Rachel fluttered her long eyelashes after the makeup artist finished powdering her face and looked in my direction. "Jules, come over here," she said, beckoning me.

As I approached, she greeted me with excitement showing in her eyes.

"Rachel, you look fabulous! What has it been, like three years since your wedding? The gown still fits you like a glove."

"It does now. I gained a lot of weight after the wedding. I panicked when I received a phone call from the magazine agreeing to use my gown in the photoshoot. I had to go on a crash diet."

"Well, it worked. You look fantastic," I said, removing a loose strand of hair from her shoulder.

"Thank you."

I could feel another sneeze coming on and sneezed three more times. Marcel walked up to us. "Bless you," Rachel and Marcel said in unison.

"Thank you," I managed to say between bouts.

"Ready, Rachel?" Marcel asked.

"Am I ever," replied Rachel.

He took Rachel by the hand and walked her over to the edge of the white paper, leaving her there to wait for his next direction.

"*Un* minute," he said, as retreated to his camera. Marcel looked through the viewfinder and nodded his head in time to the music playing in the background.

When he was happy with the camera positioning, he directed Rachel. "Darling, center yourself in the middle of the set, *s'il vous plait.*"

Rachel carefully walked onto the paper and stood over the "X" marked with masking tape. The stylist approached Rachel with a pair of white satin pumps and helped her slip on the shoes. Followed by an assistant who whisked away any signs of dust particles or smudges that had landed on the paper with a wood handle broom.

Next, Marcel handed Rachel a neutral gray test card to hold up while he performed a meter reading to measure the intensity of light reflecting on Rachel. "Okay, I need everyone on set," announced Marcel. "We've got the lighting I've been waiting for."

I decided to find a quiet corner where I could watch the photo shoot and not be in the way. My eyes were still watering from my barrage of sneezes. As I looked into the hand mirror and blotted a tear in the corner of my eye with my pinky finger, I heard Marcel counting down. *"Trois, deux, un, zero!"*

Then, I heard Rachel scream.

I looked up and couldn't believe my eyes. Two assistants carrying large buckets ran off to the side of the set while Rachel stood motionless with thick, brown liquid dripped down her face and dress.

"Absolutely fabulous!" Marcel yelled. "Now Rachel, can you mess up your hair without smudging the chocolate running down your face?"

"I'll try," Rachel said, giggling.

"Excellent. I want all the rainbow sprinkles in her hair. Now! And throw some marshmallows on the skirt. Hey! Who's got the red maraschino cherries?"

"Stop!" I yelled and ran to Rachel. "What's going on?"

"Jules, it's okay," Rachel said, reassuring me. "It's part of the shoot. We're trashing the dress."

An assistant walked up to her and ripped off her right sleeve.

"Hey, stop that!" I demanded, pushing him away. "I... I...don't understand. Why are you destroying your beautiful wedding gown?"

"I thought you knew that *Rock the Frock* is an alternative fashion magazine known for finding creative ways of breaking down the tradition of the wedding gown."

I guess I was spending way too much time in the self-help aisle at Barnes and Noble, and too little time in the bridal section. "I most certainly did not."

"Well," Rachel explained, "this feature is all about hurt brides—to help them get their revenge in the most creative way. After experiencing the devastation of a failed marriage, destroying the dress with creative materials is a form of art therapy meant to release anger and disappointment. The experience should allow me to feel happy and free again. So for my recovery theme, I've chosen to trash my gown with an ice cream sundae."

Was that all it took to get over a failed marriage? If I'd trashed my dress, I could have saved a lot of time and energy on counseling that did nothing but rehash the pain. Paying to feel pain didn't seem right, so I gave it up quickly. Still, I couldn't wrap my head around this new concept. The idea of destroying this magnificent gown upset me. I felt connected to each of my works of art, and I didn't appreciate having it ruined for the sake of Rachel's mental recovery—and right in front of me, too.

"I need Rachel's hair a lot messier before we add the salted caramel," shouted Marcel. "*Merde!* Where's the whipped cream? Come on people!"

"But you loved the gown," I pleaded. "Remember? We spent months hand sewing it for you."

"I'm so sorry, Jules. I don't know what to say. I'm trying to heal, and this is the way I need to do it."

"People, we are losing the light. Give Rachel the cherry."

After the hairstylist carefully placed salted caramels in her hair and sprayed whipped cream around Rachel's neckline, mimicking a pearl necklace, the stylist handed Rachel a maraschino cherry dipped in dark chocolate. The preserved fruit now looked like it was wearing a tiny tuxedo with a bow tie and buttons made from chocolate.

Rachel raised the cherry over her head and opened her mouth as if she was about to take a bite.

I was so blown away by this act of gratuitous destruction that I didn't hear Zoë until she shook my arm. "Jules, you need to get back downstairs right away."

"But…" I said, pointing to a chocolate-covered Rachel.

"I'm serious. It's bad."

I paused long enough to pay homage to the trashed Juliana Belle gown before leaving the roof top. As I made a mad dash for the fitting room, I once again noticed flashing lights coming from underneath the door of Paige's fitting room.

I tried opening the door, but something was blocking my entry. The flashing stopped by the time I forced my way inside. With growing skepticism, I eyed the wide optical zoom lens camera in Wing's hand.

"Excuse me. What's going on in here?" I demanded.

They looked at me with such incredulity, as though I were the one behaving inappropriately.

"Uh, nothing. Mom was taking pictures of my favorite dress," Paige said, nervously. "To help me remember what I've tried on."

I looked around the room. The dressing room was crammed full of gowns. Petticoats hung from wall sconces and mounds of netting and gowns laid crumpled on the floor. There were at least ten more gowns in the room than when I'd left it earlier. I was shaking with anger as I glared at Wing.

And then it hit me. I finally remembered why Wing looked so familiar. Wing was my mom's worst nightmare. She was the seamstress from hell.

Wing had worked for my mom when I was a little girl. The entire time Wing sewed for us at the shop, she was secretly trying to open her own business and was using mom's connections to further her career. One day, Mom caught Wing stealing fabrics and customer files.

How could I have possibly forgotten her? Especially after the way Mom had pulled Wing out of the boutique by her long ponytail?

And here she was again, twenty years later, now trying to steal *my* ideas. I grabbed the camera from Wing's hands. "Paige, I need you to leave my store immediately and take your fake mother, sneaky seamstress with you." I opened the back of the camera and pulled out the roll of film like it was a long ribbon.

"But... I... I don't know what you're talking about," Paige cried. She was trying for innocence, but I wasn't buying it.

"Wing, my mom's in the adjacent fitting room. If you don't leave this minute, I'll have her escort you out of the shop. I can promise you that this time you won't have a single strand of hair remaining on your head. If I *ever* see you in here again, I will make sure to tell every bridal store in the state to be on the lookout for you and your thieving, copycat schemes. Off you go."

Wing didn't wait for her client. She slithered away without a word.

I turned to the crying bride. "Well, just count your blessings this woman *isn't* your mother! Goodbye, Paige," I said as I left the room.

Now that I was officially cleaning out the fitting rooms, I marched into my mom's to see if she had kept her promise. She was standing in front of Olivia, feeling her aesthetician's ample breasts over her sweater. I felt flushed with embarrassment and crossed my arms in front of me. "Hey!" I said, wincing. "What's going on here?"

"Oh, Jules!" Mom gasped. "Aren't these the most fabulous breasts you've ever seen?"

"Aww, thanks, Bianca," Olivia said, beaming. "Remind me to give you the name of my plastic surgeon."

"Would you like to touch them?" Olivia asked me. "I

don't mind."

I held up my hands. "No, thanks. I'm good."

"Jules, touch them!" Mom barked. "I need your opinion on size. Do you think I should get these or go bigger?"

I gave Mom my best don't-mess-with-me look. "Why? Is Olivia selling them?"

She glared at me. "Stop joking around. I'm serious."

"Why would someone your age want breast implants?" I said, shuddering.

"For your information," Mom said, "women my age get breast implants all the time."

"And if these women were to paint their dentures green, would you?" I asked.

"Don't be silly, Jules!"

"I'm being completely serious, and I've changed my mind about what I said earlier. Some people *can* achieve perfection. You clearly have. So don't mess with it."

Mom paused, then added, "It's hard to argue with perfection. I guess a boob job is a silly idea. Maybe, I'll get my belly button pierced instead!"

I groaned and headed out of the fitting room.

CHAPTER 7

"Jackie Boy, what are you wearing? A fishing net?" Rocco laughed and pointed to an orange fisherman's net hanging from the restaurant ceiling.

"No. It's a poncho!" Jack said, a blush starting at his neck and quickly moving upwards. "My friends at the shop made it for me. They said orange looked good on me."

"A poncho, huh? You're supposed to be wearing a Black Hawks jersey, not a poncho, kiddo. You need to get out of that bridal shop and away from that hot nanny sometimes," he said, running his fingers through his thick, neatly combed back salt and pepper hair.

I glared at Rocco and his stocky, five-foot-seven frame, with a hint of a spare tire forming around his waist. I knew Tatiana flirted with anything in pants, but what a stupid thing for him to say to a little boy. Fortunately, Jack didn't understand his last comment. He was too busy glaring at me. "Why did you make me show him? I told you he would think that ponchos are stupid." Jack whipped off the poncho and threw it on the ground.

After talking to my mom, I had thought it was time for Jack to meet Rocco, but maybe it was still too soon. I did want him to spend time with more men and less time with the seamstresses. "Hey, pick that up," I told him.

"No, I don't like it."

"Of course, you do. You were so excited when the girls gave it to you."

"No, I wasn't!"

I let that one drop and picked up the poncho; I had to save my energy for the next battle. Dinner at a sushi restaurant Rocco had picked. Because Rocco didn't have children of his own, he didn't understand that Jack ate hot dogs and pizza and wasn't a forty-year-old tough Southsider, who loved sports. But instead of causing a fuss, Jack just sat quietly poking at some oyster crackers, as Rocco tried to engage him and tell Jack about his day and the new fruits he just got in from Indonesia. When he arrived at our apartment earlier this evening, Rocco brought Jack a whole crate of coconuts, but Jack hated coconut. (Even if he'd liked them, I had no idea what we'd do with an entire crate!) Rocco was trying, but he just didn't know how to connect with someone who was one-quarter his size who had absolutely no interest in Mangosteen (a tropical fruit from Indonesia the size of a tennis ball—I didn't know what it was either before I met Rocco).

"Jack, why don't you tell Rocco what you're going to be playing this summer?"

Jack just shook his head.

"Come on, honey," I prodded.

"Violin," Jack grunted.

"I'm sorry. I must not have heard right," Rocco said though he was obviously teasing Jack. "You didn't say the violin, did you? You must have meant to say football."

"I hate football," Jack said, the teasing going right over his blonde curls.

"What?" Rocco said. "Come on, guy, violas are for wimps."

"It's not a viola. I said v-i-o-lin." Jack took his stand and sent another glare at me.

"Whatever, Dude. Just remember that you want to be playing on a football field and not marching around one with a pair of cymbals."

"But I don't want to play the cymbals," Jack corrected Rocco.

"Rocco, knock it off," I said. "You're taking the teasing too far."

"Relax, Jules. He's a boy. He can take it. We're just having some fun. Right, pal?"

"I'm *not* your pal," Jack mumbled.

"What was that?" Rocco asked Jack.

"I said, 'I want some pie," Jack told Rocco.

Rocco cocked his head to the side. "They don't have pie in a sushi place. Here, try some of this spicy tuna roll."

The evening never got better. Jack eventually resorted to a stomachache; he actually did look sickly enough for me to check his forehead. No fever, but he began whining and told me he was going to throw up.

"Hey, stop with the babying," Rocco snapped, his disappointment with the lousy evening showing.

"That's not helpful, Rocco," I said.

"Well, Jack started it."

"Hey, Rocco, are you five years old? You're not in competition, you know. He's a kid who needs his mother. I'd better take him home."

"Okay, okay, I get it." Rocco ruffled Jack's hair. "Hey, kid, this is kinda new for me, too. I'm sorry if I came on too strong. Can we try this again sometime?"

Jack nodded, a doleful look on his face.

"Maybe we can go to the aquarium next time. Your mom tells me you like to fish."

Jack looked at his untouched plate of sushi and grimaced. "Not anymore."

I apologized for cutting the evening short and herded us toward the front door. Jack looked down at his feet as we left the restaurant, but I could have sworn his expression changed from sick to satisfied once we were out the door and headed home.

His attitude was much better that night during Jack's bedtime routine. Since he didn't like sleeping with his door closed, it was my job to block his bedroom doorway each night with a tower of stuffed animals. The barricade also kept Needles out of the bedroom.

Jack wasn't the kind of kid who slept with one special stuffed animal. He loved all of his Beanie Babies equally. At bedtime, we carried a large wicker basket of Beanie Babies over to his bed and shoved each of the critters under his red car bed sheets. Then, Jack climbed in to join his friends.

That night, Jack wanted me to stay with him until he had fallen asleep. I happily obliged and stretched out on top of the lumpy blanket next to him and began reading him one of his favorite bedtime stories. In between pages, I glanced over to see if he were still awake. He fought bravely to keep his eyes open, but his eyelids finally began to droop.

I kissed him on the forehead and said, "Best dreams, no bad dreams."

He repeated, in a little singsong voice, "Best dreams, no bad dreams," and fell into a deep slumber.

I stayed a while next to him, watching Jack's ever-changing expressions as he slept. Being Jack's mother was the most rewarding role of my life. I loved my sweet boy more than all the sparkling rhinestones on Miss America's dress. When he was born, my life had changed. I felt a deep sense of peace the first time I cradled him in my arms and entered into a new world where I would never be alone again.

Usually, I'd tiptoe out of his room after he nodded off, but this time, I was so sleep-deprived that I fell into a deep slumber right next to him.

The next morning around five-thirty, the sunlight streamed in waking me. I felt a crick in my neck from sleeping in the little red Corvette bed. As I laid motionless next to Jack, my heart was pounding at a terrific rate. Something about William's call nagged at me as I pulled myself into full wakefulness.

I tried to think it through. I hadn't heard from William since that call. Maybe he wasn't serious about his intention to share custody after all. I wanted Jack to get to know his father, but I also wanted to protect him from a narcissist who would never follow through with anything—and I'd have to, once again, pick up the pieces.

I couldn't lay in bed any longer trying to figure out William's next move. But when I tried getting out of bed without waking up Jack, somehow his Lego submarine ended up right under my feet, and I knocked it over. It broke into hundreds of little pieces. The Legos shattered. I was less concerned about the multiple puncture wounds on the bottoms of my feet and more annoyed about spending what little free time I had rebuilding the ship before Jack noticed I'd ruined his three-month project.

I grabbed a pillow from the bed and pulled off the racing stripe pillow cover. Using my arm like a squeegee, I shoved the Lego pieces into the case and under the bed. After I had cleaned up the remaining toy pieces, I heard my cell phone ringing somewhere in the room. I sprang up and ran on the balls of my feet in search of the phone.

Then I heard Jack's voice. I must have left the phone in his bed last night.

"Hello? Oh, hi Nathaniel. Uh, no, she can't talk right now. She's not here."

"Jack, give me the phone," I said, extending my hand.

Jack hopped out of bed, trying to get away from me. "No, Mommy's not coming in today."

"What?" I said. "Hand it over, Jack," I begged as I chased him around the room.

Jack giggled as he continued speaking with Nathaniel. "She's going on vacation to her favorite place in the whole wide world. Great America."

"Jack! Please!" I tried to grab the phone, but he managed to slip out from underneath me as I tackled him.

"She loves The Wizzer the most. And then, Mommy and Bugs Bunny are going to ride the train around the park. And then, she's going to stuff her face with cotton candy and churros." Jack laughed and ran inside the play teepee in his room.

I climbed in after him. "Give me that phone, young man." I finally secured the phone. "Nathaniel?" I could barely get out his name; I was so out of breath.

"He hung up," Jack said, with a devilish grin.

"What did he want?" I asked Jack, still crouched inside the teepee.

"He said he just wanted you to know that your first two appointments had switched to a different day, and your next appointment was at three."

"You're pretty good at taking a message, Mister. I could sure use a new receptionist. Do you want the job?"

"Nah, I think I'll stick to being a CIA agent."

"I understand. Wanna go to Great America?"

"YEAH!"

I was glad to play hooky from work matters for a bit. Or at least mull them over from the top of the American Eagle.

CHAPTER 8

" *Does this make me look fat?* " Those words, uttered by legions of clients over the years, were spoken this time by Fallon Hood, mother of Taylor Hood, who had been selected by the distinguished ball committee to participate in this year's exclusive debutante ball. Cotillion season had descended upon Chicago once again.

Naturally, I was thrilled when Fallon asked if I would design Taylor's gown. Since I'd always considered a debutante gown to be a bridal gown in disguise, it wouldn't take much imagination for me to create a princess ball gown for this future society star.

Fallon and Taylor were my favorite mother-daughter duo. I always looked forward to their appointment and had a warm feeling in my heart whenever I was around them.

Fallon had done a wonderful job teaching her daughter impeccable manners. Taylor was a soft-spoken, willowy teen who exhibited a genuine kindness. Not only did Taylor bake delicious chocolate chip cookies for the staff to enjoy, but she sent lovely thank-you notes after every fitting.

I affectionately referred to Fallon, an effervescent former actress, as a goddess. She had the flawless complexion of an airbrushed soap-opera queen and green cat-eyes that she elongated with liquid liner. Her neck was long and wrinkle-free, and she had full, red lips that she religiously kept inflated with collagen. If push came to shove, she could stand to lose ten pounds, but she said she would rather die than give up eating chocolate.

Last summer, I designed two stunning dresses for the wedding of her son: a rose-colored mother-of-the-groom gown for Fallon and an aubergine bridesmaid's dress for Taylor. Having worked with many different body types over the years, I was known for my fashion tricks to make a woman appear instantly thinner.

Fallon counted on me to make her Rubenesque frame look ten pounds lighter without her feeling any hunger pains. But she still looked to Taylor for moral support every time she asked her daughter, "Does this make me look fat?"

Of course, Taylor always reassured her mother with her sugar-spun voice, "No way, Mummy. You look beautiful."

I wished that more of my entitled clients were more like Fallon and Taylor. The thing I disliked most about my job was working with spoiled, disrespectful daughters, happy to point out their mothers' muffin tops.

Fallon had called yesterday, begging me to fit Taylor's appointment in for today. She frantically explained that an unexpected sorority party popped up on Taylor's social calendar. She was leaving for college a week earlier than expected and wouldn't be home again until Thanksgiving. Fortunately, Taylor's dress was close to ready for the second fitting. Apprehensively, I penciled in Taylor's final fitting for Saturday at noon and prayed that it wouldn't make me late for my only other appointment that day—one that could either make or break my career. I'd blocked out an entire day for this appointment, something I'd never done before.

A few months earlier, I'd spent my entire emergency fund on a full-page ad in *Modern Bride* magazine. I knew that for national bridal chains, this would be no more challenging than placing a classified ad in the *Reader*, a local freebie paper. But for me, it was a huge investment.

I spent weeks agonizing over the risks. Should I run a

series of smaller ads that would end up costing the same amount as the one-time, four-color, full-page ad? Would the advertisement really introduce my company to a nationwide clientele, as the ad sales executive swore it would? Or, was I risking everything and unnecessarily extending myself over budget? In the end, the thrill of recognition appealed more than financial solvency. I signed the contract for advertising space in the February issue of *Modern Bride*.

Thankfully, the ad scored a huge success, and I finally saw the business begin to grow and thrive. I felt such pride that the ad appeared on the page next to the legendary bridal designer, Carolina Herrera. But my excitement fizzled once the invoice came in the mail. My hand shook as I wrote the check for the final payment. For the first time in my career, I was certain that I didn't have enough money in my checking account to cover the payment. I had to find a way to get money in the account before that check arrived in the *Modern Bride* mailroom, or my bounced check would surely ruin my reputation in the bridal publishing world.

That night, I took a jar full of pennies to the Old Water Tower landmark fountain and threw the coins into the fountain. I kept wishing for a miracle and made a promise to myself that I would never do something so stupid again. After I'd thrown the last penny into the shallow water, I started to worry. A homeless man, holding a chewed-up Styrofoam cup, was creeping up to the fountain. No way was he going to steal my wishes! I gave him ten dollars to leave my pennies alone and shooed him away. A fat lot of good it did me. I still worried that after I'd left, the man returned to the fountain and fished out all of my hard-earned wishes.

But he must have left my pennies alone because the following morning I received a phone call from the administrative assistant to Melvin Carter, one of the wealthiest men in America. His secretary called to schedule an appointment the following Saturday for Melvin's wife,

Blayne Carter. I recognized the name immediately because fashion publicists from every magazine, newspaper, and tabloid were predicting that their daughter Alexa's upcoming wedding would be the biggest celebration the Manhattan social scene had witnessed in years.

The Carters and Alexa were making a special trip to Chicago on their private jet to take a tour of my establishment. I was *shocked*. Weren't there countless famous, talented designers in New York City with access to the best fabrics and the latest runway collections? Why come to Chicago when they had everything they needed right at home?

His secretary informed me that Blayne Carter became interested in learning more about my store after she asked some of her society friends, on different occasions, who designed their fabulous dresses. After repeatedly hearing Juliana Belle, she recognized my name in *Modern Bride* magazine. Blayne didn't want to go down the predictable go-to designer list of names; she wanted a unique and memorable experience for her daughter.

So, Blayne was flying in to meet with me in person to make sure I was capable of designing the sizable number of dresses in the bridal party. The members included the mothers of the bride and groom; ten bridesmaids; two flower girls; the grandmother of the bride; and the great-grandmother of the groom. Needless to say, I needed everything to be perfect for the Carters' first visit to Belle's Bridal Shop.

So far, everything was running on schedule for the Carter family's one-thirty arrival. But the stress level was rising rapidly as Calvin, the window designer, and Basil, the florist, decorated the shop. Instead of spreading their decorating magic throughout the store to make it sparkle, the two men were bickering with every interaction. Staple guns, tall bamboo trellises, and naked mannequin body parts covered the floor like booby traps (no pun intended).

It was a scientific fact that flowers and plants helped

improve mood and boost brain power. Even though I could always use more brain cells and enjoyed the sweet scent of blooming flowers, today I felt like I was working in a Venus fly-trap. Basil had gone completely overboard decorating the shop. The massive assortment of flowers he arranged for the work table was sucking all of the oxygen out of the air and making me lightheaded.

And then there was Jack's unexpected appearance. Tatiana had "the most important modeling tryout" of her life. At first I was irritated, but then I remembered how important everything seemed at her age. How could I say no? She dropped him off at the store, and lucky for me; Jack easily kept himself busy. He chatted with the seamstresses in the workroom and Big Wheeled around the shop.

Earlier, I'd explained to him that today wasn't going to be one of those days. He had to be a good boy and play quietly in Mommy's office. I also told him under no circumstances was he to bring Gus, his spotted leopard gecko to work. He was great at taking care of Gus—except when Gus decided to pull a disappearing act. On those days, shrieks from the workroom alerted us to the fact of where Gus had gone wandering—often up one of the seamstresses' stubbly legs. It seemed he felt at home there; the scenery, from his point of view, must have reminded him of the thick, prickly cacti he used to call home. The seamstress would run around, kicking and screaming until Gus finally untangled himself from her overgrown stubble and fell out from underneath her floral peasant skirt.

The commotion would send Jack running into the workroom with Gus's terrarium and a bottle of extra-strength aspirin for the seamstress. But not today. Gus was not going to be causing any problems because he was safe at home.

My biggest challenge was going to be keeping the peace between Basil and Calvin. The last time they worked together, Basil made a pass at Calvin. Naturally, Calvin overreacted and sued Basil for sexual harassment. Calvin agreed to drop the charges only if I agreed to provide a sexual-harassment training program for all of my employees. Since most of them spoke hardly a word of English, the lecture series looked more like a naughty game of charades than an informational seminar. Afterward, Basil became severely depressed and refused to work with Calvin. The problem with fresh florists is the same as fresh flowers. When they begin to fall apart, you don't want them around anymore. I wished I had the nerve to fire Basil and invest in silk flowers. As of yet, I didn't have a backup plan and begged both men to make today the exception to the rule.

And, of course, the phone began to ring incessantly from the moment I sent Zoë out for Jack's lunch. To make matters worse, I had a walk-in customer looking for a tiara to complement her veil. I kept my energy high by running back and forth to my office every couple of minutes to take a breather from the chaos.

I sprinted into the office for the third time. "Jack," I begged, "please turn down the television set. I can't hear the music playing on the overhead speakers in the showroom."

"Sorry, Mommy," he said, his expression downcast. "I'll give myself a timeout."

One look into those kind blues eyes of his and I couldn't help but smile. "That's okay, kiddo," I said, messing up his already-messy hair. "Really. It's fine." What a kid. Whenever he thought that he had misbehaved, he took it upon himself to take a timeout. Well, most of the time.

"Jules," Basil said, knocking on the door. "Calvin is being such a sh…"

"Basil! Language!" I said, pointing to Jack.

"…shitake mushroom," he said, changing course more quickly than I'd given him credit for. "Can you please talk to him?"

"Yes, but I need to check on Taylor first. Can it wait?"

"I suppose," he said, turning on his heels to leave. "But

there's no telling what that stupid mushroom head will do next." He waved at Jack as he left.

I looked at Jack and we both shook our heads.

"Way too much drama," Jack said, making us both laugh.

After giving him a big hug, I returned to Fallon, who was busy taking candid pictures of Taylor's fitting for her debutante scrapbook. Taylor looked regal in her ball gown appliquéd with blossoms and petals as she stood on the pedestal in the middle of the showroom.

"Smile, Girls," Fallon snapped another picture. "Wow, I've never noticed how much you two resemble one another. You and my daughter could pass for sisters, Juliana."

"I wish," replied the *only child* in me.

"Jules, stand behind Taylor; that way we can see the gown better," Fallon begged.

I poked my face out from behind Taylor's back and forced a practiced smile. Unlike Wing's sneaky snap photo shoot, I didn't mind in the least that Fallon was taking photos, but I could have lived without the steady camera flashes. Another flash went off, and more tiny little black spots eclipsed my vision. Thank goodness the camera began to buzz while it rewound the film.

"Oh, no. Time to change the roll," Fallon sighed. How many rolls of film had she brought with her?

I was almost finished with Taylor's fitting when I glanced back to see a couple of walk-in customers enter the shop. As if the camera flashes weren't enough, I was nearly blinded by the glare from the woman's thick canary diamond ring and bracelet, which matched her bright skin-tight yellow turtleneck, pants, and matching pumps. You could tell she was an attention seeker.

The man, on the other hand, didn't look like he craved attention in the least. He was an ordinary-looking fellow in his late fifties. He wore wire-framed glasses, a burgundy striped tie, and an understated dark suit. Age-wise, they looked like father and daughter, but there was little question about the nature of their relationship. Even though I would have loved to work with them just to find out their story, there was simply not enough time. I needed to finish the fitting as quickly as possible with Taylor. I couldn't afford to turn away any potential client, though, and fortunately, Nathaniel was ready to help.

The zoo-like atmosphere got even crazier when Max Marshal, the producer from the Style Network, finally showed up for his surprise visit. Sitting semi-reclined in the tan suede massage chair in the "Groom's Corner," he was scribbling in his notepad as he watched my every move. Of all the days, hc happened to choose today, the most atypical day, to observe my normal daily interactions with my staff and clients.

I'd created the "Groom's Corner" after one too many men entered my store looking uncomfortable. It didn't matter how powerful or worldly they were; somehow the sight of expensive women's bridal apparel made men shrink in size. The "Groom's Corner" allowed fiancés, fathers, and husbands to sit back and relax. Or check the latest business news or stock market results on CNBC on the wall-mounted television set. I had the latest copies of *The Wall Street Journal*, *Sports Illustrated*, and *Golf Digest* (though the *Cosmopolitan* magazine tucked between the magazines always seemed to be the one left open) neatly arranged on the coffee table. I also kept a small bar stocked with sodas, beer, and snacks nearby.

I got the idea for the setup while shopping for a couch with Jack. Surprised that not a single kid was jumping from couch to couch in the furniture store, I noticed the colorful sign for "The Kid's Corner" outfitted with video games and pinball machines to entertain them while their parents shopped. I figured the concept would also work well at my shop, and it had. The "Groom's Corner" made it much easier to complete the sale with the female clients, but allowed them to still have him near enough to offer an opinion when asked.

By the time Zoë arrived with the McDonald's Happy Meal and small vanilla shake for Jack, Nathaniel was still busy helping the drop-in customer. I noticed that he was carrying an expensive handmade silk negligée set to the fitting room. Before entering the room, he gave me a thumbs-up.

"Good job," I mouthed to him. He was familiar with the new set of rules I'd recently established. No one was to leave the store without buying something. I didn't care if it was an evening gown or a hair barrette. I winked at Nathaniel and signaled Zoë to help the customer who was trying on tiaras and veils.

Jack, who could smell McDonald's a mile away, ran out and snatched the food from Zoë's hands and ran back into the office.

I looked around to check on the male guest who'd come in with Nathaniel's prospect. I noticed he had no interest in hanging out in the "Groom's Corner" with Max while his friend tried on negligées in the fitting room. He appeared quite comfortable meandering around the shop, looking at all of the accessory display cases. As long as he was looking, there was a good chance he would be buying, so I didn't give him a second thought. I went back to Fallon, who was in the throes of planning the Cotillion after-party.

"So, as I was saying," she said, "the string quartet could be set up in the foyer. I think it's a lovely way to welcome our guests."

"I agree," Taylor added.

"What would you prefer, a quartet or a harpist?" asked Fallon.

While Taylor and Fallon discussed the details of the party, I made a small adjustment to the plunging neckline of Taylor's bodice. It was a little too low cut and would not conform to the Cotillion rules.

As I was finishing pinning the fabric between her breasts, I looked over at a rack of sample gowns in the far corner of the room. I could have sworn that one of the white silk gowns was moving. I assumed Jack was playing his camping game again, and the dress was his pop-up tent. I was about to shoo him away when I glanced down at the floor. Instead of finding a pair of glow-in-the-dark Velcro sneakers, I spied a pair of men's black leather tasseled loafers.

"Taylor, will you excuse me for a minute?" I said and headed for the rack of gowns. En route, I heard the window designer's high-pitched shout coming from the front window. I immediately changed course and ran over to see what was happening.

"Basil, get those stinky pink flowers out of here this instant!" Calvin yelled, kicking aside the flowers on the floor.

"How can you say that about my Red Canna blooms? Leave my fragile flowers alone! Why don't you get rid of your butch-looking mannequins," Basil said, pushing over a mannequin.

"Well, at least they don't shave their chest to go clubbing every Saturday night," Calvin said, smirking.

"How dare you!" Basil lunged at Calvin.

"Enough!" I said and broke up the fight. "First of all, please, watch what you're saying. Jack's in the other room."

"Sorry, Jules, but Calvin is acting like such a sh…"

I glared at him. "Not again, Basil." I grabbed Calvin by the wrist and looked at his watch. "It is now 12:38 PM. You have exactly ten minutes to finish your display and clean up this mess. And Basil, take your delicate Canna petals and put them back where they belong."

I grabbed a can of air freshener and turned on my heels, leaving the two of them staring at each other with sheer contempt. I began spraying away any smells of the French fries, replacing it with the lovely scent of magnolia in preparation for the Carter family's impending arrival.

I'd forgotten all about the bobbing white silk gown and began to walk back towards Taylor when I noticed the tasseled loafers again—this time on the floor behind the antique jewelry display case. The back of the case covered the man from his waist to mid-thigh. However, I looked down and noticed that his pants pooled around his ankles.

At that moment, Jack sped out of the office holding his favorite racecar and began dragging it over every flat surface of the store. My motherly instinct informed me that his next test track was going to be the jewelry case.

Running from the opposite direction, I catapulted over a mannequin head still lying on the floor, and picking up the pace, leaped over a large glass bowl filled with roses, and just missed the portable steamer before I met up with Jack in front of the case.

Jack had been raised around many diverse—even unusual—people at the shop and was paying no attention to the man.

"Look, Mommy," he said as he moved the car back and forth on the glass display case. "The car's driving on thin ice. Wanna see me make it go really fast? Oh no, it's out-a-control! Watch out, ahh," he yelled as he launched the car off the case and plummeted toward the floor.

I grabbed Jack's tiny hand before the car could crash and burn in the pile of pants on the ground. "Jack!" I said, a little too harshly. "Did you finish your lunch?"

"Not yet, I'm busy racing."

"Well, race to the office and finish your lunch before it gets cold. Please."

"Okay, Mommy."

Jack turned his sports car into an airplane, and after a couple of loops, they both landed safely in the office.

Finally, I could confront the sick bastard in my store. But he'd disappeared again. I looked around the store but didn't see the leather tassels anywhere.

Nervous about the mystery man, but with a dozen things to finish before the Carters arrived, I checked in first with Taylor. Luckily, all I had left to do was pin the hem of her dress.

I knelt by her white shoes with cute rhinestone buckles and began pinning the back of the gown. Every so often, I glanced in the mirror to check if the front length of the dress was even with the sides. During one of my hem checks, my eyes caught a glimpse of the black loafers once again. From the shoes, my eyes traveled up the navy wool pants, which, mercifully, were belted once again around his waist. I couldn't believe my eyes; I froze, afraid of what would happen next.

Mr. Tassels was standing by the French armoire holding a mid-size flower bouquet of Red Canna blooms in one hand and staring lustfully at Taylor. I had always thought of Taylor as a sweet and innocent young girl, not some temptress. She had soft features, fair skin, and deep blue eyes. Her blonde hair, flat-ironed straight, fell just above her shoulders, and her tanned body was thin but curvy. No way was I going to let this guy deflower her in his mind. Fortunately, Taylor was so immersed in conversation with her mother that neither she nor Fallon noticed anything going on around them.

I pretended to go back to hemming the dress, but I felt the heat of my anger. I couldn't believe it. With a store full of people, was I the only person to see what was going on here? I had a feeling that Mr. Tassels was practiced at the art of deception. This interloper, who snubbed my Groom's Corner, was now turning my beautiful shop into a house of sin right before my eyes. As much as he tried to block what he was doing with the hand holding the bouquet, I could clearly see what Mr. Tassels was up to.

"Please stop. Please, oh please, stop," I muttered to myself. I knew I had to do something, but what? Before I could make a move, I heard Taylor scream.

"Oh my God. It's SO gross!" Taylor exclaimed.

I was too late. My stomach heaved.

"Mom, it's like the most disgusting thing I've ever seen. It's so big and slimy!"

"What are you talking about, dear?" Fallon asked her daughter.

"And spotted!" added Taylor, crossing her arms in front of her.

"That's it, I'm calling the police," I said, frantic for a resolution.

"Stop it! Both of you," Fallon demanded. "Stop with the overacting right now."

Fallon was in full mom mode and the voice of authority. Taylor and I stopped.

"Seriously, it's just a cute little gecko," Fallon said, laughing and pointing at Gus. "He's not going to hurt you. Look, he's just sitting there, minding his own business."

Sure enough, there was Gus, sprawled out on a pincushion on the table next to Taylor.

"Forgive me. That's my son's gecko," I said, apologetically. "He's not allowed at the shop. Jack must have snuck him into his backpack again."

"Come here, Bad Boy," I said, as I picked Gus up by his tail and put him in an empty shoebox lying on the floor. I closed the box and poked some holes in the box top. "I'll deal with you later," I said, pushing the box underneath the worktable.

Taylor and Fallon went back to their party talk. And I refocused on Mr. Tassels. He was well into his performance when I released the dress, letting it fall to the floor. I stood and prepared myself to kick Mr. Tassels out. Capitalism has its limits! Both Fallon and Taylor looked puzzled by my actions.

My heart raced as I walked up to him, ready to kick him in his twig and berries.

"Hey, what's up?" Jack asked. He'd come out of the office and was standing in the middle of the doorway with his hands on his hips. "I can't find the ketchup, Mommy."

"In the office, in the mini fridge," I said pushing him back inside and trying to block his field of vision. "Ketchup's on the right-side shelf."

"Okay, okay. I'm going," he said, rolling his eyes.

I heard Fallon whisper to Taylor behind me. "Jules doesn't seem herself today."

"Yeah, I know," Taylor said. "I wonder if something's wrong."

I was about to explain myself when Mr. Tassels' girlfriend came out of the fitting room, Nathaniel following her and shaking his head.

"Thank you, just looking today. We'll be back again," she said casually. She held out her hand to Mr. Tassels. He took it, and they strolled out of the shop. He had the nerve to wink at me as he left.

"Please, don't ever come back," I said under my breath.

"Ms. Belle, are you okay?" asked Taylor.

"Absolutely," I said. "Does anyone have the time?"

One-fifteen, a chorus of watch-wearers informed me. Half the day was gone and neither Nathaniel or Zoë had made a sale. Zoë's client had left after uttering those cringe-worthy words: "I'm going to have to think about it."

In the meantime, Jack had fallen asleep on a pile of cashmere fabric in the office, and Calvin and Basil had done a remarkable job with the store and were now out to lunch together. Go figure.

Max Marshal was packing up as Blayne Carter, and her entourage arrived at one-thirty sharp. She was impressed with the store, staff, and the design. However, she remarked that the flowers gave her hay fever. Nathaniel was more than happy to toss the flowers in the garbage.

Max vigorously shook my hand and said with a big grin, "I think I've seen plenty for one day. You're perfect for the Style Network. I'll be in touch."

A few weeks after the Cotillion, Fallon sent me a professional portrait of Taylor in her fairy princess gown. To my surprise, she included some press photos and candids of Taylor's final fitting in her thoughtful thank-you note. She mentioned there was one particular picture she thought I'd find interesting.

The picture, in wide format, captured Taylor smiling at the camera as I pinned her skirt. To the left of us, Max Marshal was reading the *Cosmopolitan* magazine. Off to the side, Jack used ketchup to finger-paint the showroom wall. To the right of Taylor, Basil had Calvin in a headlock. And in the far-right-hand-corner, by the armoire, Master Bator Von Tassles was grinning from ear to ear as he watched the fitting with his ol' one-eye peeking out from his open fly. And people wonder why I don't design men's formalwear!

CHAPTER 9

"Come on, Jules, please hurry up. The dress still isn't fitting right."

I was glad that Penelope and I had decided to slip away to the cathedral's bathroom to make this urgent repair in private. In the restroom sitting area, I got down on my hands and knees and crawled under the skirt just minutes before the wedding ceremony was about to begin.

"Can you see anything?" asked Penelope.

"I'm trying, but I can't see through all of the rows of crinoline." I began peeling away the many layers of tulle netting as though the gown was a gigantic onion.

"Well, it's driving me crazy," Penelope said, yanking on the skirt.

"Hey, stop that!" I yelled, as my left false eyelash got stuck in the netting. I brushed away the mesh fabric that ripped off the fake eyelash.

"That's just great," I said, blinking a few times.

"Oh, you found the problem?"

"Nope, not yet."

"Do you think it's possible that the netting got tangled up with the slip?"

"I doubt it. Hold on, I'm going to try to get a closer look." As I burrowed my way up Penelope's body, the crinoline tore away at my expensive chignon hairstyle. I continued to push the netting away, trying to see what had Penelope Van Zealand's panties in a bunch, literally.

"Good news. I can see the garter now, and it doesn't look like that's the problem," I said.

"Keep looking," she demanded.

"Can you please stand still?" I begged her, trying to regain my balance. I slipped off my satin pumps to get better traction as I continued to guide my way through the fabric towards the back of the dress. About halfway there, my oversized teardrop chandelier earring caught on the tulle netting.

"Ouch!" I yelped, jerking my head away. The motion caused the earring to rip from my earlobe and get tangled in the netting. I decided to leave it there, along with my eyelash. Honest to God, I felt like a fly in a massive silk spider web.

"Are you okay, Juliana?"

"Just fine," I said.

As I knelt in my champagne-colored evening gown, the bugle beads dug into my knees. I shifted and pushed the lining surrounded by yards of tulle towards Penelope's hips. "Did that help any?"

"No, it's still tangled up in something."

"Why don't you take off the dress?" I yelled out from between her legs.

"I don't have time. The ceremony is about to begin, and the photographer is waiting to get a few candid shots before I walk down the aisle."

"Thank goodness the photographer's missing out on this little photo op," I said under my breath. "Oh, here we go."

"What is it?"

"By any chance, are you wearing rhinestone panties?"

"Oh, wow. Is that what's going on? The tulle probably got hooked on one of the stones," she said matter-of-factly.

I closed one eye to get a better look. "Yup, I believe that's the culprit."

"Oh, thank God! Now, be very careful when you unhook it. I don't want my panties to rip."

My job never failed to surprise me. Is this what it meant to bend over backward for a customer? I truly didn't get paid enough to deal with my clients' crazy requests.

After I extracted myself from Penelope's wedding gown, I made sure that both the dress and the bride looked perfect. Once I gave Penelope the thumbs up, the happy bride darted to the entrance of the church, ready to take her walk down the aisle.

I was about to leave the bathroom when I caught a glimpse of my reflection in the mirror by the sink and wanted to cry. My hair and makeup were a disaster, and my gown was wrinkled. Not to mention that I was only wearing one earring because the other one was still being held hostage in Penelope's gown. I needed to pull myself together quick before I missed my bride's walk down the aisle. I decided to go with the single statement earring trend, combed back my hair, peeled off the other false eyelash, and headed out the door.

Times like these made me feel like the bottom person on the totem pole. Even though I traveled in the same social circles, looked the part, and could nab a reservation at the trendy new hot spot in town—the reality was somewhat different. My clients wintered in Palm Beach while I made road trips to the Wisconsin Dells Monsoon Water Park. At the end of the day, I was just a privately owned small bridal business owner competing against a huge corporate bridal world.

The bridal industry's revenues kept rising higher than the Sears Tower, and big companies were now the main players. I couldn't afford any mistakes or mishaps because I could easily lose a bride to my sizable competition. Sometimes, I felt more like an actress, who must outperform her competition to get hired for the next role (which was one of the main reasons I had to keep my failed marriage and cynical attitude about the institution of marriage to myself).

In my case, the next big show was the latest society wedding. Even though Blayne Carter hired me to design her daughter's entire wedding party, that was yesterday, and I knew I couldn't rest on my laurels. Today, I had to be *on*, full of energy and vision. It didn't matter what else I had going on in my life; I needed to get to the ceremony on time to watch my dress get married.

Still feeling sorry for myself, I found a place to sit in the back of the magnificent cathedral with the beautiful stained-glass windows. Alone as usual. I didn't want to ask Rocco to accompany me because we hadn't been dating long enough. Besides, he had already told me that he hated to, in his words, "wear a gorilla suit."

I got a warm feeling inside as I watched the groom enter, followed by his best man, groomsmen, and bridesmaids to the sound of hymns sung by the sixty-member boys choir.

Following a long pause, Penelope made her grand entrance wearing the Victorian white duchess-silk gown abundantly appliquéd with original 18th-century lace and scattered pearls. Her blonde updo was lightly covered by a sheer royal-length veil made with hundreds of hand-embroidered sequins, glistening now in the sunlight streaming through the colorful windows. My heart beat quickly as I watched her carry a bouquet of tightly arranged French nosegays, bluebird roses, and scented geranium leaves that befitted a storybook heroine. Penelope looked radiant as she floated past an ocean of pastel-colored flowers, down the white-satin carpeted aisle on the arm of her father to the "Wedding March" from Wagner's "Lohengrin."

As I watched the breathtaking train trail behind Penelope's small frame, I was embarrassed to admit that I felt a small pang of envy. I worked with women on a daily basis who enjoyed an extravagant lifestyle and rarely felt jealous. But it was different with Penelope. During every appointment, she shared the latest news about her dream wedding to Tad, aka Prince Charming. I tried my hardest to act enthusiastic, but inside a dull ache grew in my heart.

Once the hour-long ceremony was over, I left the church and headed over to the lavish, six-hundred guest reception at The Drake Hotel, overlooking Lake Michigan. For the first twenty minutes, I watched waiters dressed in white dinner jackets busily passing trays of chilled caviar. Again, those pangs of sadness grabbed hold of me.

During the remainder of the cocktail reception in the polished mahogany foyer with the hand-painted ceiling, I positioned myself by a large palm tree and sipped sparkling champagne while listening to the strolling violinist. I managed to situate myself in a great spot where the waiters came out with fresh hors d'oeuvre trays every few minutes. I stuffed myself with delicious duck pâté canapés and enjoyed the big-band orchestra that eventually took the place of the violinists. As I listened to the music, my mood altered, and I started to feel grateful I was able to attend such a magnificent wedding.

I walked over to pick up my place card, curious to find out at which table I'd be spending the remainder of the evening while making small talk with the other principle members of Penelope's entourage: her life coach, interior decorator, and yoga instructor. The other key members of "Team Penelope."

At first, I felt honored to be included on the exclusive guest list—until I realized the real reason I always received an invitation. Surprisingly, it wasn't for my natural conversational skills. It just so happened that I played a crucial role in the wedding. I was the official wedding gown's guardian.

Before I could grab another canapé from the waiter, I spotted Penelope out of the limelight for a change. She motioned for me to come over to her.

Guardian of the dress, reporting for duty! I set down my glass and made my way to her.

"Hey, Jules. Would you mind helping me with my bustle?" she asked.

"Of course. There's a restroom around the corner."

"Oh no. We're not doing that again," said Penelope, as she grabbed me by the wrist and pulled me into the large reception area.

"Right here?" I questioned her.

"Sure, why not? It should take only a minute."

While I straightened and struggled with the bustle, Penelope could barely stand still.

"Delilah!" she called out to a beautiful young brunette dripping in sequins. "Darling, you look fantastic. Meet my amazing designer. Oh, and grab Aspen and Sophie."

As the ladies walked towards us, Penelope whispered, "Jules, I'm excited to introduce you to my girlfriends."

The group of women and I exchanged greetings.

"Ladies," Penelope said, "Juliana is one of the most talented and extraordinary designers in Chicago. Can you believe she designed this fabulous wedding gown? It's a work of art, right?"

The ladies nodded in agreement.

"Delilah, you need to make an appointment with Juliana if…I mean…when you get married."

I felt grateful for the referral, but I also knew that Penelope was tricking me with flattery. Her showy display wasn't intended to shine a light on me; it was designed to attract even more attention towards her.

For the remaining cocktail hour, we continued to mingle with guests. Penelope paraded around the great reception hall like a grand dame, holding me by the hand and affectionately introducing me as, "my designer." Once Penelope finished working the room, she released me from her clutches and rejoined her new husband at the end of the reception.

At the completion of the cocktail hour, guests were directed to the Gold Coast Room by way of the velvet-covered staircase. Still holding on to my empty champagne glass, I disappeared into the slowly dispersing crowd. Being among these guests, I wanted to believe I was one of these tightly gowned, narrow-waisted society ladies. But Penelope's feigned conversations with her girlfriends reminded me that I was simply the designer behind the gown.

Inside the regal ballroom, the soft lighting from the elaborate chandeliers created an intimate atmosphere. Colonnades bedecked in cream and gold spiral vines surrounded the guests, and heavy eggshell French floral damask cloths with gold tassels covered the dining tables and matching covered chairs. The focal point of each table— the towering floral arrangements—echoed Penelope's bridal bouquet.

When the orchestra leader invited Penelope and Tad to cut the wedding cake, it was my cue to leave. I walked over to the corner of the dance floor to watch the cake-cutting ceremony and then planned on slipping away, unnoticed.

As I observed two waiters wheel in the cake, I tried to imagine Rocco and me cutting the cake. *What?* Where had that come from? I barely knew the guy. I consoled myself that I was just trying the idea on for size, which for me was a big step. The vision no longer seemed off-putting. Not a resounding recommendation but I felt a glimmer of hope. Maybe it *was* possible for me to be married, have a family, and run a successful business as a married woman.

Sure, Rocco was a little rough around the edges, but he was a good, normal guy—not a William, at all. You'd have thought I was living in the 19th century the way I made divorce a death-of-love sentence. People got divorced all the time—and kept trying—didn't they? Besides, Jack needed to have more men in his life. That poncho *was* a dead giveaway!

Once the waiters finished setting up the cake and left the stage, Penelope forcefully pulled Tad towards the center of the dance floor.

"Can somebody get me a mike?" she demanded. The unwilling groom tried backing away. "Don't you dare move, you dirty little coward," Penelope hissed at her groom.

The confused orchestra leader handed Penelope a wireless microphone.

"Excuse me, everyone," Penelope tapped on the tip of the microphone. "Can I have your attention, please?" Penelope shot Tad a nasty look.

Tad appeared sickly and pale as a ghost.

"Are you going to tell them, or do I have to do everything?" she asked Tad.

He looked down at the floor.

She stared at him in silence for a moment. "Fine, I'll do it." Penelope held the microphone close to her pursed lips. "Hello everyone. I have an announcement to make. This marriage is officially over. You can all go home now." She held out her hand and dropped the microphone on the floor causing a loud thump over the sound system.

Guests looked shocked, and loud chatter filled the room. Nonchalantly, Penelope walked over to the coconut cream wedding cake and grabbed the top layer. As she held up the topper, the entire Gold Coast Room froze. A few guests squirmed in their chairs.

"Here's to my lying, cheating, player of a husband, Tad!" She yelled theatrically. With a mighty wind up, she flung the top tier of cake at the groom.

Tad managed to duck while the cake continued its forward trajectory. The projectile hit a pillar, causing some of the cake filling to splatter onto my forehead. The terrified bandleader ran over to me and graciously handed me his pocket square. As I wiped my forehead, I watched Penelope walk over to the closest table, where she picked up a heavy lead glass vase of white rose buds. The guests at that table involuntarily ducked.

"Baby," Tad begged, "don't do anything crazy."

Penelope hurled the vase at Tad with all her strength. Her aim remained poor and the vase shattered into a million pieces all over the dance floor. Waiters began rushing around frantically, trying to clean up the shards of glass. Tad stood in the middle of the dance floor too stunned to move.

Calmly, Penelope walked over to her parents' table. "Daddy, may I borrow your plate?" Her father opened his mouth, but no words came out. She took the plate without waiting for him to respond and held it to her chest, without bothering to scrape off the remaining beef tenderloin. In one swift motion, she flung the plate at Tad's head like a Frisbee. Another near miss.

Penelope threw up her hands and walked over to her mother. "Mother, may I?" she asked rhetorically then picked up not only her plate, but also the plate of the guest sitting next to her, and took aim at her betrothed.

"Don't do it!" Tad warned.

She lowered the plates. "Okay, Tad. Whatever you say," she said sweetly.

"Good girl," Tad laughed nervously and took a step forward.

Whoosh! Like a sword thrower, Penelope flung both plates at once. Tad yelped as one of the plates clocked him in the stomach while the other one missed him by a centimeter and broke a lead-glass mirror behind him.

Now hysterical, Penelope continued to tear up the Gold Coast Room. She was throwing anything she could get her hands on. "How dare you do this to me!" she growled. "I hate you! I hate you!"

Four police officers charged into the room and surrounded Penelope. She ignored them and continued her tirade. One officer managed to grab her by the waist, but she dug her fake nails into his arm. He pulled away to find three press-on nails embedded in his arm like little pink daggers. She continued to kick and claw at anyone who came near her.

Upset guests were leaving in droves, and I became caught

in the wave of a stampede toward the exit. I pushed my way through the shoulder-to-shoulder throng, and as I was at the front of the room, I felt my knees buckle as I slipped on something slick. I landed hard on the cold, wet marble floor.

"Are you all right?" asked a concerned guest from behind me.

I waved my hand. "Oh, goodness," I said, "I'm perfectly fine." Then I noticed the dripping blood and spotted a huge shard of glass lodged in my palm. Within seconds, my body broke out in a cold sweat.

Next thing I knew, I was lying on a couch, my vision blurry, not sure how much time had passed or where I was. Dazed and confused, I sprang into a seated position and nearly fell off the couch.

"Hey, take it easy," said the police officer as he grabbed me by the arms and helped me regain my balance. "Are you okay?"

"Who are you?" I asked.

"I'm Officer Ross Reilly."

"Am I under arrest?"

"No," he said, smiling at me. "You fainted after you cut your hand on some glass while leaving the wedding. Do you have any memory of that happening?"

"Sorry, I don't recall," I said in a throaty whisper, looking at my neatly bandaged hand.

He continued, "The paramedics should be returning shortly."

I took a closer look at the bandaging. Then I peered out of the window of the lobby and noticed two police cars with flashing lights parked in front of the Drake Hotel. Nothing was making any sense to me.

"Do you remember your name?" asked Officer Ross.

"Juliana Belle," I said, extending my mummified stump. The look on my face must have confirmed what a stupid gesture that was on my part, and we both laughed. That made my head ache, but I wanted out of the hotel. "If I'm not under arrest, can I leave?"

"Well, you hit your head pretty hard on the marble floor, so I need you to stay put until the paramedics check your stats one last time."

"Do you know what happened tonight between Tad and Penelope?"

Officer Ross nodded. "But I'm not permitted to say."

"Please, Officer. I'm worried about Penelope."

He looked around the room and whispered, "Don't tell anyone that I told you. Okay?"

"Scout's honor." I held up two fingers and gave him an innocent smile.

"Apparently, the bride caught the groom with another woman."

"No!" I cupped my bandaged hand over my mouth. "Do you happen to recall her name?"

"It was something like Lila."

"Delilah?" I interjected.

"Yeah, that's it."

"Oh, how awful."

The police officer's walkie-talkie went off. "I'm sorry, ma'am, but I need to get back inside. Please wait here for the paramedics. They'll be back shortly." He handed me a bag of ice and left.

While I applied ice to my forehead, I noticed three police officers escorting Penelope through the lobby. Her hands were handcuffed in front of her, and the back hem of her gown was thrown over her head like a cape, the way gangsters throw towels or jackets over their heads in similar situations.

Officer Ross read Penelope her rights. "You are being charged with spousal abuse. You have the right to remain silent. Anything you say can and will be used against you. You have the right to an attorney…"

"Penelope," I screamed, jumping up from the couch. "It's me, Juliana."

She tried to look around, but couldn't see through her dress. "Jules, is that you?"

"Uh-huh," I said, as I ran up to Penelope and gave Officer Ross a half-smile.

He nodded his head.

"Is there anything I can do to help?" I asked.

"Yeah, get me the name of a good divorce attorney."

My client, Scarlett Smith, would be surprised to hear the new record breaking time that it took for one of my brides to hire a lawyer: not three years, but just three hours.

"Will do," I said, trying to stay close to Penelope.

"Oh, and promise me that you'll charge that slutty whore, Delilah, double when she visits your shop to buy her wedding gown. I never liked that two-faced, little bitch any how."

"I promise." I stopped walking, from shortness of breath, and watched Penelope continue to fight off the officers.

"Ma'am, let's go," barked Officer Ross.

"Oh, all right," Penelope said. "You don't have to push!"

As Penelope stepped into the waiting police car, I glanced at her yoga-sculpted rear end exposed for the whole world to see. My head throbbed, my hand hurt, our dresses were a mess, and it was the end of Penelope's fairytale's final chapter—as well, in all likelihood, to my little fantasy of starting over and getting married again.

The only good thing? With a quick flick of my wrist, I had retrieved my earring dangling from the upturned layers of tulle.

CHAPTER 10

"**O**kay, buddy, where did you hide my keys this time?" I asked.

"I don't know!" Jack shouted from his room.

"Listen, Jack, the driver's waiting for me outside. I need my keys this second or…"

Before I could finish my sentence, my cat, Needles, meowed and stood up in her kitty bed laying in the hallway. She stretched out in front of me as though she were trying to tell me something. I picked her up and saw something shiny in her bed.

"Ah, thank you, Kitty," I said, giving her a kiss on the nose and retrieving my keys from her cushion.

"I guess you're off the hook this time, Jack though we both know how those keys got there in the first place." Now that the coast was clear, Jack joined me in the hallway, his hands behind his back. I gave him a kiss, then glanced one more time in the mirror. What a ridiculous looking dress!

As I opened the front door, Jack jumped in front of me with the water gun he'd received at his fifth birthday party. "Mommy, why do you have to go to the stupid wedding? Come to the beach with Tatiana and me."

I looked at Tatiana in her string bikini. "Tatiana, it's the beginning of September, don't you think you should change into something warmer with more coverage before you leave for the beach?"

Tatiana glared at me but turned around to go change.

"You play wedding every day. Please come with us," Jack begged. "We're going to have so much fun. See…" Jack let loose with the gun.

I couldn't believe the damage such a little gun could do. My makeup was a mess, and my hair took the brunt of the spray. I looked at my watch: 1:20 PM. I was already twenty minutes late and had zero time to dry my hair and reapply my makeup. I grabbed a towel, purse, and wedding card full of cash, and headed for the door. Just as I was about to leave the house, I remembered the heart shaped baking dish of beef Wellington and made a mad dash for the kitchen.

Inside the Town Car on the long drive to Galena, I managed to reapply my makeup and asked the driver to run the heater on high to dry my hair. Flushed and overheated, I had sweated through my polyester dress by the time we pulled up to the forest preserve entrance.

I read the dusty sign out loud, "Explore Riser Woods and Experience the Prairie Life," and sighed. "Stanley, know anything about the Prairie life?"

"Not a thing." Stanley shook his head and chuckled.

"I was afraid you were going to say that," I said, laughing nervously. "Can I have another minute before I begin my experience?"

"Sure. Take your time. You might want to bring an umbrella with you."

I looked out the car window at the clouds forming overhead. "I forgot to bring one. I must admit; I'm feeling very unprepared today."

I wasn't quite ready for the kumbaya of a hippie wedding—or any wedding for that matter. Ever since Penelope's debacle a few weeks ago, I'd been thinking about the hopelessness of finding a good groom for myself. The other night, Rocco had leaned over to give me a goodnight kiss, and I actually flinched. He noticed. I noticed. But neither one of us said anything. I just awkwardly hugged him, said goodnight, and closed the door on him. I was tired of this see-saw of good and sad feelings, but I couldn't quite shake them.

When Stanley let out a big sigh, I brought my thoughts back to the wedding in the woods. I straightened my dress, checked my restored makeup, and got out of the car.

As I stood motionless at the deserted entrance to the trail, I asked Stanley, "Are you sure this is the right place?"

"Yes, ma'am."

I didn't see a sign, balloons, flowers or any indication that this was the place where Melody, my best girlfriend from high school, was about to be married. There was no music playing, just the loud lawnmower sounds of the buzzing cicadas. I was ready to get back in the car and call it a day when I heard, "Oh my God. Jules, is that you?"

Lela Thompson, the most popular girl in high school. She wouldn't be caught dead talking to Melody or me back then. What the heck was she doing here?

I started to walk over to Lela when Stanley touched my arm. "Juliana, don't forget this." He handed me my large glass dish.

"Oh, thank you. I almost forgot." I smiled and took the dish from him. "So, I'll see you back here at eleven o'clock tonight?"

"I'll be waiting right here where I dropped you off," he said.

"Thank you. See you later." I walked over to Lela, who was looking me up and down.

"Did you design the bridesmaids' dresses?" she asked.

"No, I didn't." I shuddered. Design a tiger-beetle-green-Dacron-polyester-ruffle-at-the-neck-and-butt-bow dress that made me look like a lampshade? No way. But I wasn't going to tell Lela that.

"You're in a wedding and didn't design the dresses? You

must feel sick to be wearing someone else's label."

"Actually, I'm fine with it."

"Well, I'm glad that *you* ended up with the beetle juice dress. When she insisted that *I* wear the green dress, I told Melanie that neon green makes me look sickly and that you're such a sweetheart that you wouldn't mind. So, she gave me the pink color instead. Isn't that great?"

"Yeah. Sure. I appreciate having the opportunity to wear a different color other than pink, my favorite color."

That remark just sailed right over her. "Then again, I suppose you don't make dresses for $50.00," Lela continued. "Can you believe this wedding? I don't know how they did it on a $1,000 budget, but they did. You would think they grew up as hippies and not North Shore entitled kids."

"To each her own," I said.

After going away to Madison University, Melanie rebelled against her wealthy and extravagant upbringing and wanted to live a simple, eco-friendly life. She met her soon-to-be-husband, Lenny, in college. I hadn't met him yet though Melody had told me all about him—an eccentric artist who was the complete opposite of her banker father. Lenny had resisted marriage because he refused to feed the multi-billion dollar wedding industry, but finally they decided to make a statement by having the wedding in the land of corn and soy. Tonight was going to be an interesting night.

"Yikes!" I screamed, spinning around without dropping my dish and trying to swat whatever enormous creature had landed on my back.

"Jules, relax. It was only a horsefly," Lela said, shooing it away. "Come on. Let me show you the campground."

We headed off, but my heels kept sinking into the soft dirt as we followed the trail for what felt like half a mile. I couldn't help but keep looking around for the horse fly.

"So, do you and Melody see each other often?" Lela asked.

"No, not really. I've been pretty busy running the business and raising my son."

"That's surprising. You were both connected at the hip back in the day."

"I didn't think that you even knew that we existed."

"Sure, I did. We may have run in different packs, but I knew who you were."

"Then how did you and Melody become friends?" I asked.

"Didn't you know that we went to the same college?"

"No, I didn't."

"Well, it's important to keep up friendships. Especially with Melly, she's awesome."

"I agree." What I didn't agree with was Lela calling Melody, Melly. That was the nickname I had given Melody in high school.

When Melody called me to ask me to be her bridesmaid, I felt honored and happy to hear from my old friend. After the divorce, I separated myself from almost everyone and threw myself into my career and family. I missed some of my friends and was hoping to rekindle our friendship.

We finally came to the end of the trail where tall trees surrounded an open area with picnic tables scattered in the clearing. I noticed a hand-painted welcome sign nailed to a utility pole and paper lanterns hanging from the trees. The surroundings were feeling more festive.

A hunched-over, elderly lady with white hair the color of a cotton ball, wearing a floral dress came up to me, her hands open. "Hello Dear, I'm Melody's grandmother, Sissy," she said. "I'll take that for you."

"Thank you, Sissy." And just in time. The ruffle around my neck was starting to irritate, and I could hardly wait to get rid of the heavy dish and scratch myself. To keep the budget on track, Melody and Lenny asked everyone to cook, bake, or bring wine and liquor to the wedding. I gladly handed over the beef Wellington and clawed the back of my neck.

"The bridesmaids' flowers and gifts are over there," Grandma Sissy said, pointing toward a wooden picnic table. "And help yourself to some punch. It's an old family recipe." It looked a lot like Hawaiian Punch with a few orange slices, so I passed.

I watched as Sissy put my dish down in the middle of a cornucopia of vegetables, hummus, and some mushy dishes that didn't look familiar. As I studied a platter of something that looked like fern leaves wrapped around gelatin, I felt someone grab me from behind.

"Ju-Ju-be!" yelled Melody, giving me a big bear hug.

"Melly-Belly!" I turned around and gave her another hug. I took a step back and studied the bride. "Congratulations. You look amazing."

Melody was wearing an off-the-shoulder sage lace peasant blouse with a matching multicolored tiered skirt of darkening shades of sage. She had her auburn hair pulled up on top of her head in a tight bun surrounded by a halo of yellow wild flowers. Long beaded earrings and necklaces added some drama. She wasn't wearing shoes, just a toe ring.

"Can you believe that with all of the setting up, I didn't have a chance to shower?" She sniffed under her arm. "Do I stink?" she asked, looking worried.

"You look sparkly clean to me," I said, backing away a few inches. "I feel honored that you asked me to be one of your bridesmaids. I've missed you."

"Me, too. I can't believe you're really here." Melody gave me another hug. "Where's your date? Rocco, isn't it?"

"He had a last-minute emergency at his store. But he sends his regards."

"That's too bad. Hopefully, I'll have a chance to meet him soon."

"Definitely. We'll all have to go out sometime." I, too, was disappointed to get stood up by rotten bananas. Rocco gave me a last-minute phone call telling me that his order of Argentinian bananas came in spoiled, and he and another employee had to stay and get rid of the fruit—and the smell. Truth be known, though, I think he was just getting out of the gig.

"Oh, wait. I see Lenny," Melody said, pointing to a guy wearing shorts and a Rolling Stones t-shirt, his face adorned with round, John-Lennon-type glasses and a long, thick beard and mustache. "Lenny, darling. Come over here. There's someone I want you to meet."

"You must be Jules," Lenny said, giving me a kiss on the forehead. "Melody speaks highly of you and treasures your friendship. So precious jewel, we're glad you're here to revel in our joy."

"Thank you for including me in your wedding."

"Wouldn't have it any other way. Often, friendships fall away like rose petals, and we need to keep our roses intact. Isn't that right, my love?" Lenny put his arm around Melody's waist.

"Jules, isn't he amazing?" asked Melody, hugging him back. "Lenny's poetry brings people together."

I nodded in agreement. Lenny had made a big impression on me. Not only was he insightful, but also he reminded me how much I valued my friendship with Melody and from now on, I was going to make sure to spend more time to my dear, old friend.

"Jules, would you please excuse me?" Lenny asked, interrupting my thoughts. "I need to round up our guests for the ceremony."

"Of course. It was a pleasure meeting you, Lenny."

Before Lenny left, he took Melody in his arms, dramatically dipped her, and gave her an enormous kiss. Then he stood her back up, laughed, and left her standing speechless with a big grin on her face.

"Wow!" I said. "Lenny's wonderful."

"He truly is. I'm so happy, Ju-Ju-Be."

I smiled at Melody. "It's almost time."

"I can hardly wait. Go get your flower bouquet and meet us at the big willow tree by the lake? That's where we'll be exchanging our vows."

"How romantic. Be right over."

I was delighted to be back in touch with my dear friend, but her choice of setting wasn't working out for me. The handpicked flowers from the park, including something that looked suspiciously like poison ivy, had me worried. I'm pretty sure there were no poisonous weeds in the bouquets, but I wasn't taking any chances. I took one of the larger leaves from a violet and pulled those questionable leaves out of mine. I was also expected to wear a flower headband (no sign of poison ivy!). My bridesmaid gift was a homemade bottle of patchouli perfume—some things never change.

By now I could hear distant thunder as I walked to the ceremony spot and felt a few raindrops on my face as I took my place next Lela, who was saving me a spot. The intimate ceremony lasted only ten minutes. The entire "service" consisted of Melody and Lenny staring into each other eyes. No one spoke a single word during the ceremony. The minister explained before the start that Melody and Lenny would make their connection known spiritually by reading each other's thoughts. The minister, bridesmaids, and groomsmen just stood in silence "feeling" the moment. The short shower soon ended with a rainbow. While everyone was feeling their inner light shine from the energy of the arch, all I was feeling was a rash I imagined was spreading all over my body as I stood there drenched from the rain. I scratched away through the ceremony and was delighted when it was over. How did I know when the ceremony was over? A friend of theirs—Sky—played on his guitar, "True" by Spandau Ballet.

As if the polyester and patchouli weren't already playing havoc enough, I was getting bitten up by mosquitos. All I wanted to do was go home. Besides, I knew I wouldn't get much quality time with Melody or Lenny at the reception;

that would come after their honeymoon, assuming they believed in *that* tradition.

I tried calling Stanley, but there was no cell phone reception in this godforsaken paradise. Somehow I'd have to wait patiently until eleven o'clock. I scratched my neck some more. Then I remembered I had a few chewable allergy pills in my purse from a recent episode Jack had with a wasp's nest. I dug around in my purse, popped a couple in my mouth, and hoped that would help.

I kept checking the buffet table to see if anyone had touched the beef Wellington. After I spent weeks, (okay maybe only a day) looking for a cute heart shaped serving dish, it was disappointing to see that the dish remained untouched. After a few minutes, I overheard a woman say, "Can you believe someone had the nerve to make a beef dish when practically everyone here is vegetarian?" So much for my attempt to reconnect with old friends. Why didn't anybody tell me?

I tried talking with some of Melody and Lenny's friends, but I didn't know what to say. Nice soybean casserole? I hadn't touched it. Beautiful dress? I wasn't going to be impolite, but that didn't mean I had to lie about liking the bridesmaids dresses. I did, however, like Melody's dress and felt happy for her that she could wander around on her wedding day feeling so comfortable and breezy, and not have to carry around a fifty-pound dress in five-inch stilettos. I also enjoyed watching people having a good time, dancing and sitting in the grass around a fire, listening to the guitarist playing some old tunes on his acoustic guitar.

After several people had offered me a joint or a shared beer bottle, I decided I would be safe with Grandma Sissy's punch. I was finally starting to enjoy myself at this Woodstock wedding. I saw Melody, standing alone, swaying to Sky's music. Good time to grab a minute or two with her.

"I'm so happy for you and Lenny," I said, giving her a big hug. "And I'm glad to have my old friend back."

Melody laughed and hugged me back. She truly looked happy.

"What do you think of the bridesmaids' dresses?" she asked.

I cleared my throat. "They're great."

"Is that all you can say after *you* were the inspiration?"

"What do you mean?"

"I can't believe that you don't remember. I modeled the bridesmaids' dresses after our matching prom dresses. Yours was pink, and mine was green."

I must have blocked that out. No, I *know* I blocked that out. Melody didn't seem to notice because she'd moved on to a new topic. "Hey, here's someone I want you to meet. He's a very nice, single doctor."

By now Melody was pulling me over to a handsome man named Dr. Kyle Fitzpatrick. At least I think he was handsome; I tried to focus on his face, but all I could see was two pairs of green eyes, his lips, and a lot of brown hair. Time to get some glasses.

"Juliana, can I get you a drink?" he asked after the introductions when Melody had moved on to speak with some other guests.

"No thanks, I'll just have some more punch."

Kyle returned with two cups of the red stuff. He was nice enough to join me as we stepped back in time, drinking after-school punch.

"Thanks," I said. "So, Melody tells me you're a physician. What kind of doctor are you?"

"I'm a proctologist."

I burst out laughing. "Oh, that's funny."

"I'm not joking," he said, with more than a little irritation.

"Oh, sorry. You're right, that's no laughing matter." I locked my lips to stop laughing. "Any hoo, we have a lot in common."

"Are you a doctor, too?" he asked.

"No, but my ex-husband's an ass." I started laughing

again. What was *wrong* with me? Maybe I was having an allergic reaction to the antihistamines?

He shook his head.

"Do you know the reason he's my ex-husband?

"Because he's an ass?" he said, trying to beat me to the punchline.

"Exactly. One day I got a phone call from a woman named Candy, telling me that William slipped and fell in a hotel shower and was in the hospital with a concussion."

"What happened?" he said, sounding as though he already regretted asking.

"Apparently, Miss Candy Cane was shaving his back when she accidentally dropped the razor and hit his foot. He flinched and slipped on some soap suds."

"How awful," he said.

"Yes, he's hairy like an orangutan. I've never seen anything like it."

Kyle shook his head. "I meant the fall, not his back."

I ignored his last comment. "Do you know how many times I've asked him to shave?"

"No, can't say that I do."

I glanced around. "Thousands of times."

"Thousands?"

"Well, maybe hundreds. Frankly, I stopped counting."

"I'm pretty clear on his back being hairy. Can we please move on with the story?"

I paused to think about it. "Major league hairy, like a shag carpet!"

Kyle shook his head.

"But I digress; after I hung up the phone, I couldn't get the sound of her voice out of my head. I wondered what did she have that I didn't have? The answer was obvious."

"What was it?" he asked.

"My husband."

"And now he wants back into my son's life. What if he abandons him the way he did our marriage, and I'll be left to clean up all the pieces?" I seemed to be having a difficult time speaking. "Do you know how hard it is to live in the world of nothing but brides, brides, and more brides after you've gone through a divorce?"

"Must be rough."

"All I want is a happy ending. Like my dear sweet Aunt Audrey."

"Is she dead?"

"No. She's not dead, Silly. I mean she got her happily ever after."

"You're saying your Aunt Audrey lived a fairy tale life?"

"That's right." I swallowed more punch. The stuff was actually quite good. "Come to think of it, so did all my friends, parents, and my UPS delivery driver." I sighed sadly.

"I don't think I'm the right kind of doctor for you. You need a shrink. I'm going to move to another table now. Take care, Jules."

I yelled after him, "Hey, where do you think you're going? I haven't finished telling you about my Aunt Audrey."

Melody came running over. "What's all the commotion about?"

"Dr. Mitzfatrick over there doesn't like my Aunt Audrey," I said. "Nice guy, right?"

Melody seemed concerned. "Does he know your Aunt Audrey?"

"Nope," I said, shaking my head back and forth quickly.

"Oh, boy. Someone's had a little too much moonshine for one night. I'm cutting you off."

"Moonshine? What're you talkin' about? I haven't had anything to drink all night. Just some of your granny's punch. It's deee-lish," I said, raising my cup and toasting to no one in particular.

"Yes, Granny Sissy makes the best corn mash moonshine you'll ever taste. It's around 190 proof."

"Oh. I see. Well, you know, I think I need to go home."

"Jules, you're in no shape to drive. You're welcome to crash in one of the tents."

There was no way I was staying here another second, much as I loved being with Melody. My idea of camping was staying at a motel, not a campground full of bugs and port-o-potties. I needed a hair dryer, a bathtub full of calamine lotion, and a bottle of extra-strength aspirin for a raging headache that would be coming tomorrow morning. And Stanley.

As I hiked back down the dark trail, my head spun faster. I held my cell phone up towards the stars, trying to see if I could get any reception bars. I even tried climbing a large rock, but still no luck. At one point, I stepped in a mud puddle that felt like quicksand and had to leave my dyed olive pump behind. When I finally reached the parking lot, no one was there.

I must have fallen asleep on the bench, because I woke up with a start, about to grab my mace key ring when I realized it was Stanley, on time, 11 PM, as promised.

As he helped me get into the car he asked, "Juliana, do you know that you're missing one shoe?"

"Yes, Stanley, I'm missing a lot more than that. Now, please take me home."

As we bumped along toward the highway, I had the sinking feeling that there was no Prince Charming wandering Riser Woods, carrying an olive slipper, in search of the loveless woman driving away wearing the matching muddied olive pump.

CHAPTER 11

Starting at age three, I was forced to attend the yearly employee Christmas party. Honestly, *party* was not an accurate word to describe the painfully miserable time shared by all. It was more like a funeral.

Most of the scamstresses were Eastern European women who moved to America to support their large families back home. Typically, their husbands or another family member stayed behind with the children while these persevering women worked endless hours to send home practically every penny they made. Some remained in America for years before returning home to their families. And that meant they missed seeing their children grow up, they lost touch with family and their relationships with their husbands suffered.

Because the holiday season was already fraught with emotion, this was the most difficult time of the year for my staff. Early on, Mom and I tried to jumpstart the holidays by creating a joyous work environment, and I now carried on the tradition. Calvin decorated the workroom, and I hung monogrammed stockings for each staff member. I kept cheerful holiday music playing on both floors of the shop and stocked the lunchroom with an endless supply of Christmas cookies. Despite all these efforts, the Christmas spirit was hopelessly missing.

By the time the Christmas party rolled around, the ladies

had resorted to their typical martyr mindset. They refused to smile or even try to have a good time. Over dinner, they passed around family photographs, lamented the state of their marriages, and talked about tragic stories in the news. And they had what a friend of mine called an "organ recital" —conversations about gory operations, faulty gallbladders, and terminal illnesses.

For years, I wracked my brain to come up with the perfect Christmas party theme that would transform the mood. The closest I ever came involved a "Meet and Greet" with Santa. But when the seamstresses sat on the big guy's lap, they turned the occasion into a full-blown psychiatric session. Needless to say, Santa left with a terrible migraine and a severe groin pull.

Never again would I go through the trouble of arranging transportation for the ladies to eat dinner at a Polish banquet hall or a Russian tearoom. Nor would I hire a fortune teller after they forced her to predict only future tragedies!

And yet, hope must spring eternal because as I geared up for this year's Christmas party, I was determined to make it memorable. Tonight's potluck dinner was going to be different. I took a deep breath and walked into the workroom.

There wasn't a lot of extra elbow room here, and a lack of personal hygiene quickly became apparent—and problematic. Somebody forgot to wear deodorant. Others failed to use the mouthwash I stocked in the restroom. By this late in the afternoon, these lapses had affected the mood of the entire room. So, too, would the announcement I was about to make.

As I made my way through the tight quarters, the seamstresses stopped working and began shutting off their machines and collecting their belongings, ensuring they'd be ready to split the minute the "party" was over. I stopped in the middle of the room and glanced at the large clock that hung on the wall and said, "The day's not over yet, so please put away your time cards. I still have some announcements to make before our holiday dinner together."

They stopped and turned their attention to me.

"I have some important news I need to share with you," I said. "I'm sorry to have to do this now, right before the Christmas party, but it simply can't wait."

Silence.

"I just completed our annual review, and our revenue projections are very disappointing. It seems that production time has been growing steadily. Garments that should take only six weeks to finish are taking up to nine weeks." As I spoke, I maintained a steady and stern voice.

The staff looked at me as if I were out of my mind. I had never spoken to them in this tone before.

"Furthermore, there are still too many conversations going on in the workroom, which is slowing everybody down and not allowing you to stay focused on sewing. Plus, it gives you more of an opportunity to bicker. Especially after the yardstick incident." I looked at Olga and Svetlana and knew everyone immediately recalled the incident at last year's holiday dinner when Svetlana tried knocking out Olga with a yardstick for having the audacity to call her homemade pastila store-bought. I continued, "I've noticed less camaraderie and substantially more arguing between the cutters and sewers." I paused. I thought how ridiculous this sounded and had to squelch a smile as I visualized the cutters and sewers snapping their thimbles like they were dueling characters in "West Side Story."

"You've left me no alternative but to hire a workroom manager, Stone Stafford, to bring some discipline back to our business."

The group gasped in unison. Loud chatter filled the room.

"Ladies, ladies. And gentlemen. Silence, please. If you have something to say, you can speak with me directly, later. Now, please let me finish.

"I have invited Mr. Stafford to the Christmas party

tonight. He will be performing a short ice-breaking activity before dinner. So, please give him your undivided attention and make him feel at home." I looked around the room and saw some very upset faces.

As I headed for my office, Natasha, my gaunt, seventy-two-year-old Russian seamstress, pulled out a ring of keys from her purse and threw them hard onto the surface of her sewing machine. The loud clatter got everyone's attention. From the start, I knew that Natasha was going to be a problem. She'd been with us for ten years, coming from a small peasant village of Obshchina just after the Soviet Union collapsed. She was one of the toughest Eastern European babushkas I've ever met, and she intimidated everyone with her hard facial features and lack of humor.

Over the years, she'd tried to intimidate both Mom and me on many occasions, especially for the first few weeks after I took over the business. But I knew that if she ever caught me breaking even a hint of sweat, I would be dead meat. I had to put on a strong façade, or she'd eat me for Russian supper.

I faced Natasha. "Is there a problem here?"

Natasha's dark eyes, surrounded by shimmering blue eyeshadow, pierced a hole in my head. "I go home. I no stay for party," she said with a smirk.

"If you don't wish to join the party, you're welcome to leave. Now, put your keys back in your purse and finish cleaning up your work area. That goes for everyone because I expect all of you to gather in the showroom in fifteen minutes for our group picture." I walked out of the workroom and left the girls to stew. I couldn't have been more pleased.

At the appointed time, a very unhappy group of women and men gathered in the showroom. I refused to let their mood affect me. I set up the camera on a tripod and asked, "Why don't we take our group photo by the window decorations?"

Just then, a handsome, muscular young man walked into the store. I saw more than a few eyebrows raise. I walked over and extended my hand to meet his. "Stone, welcome. So glad you could make it."

"Thank you for inviting me, Ms. Belle." He smiled broadly. He had a nice smile.

I took him by the arm and led him into the store to meet the others. "Everyone, say hello to Stone Stafford."

"Hello," the group replied as one, barely making an effort to sound welcoming.

I tried to sound upbeat. "Stone, we were just about to take our annual group picture. Would you care to join us?"

"Sure."

I heard some scoffing remarks in Polish coming from the group. I sat Stone between Berta, my sixty-one-year-old seamstress, who'd lost her third finger in a freak ironing accident, and Elizabeth, who'd recently begun faking blindness in her left eye.

"Come on, you two," I said. "Make some room." Stone draped his long arms over both ladies' shoulders, practically cupping their big bosoms.

As I struggled to get everyone to fit inside the camera frame, I noticed Elizabeth kept glancing down at Stone's hand and laughed to myself. I always knew she was feigning her waning eyesight. In reality, she had a lazy eye that she used to her advantage whenever she felt, well, lazy. Luckily, I was in a good mood. Otherwise, I might have finally called her out on her bogus blindness.

I looked at the unhappy crew and set the second timer. "Okay, everyone," I said, speaking loudly, "remember to smile."

I snapped a few more pictures and then asked the group to gather around the dinner table. As the girls took their seats (including Natasha), I could hear them whispering in a mix of Polish and Russian. They were none too pleased with the thought of taking orders from a twenty-five-year-old boy.

Stone stood in the corner of the room, waiting for a proper introduction. He looked a little worried as he glanced at the older, heavyset women. I felt both sorry and nervous for him. To be honest, I was a little nervous myself as I walked up to the front of the long banquet table decorated with poinsettias and votive candles.

"Okay, everyone. Before we begin this lovely dinner that you worked so hard preparing, it is my pleasure to introduce Stone again—as your new workroom manager." Stone walked over to join me. We shook hands, and I stepped away.

"Hey. How is everyone doing?" he said, full of professional good cheer.

No one answered.

He glanced around the room and gave them a nervous smile. "Ms. Belle never mentioned that I would be working with such a gorgeous group of women—and some good-looking guys, too." He nodded at Nathaniel and Basil, who smiled; Phu and Calvin looked as though Stone had already ruined their holiday.

Really, Stone? I thought. *Gorgeous, you say? So this is how you're planning on winning them over?*

Maybe he wasn't very smart, but at least he had his good looks going for him. Stone's chiseled features accented his soft brown eyes. His thick dark hair swept back from his forehead, emphasizing his strong jawline with the slightest hint of a five o'clock shadow. He wore a tight black button-down shirt that accentuated his large shoulder and chest muscles, and his rolled-up sleeves clung so closely to his massive biceps they looked as though they could cut off the circulation to his arms. His tailored black pants showed off his tight gluteal muscles, among other things.

"Juliana…Jules?" Stone said, repeatedly.

I realized I had been caught staring and began to blush. "Yes?" I asked, flustered.

"Would you mind turning on the music?" Stone stage whispered. "It might improve the mood."

"Of course." I walked over to the stereo and hit Play on the CD player. It started with a regular dance track, gradually picking up the tempo. Then the lyrics began: "Do you want it? If you do, then shake it, baby!" By now, the tempo was rocking.

Stone whipped his head around, and like a tiger circling his prey, his mouth widened into a real smile this time, as he lithely walked around the banquet table. "I'm looking forward to meeting each and every one of you tonight." He stopped and nodded at Natasha. "What's your name?"

"I...I...I dunno," she stuttered. "I no speak English."

"No problema. You don't have to say a word." He took her hand and helped her out of her seat. Still holding her hand, he grabbed an empty chair with his other hand and dragged it behind him. Her leather sheepskin and wool slippers slid along the floor, foiling her efforts to resist his advances. The others watched, mortified as he spun the chair around and gently pushed Natasha to a sitting position.

"Come on, darlin'. Don't worry, I won't bite," he said, grinning. "Well, maybe just a little, if you're naughty."

Natasha wore a red-patterned, two-piece polyester dress with an elastic waistline and a crochet-lace-trimmed collar. To make merry, she'd added a large green and red wreath brooch and matching earrings.

Stone gently removed her glasses and let them dangle freely on the gold eyeglass chain. He softly smiled as he raised his hand to her head and unclipped the red plastic banana clip, allowing her gray hair to fall around her shoulders. A small squeal escaped her lips as he ran his fingers through her hair.

A gasp swept through the room.

Stone paid no attention to anyone but Natasha. He took her chubby, little fingers and placed each of her hands on his thighs. She pulled her hands away instantly, as though his thighs were as hot as her dressmaker's iron. Again, he slowly took her hands and placed them back on his thighs.

"Now, keep em' there!" he ordered.

This time, she listened. Her eyes bugged out as she watched him slowly unbutton his black silk shirt. Berta, conservatively dressed in a tailored blue jacket and trousers, made the sign of the cross, and I began to worry about my decision to hire Stone. I decided to give it another minute; then I'd pull the plug.

But as we all watched, transfixed, I began to notice that the employees were smiling, pointing, and nudging the person next to them. After Stone had removed his shirt, he swung it over his head and threw it at Olga's face. She carefully began folding the shirt, after giving it a little sniff. That's when we noticed that he was wearing full shimmering body makeup, which made his skin look very tan and smooth shaven everywhere. As a bonus, his silky-smooth chest could do tricks.

We watched in amazement as his pectoral muscles undulated in front of the now pale-faced Natasha. Up down, up down, they danced. Then he took Natasha's hands and placed them on his pierced nipples. Her body slumped over as she pleaded with him, "No more, no more."

He raised her chin to meet his gaze and kissed her passionately on the mouth before setting her free. While she stumbled back to the table, she received a couple of high fives. Eventually, Natasha found an empty chair and began fanning herself with a napkin. Lucie, the warm, petite Ukrainian pattern-maker, handed her a glass of champagne, and they clinked glasses. That made me happy. I'd brought out the same bottle of champagne every year, only to return it, unopened, to the liquor cabinet.

Stone gave me the thumbs up to switch tracks, and old-fashioned bump-and-grind stripper music replaced the party music. I figured that by now, the ladies were putting the pieces together that Stone was not the new workroom manager with a raging senior-citizen fetish, but this year's hottest Christmas present.

Stone turned his magic on to straight-faced Berta. As he pulled off his pants with one single tug and began pumping his pelvis towards her, the others cheered madly, including Phu, who, by day, was painfully shy.

While Stone continued to pulsate in his boxer briefs for Berta, I thought back to earlier this afternoon. I couldn't bear the thought of another depressing potluck Christmas party. Especially after that pastila-and-yardstick situation last year. No way was I going to let this year's party devolve into the usual bickering, with everyone criticizing everyone else's cooking. If I couldn't lift anyone's spirits this year, I swore to myself that this was my last attempt at a party.

I sought some inspiration from the Yellow Pages and let my fingers do their proverbial walking to the entertainment section. I worked my way through A to E, where I spotted an ad in big bold letters "Exotic Entertainers Chicago—male strippers are just what your party needs."

As soon as I hung up after booking my first ever Workroom Manager Stripper, I regretted making the call. The absurd sexual harassment seminar the staff had endured sprang to mind. Would Belle's Bridal be accused of that again? Would my employees have a sense of humor? Or, would I be flying to Romania the next day, looking for new seamstresses because my staff quit?

Out of all the scenarios I thought would unfold, I never expected this to happen. When I looked back at the spectacle, Olga's legs were straddled around Stone's waist while the back of her head met the front of his face.

It was while Stone was lifting Olga up and down like an elephant's trunk that my mom walked into the shop. She took one look at Olga making trumpet sounds as she rode between Stone's thighs and said, "I'm not sure what's going on here, but I know that your father wouldn't approve of me staying." She smiled mischievously. "So, make sure to take lots of pictures." She flung her fur stole around her neck and left.

By the time the door closed behind her, things had gotten even more rambunctious. Stone had Elizabeth down on her knees. Without much prodding, he pushed her face into his crotch. She must have latched onto one of the buttons on his briefs, because as she pulled away, she had his briefs between her teeth.

Stone looked down at her and said, "Would you like me to take them off?"

Still holding the button in her mouth, she nodded.

"Well, you'll have to let go."

She opened her mouth, and the briefs sprung back around his hips. Elizabeth stuck out her tongue for all to see. The button was sitting on the tip of her tongue like a Tic-Tac. Everyone applauded her victory.

"Can you help me take them off?" Stone asked.

Still on her knees, she slowly pulled off the briefs, now eye level with a shimmering gold lamé G-string.

"Everyone, GIVE him dollar!" demanded Olga, and waved a dollar at Stone.

Oh, this was all going so very, very wrong, I thought to myself.

He took the dollar bill and rolled it into a tube. After placing the tube in Olga's mouth, he pulled the G-string out away from his body. She slid the dollar into his G-string like it was a straw, and she was extremely thirsty. The girls and the guys alike applauded.

Stone continued down the line of women. He chased an asthmatic Victoria round and round the table for a while, eventually letting her sit down to take a puff of her inhaler. He then motioned Svetlana to kneel on the floor.

I looked up and noticed a crowd was forming outside the front door. The folks at Purr Salon, the trendy hair salon next door renowned for its beautiful staff and blowout parties, must have heard all the commotion. And I was glad.

Just last week my hairdresser was telling me all about

this year's fabulous private party the salon owner was throwing at a hot local nightclub. When she asked me what I had planned for my staff, I didn't have much to share. I sure wasn't going to say, "A potluck!"

So when I saw my hairdresser's face scrunched down towards the bottom of the door, I laughed. As I walked over to the door, they motioned me to let them inside. Instead, I pushed open the mail slot and said, "Sorry, private party," and pulled down the shade.

I stood by the door and took in the festive holiday splendor. Stone was beginning to wind down (thank heavens!), and some of the girls had turned their attention to drinking and laughing as they ran around the usually staid workroom. Some were wearing tiaras and dancing with mannequins while others were complimenting each other on their delicious food and swapping recipes. It was a joyous sight to see.

I was about to make myself a plate of food when my cell phone rang.

"Hello."

"Ah, yes. May I speak to Juliana?"

I looked at the cell phone, before answering, "For god's sake, William, it's me, Juliana. You're calling me on my cell phone."

"I was calling to talk to Jack," he said.

"He's at home."

"Can you speak up, I'm having a hard time hearing you." The music was blaring.

I covered the receiver as I spoke. "He's not with me. I'm at work. He's at home with Tatiana."

The girls began chanting in the background. "Take it off, take it off!"

"Sure doesn't sound like you're at work to me. Sounds like you're at a strip club."

I rolled my eyes. "That's your stomping ground, not mine."

"Well, wherever you're at, sure doesn't sound like a healthy environment for a kid."

"Like I said, Jack isn't with me. Call him at my house, if you wish. Goodbye, William."

After I had hung up the phone, I started to feel uneasy. But then I thought, dammit, I'm not letting that man ruin another good time for me. I pulled myself together and walked over to Stone. I looked at my watch and realized that he had stayed an hour longer than the original booking time. I collected his clothing strewn about the room and managed to pry him away from the ladies.

"Thank you so much. You've been an incredible sport," I said, walking him to the door.

"My pleasure," he said. "Those were some of the coolest dancing grannies ever."

"Were they your oldest clients to date?" I asked, handing him his shirt, which smelled of cinnamon and citrus fruit scented cologne.

"Definitely. But, hey, it's all part of the job," he said, as he slipped the shirt over his sweaty torso.

I felt self-conscious handing him his pants. He smiled, and my stomach dropped.

"Anytime you want a private dance, Juliana Belle," he said, lifting an eyebrow, "just give me a call." He handed me a business card.

My face felt flush. "Goodbye, Stone. And thanks again."

Once Stone left the shop, I walked over to Natasha and put my arm around her shoulder. "Well, Natasha, aren't you glad you stayed after all?"

She smiled a big, snaggle-toothed grin. "This best Christmas party ever. Can't wait for next year—but hey, why wait? Let's do at Easter!" Everyone cheered in agreement.

Natasha wrapped her matronly arms around me and pressed my face into her big, ample breasts. "But...next time, he no haf gold stringy-string, okay?"

"Okay. No stringy-string next time," I said, laughing and

trying to squirm out of her stronghold.

"Ah, you know vat?" Natasha poked her temple with her index finger. "Never mind, I tell him when he come to vork next week. Our vonderful new sexy manager," she said with a hearty Russian laugh.

Well, *von't* they be disappointed on Monday?

CHAPTER 12

Dress, check. Petticoat, check. Bridal corset, check. Veil, you bet! I went down my mental checklist. Next, I inspected the gown for any hanging threads and fabric creases. Finally, I secured the off the shoulder satin and embroidered lace princess ball gown to a cardboard bodice form and gently slid the dress inside a large white garment bag with Belle's Bridal Shop branded in gold script. Smiling, I traced my finger across the embossed letters.

With one big heave, I hung the weighty gown on the front of the office door and pulled up the long zipper. I still had to find the missing antique tiara, which I had misplaced somewhere in the store before I could give the dress my final stamp of approval and move it to the customer pick-up area for Hazel Nutt's 1:00 PM appointment.

But before I could begin the scavenger hunt, I had to pull together a collection of wedding dresses for today's charity fashion show luncheon at the Fairmont Hotel. My first appointment of the day had just arrived as I finished securing the last garment bag to the collapsible rolling rack I had set up by my office.

"Well, *hello*, Katie," I cooed, as I regarded my three-and-a-half-foot, four-year-old client bedecked with golden ringlets and pink polished nails.

Katie had her arms wrapped around a large doll that

looked like her twin.

"Are you ready for your fitting?" I asked.

"No!" she spat, as she hid behind her mother's skirt.

"Sorry, Jules," said Astrid Conway, Katie's mother. "Katie's been very naughty today, but she promised to behave during the fitting."

Astrid gave Katie a sidelong glance. "Right, Katie?"

No response.

I gave Katie a warm smile and asked, "Would you like to come with me and try on your lovely flower girl dress?"

Katie shook her head back and forth.

"It's all right," Astrid said in a fake singsong voice. "Do you remember your promise?"

Katie continued to shake her head. "No."

"Well, then I'll remind you. If you're a good girl, Jules will make a matching dress for Missy Squatpump."

I looked at Astrid, who was now nodding at me frantically.

"Oh, yes, of course, I will," I said, holding out my hand. "Katie, may I see Miss Squatpump."

"It's Missy Squatpump!" she corrected me.

"Sorry, may I see Missy?"

"Nope." Katie clutched Missy tightly in her arms.

"Katie Conway, you show Jules Missy Squatpump this minute," Astrid insisted.

"Fine," Katie said with a grin, throwing the doll at me.

I was able to catch the dolly before she plummeted head first into my stomach. As I grasped it, the doll gave off a pungent odor that reminded me of, well, never mind. When I stared into Missy's eyes, I had a flashback to my life before being a mother.

Before Jack came into my life, I never held an infant and had any idea how to change a diaper or feed a baby. Plain and simple, I felt nervous around anyone shorter or more emotional than me.

Everything changed when I had Jack. And now that he was five years old, I've become more relaxed around children. My plan was to stay calm and win over Katie's affections. I held up the stinky doll and looked into her big green eyes. "Welcome, Miss Scuttlebutt," I said. "I'm happy to have you for a client."

I glanced over at Katie to see how I was doing. I could have sworn that I saw a tiny smile beginning to form in the left corner of her mouth.

"It's Squatpump!" she reprimanded me. "And I told you, it's MISSY."

"I'm terribly sorry," I said apologetically to the doll. "May I call you Missy?" I forced the doll to nod.

Katie listened intently to our private conversation.

"Missy, what beautiful eyes you have." I held the doll's mouth to my ear. "Oh, why thank you." I giggled.

"What did she say?" Katie demanded.

"Missy said that I have beautiful eyes, too…and a lovely dress."

Katie scowled.

"Okay, fine," I said. "She didn't mention anything about the dress. She did say she would let me take her measurements—but only after your fitting."

Katie gave this some thought and seemed to come to an agreement. "I agree with Missy," she said. "I don't like your dress either!"

"But Missy never said that!" I responded defensively. Great. Now instead of using my ventriloquist skills to get Katie into the fitting room, I was acting out a scene from "Mean Girls."

"I want you to make Missy a pink dress, with lots of bows," Katie said.

"Absolutely."

"But it has to be pink, 'cause pink's my favorite color."

"Well that's a coincidence," I said. "Pink happens to be my favorite color, too."

"You're too old to like pink."

"Okay, enough of the small talk." I placed my hand on

her shoulder. "Wave goodbye to your mommy, and let's get started."

As I led Katie towards the fitting room, I prayed that Nathaniel had refilled the crystal candy dish with chocolate kisses. To get through the fitting with this tiny terror, I would be using those magical silver bells as bargaining chips. But the odds were against me. Only safety pins, scotch tape, and gray wisps of lint filled the dish.

I began fitting Katie's dress: a yellow gauze tutu belted with an enormous daisy affixed to the back of a green gingham belt. Just as I was pinning the hem, Nathaniel called out, "Jules, the fashion show coordinator's here to pick up the gowns."

Katie looked up at me, squinting her light green eyes, and said, "If you leave me alone in here, I'll scream."

I regarded the pouty little girl and took her threat seriously. "I'm in the middle of a fitting and can't leave the room," I called out. "But the gowns are hanging by my office. Can you please roll them to the elevator?"

A few minutes later, Nathaniel knocked for a second time. "What is it now?" Katie shrilled.

"Sorry to keep bothering you," said Nathaniel. "The dresses are too heavy for the coordinator to manage alone. What do you want to do?"

I let out a heavy sigh. "Go with her to the hotel and stay there to help with the setup," I pleaded.

Katie stomped her foot and pulled my hair.

"Ouch, let go now," I said with a pain-induced edge to my usual tone.

"Great! I'll go now," he said, obviously excited to help with the show.

One problem solved. Now, how could I find a way to tame this child?

The interruptions stopped, and I managed to find a way to finish Katie's fitting without any more tantrums or snide comments regarding my age. When she emerged from the fitting room, Astrid looked surprised.

"Wow, that seemed to go well," Astrid said.

Katie forced a smile. "Thank you, Miss Belle. That was fun."

"I had fun, too," I said, only partially lying.

Astrid looked around. "Where's Missy?"

Katie turned to me and crossed her arms in front of her chest.

"Oh, I forgot about Miss Squatpump," I said. "She's still in the fitting room looking through a magazine. I'll get her for you, sweetheart."

I could hear Katie whisper "Missy" followed by an unmistakable stomp of her foot as I walked into the fitting room, where I was holding the doll hostage. Carefully, I removed the tape from Missy's mouth, cut the thread that wrapped her wrists, and unpinned her dress from the chair. A few seconds later, I returned Missy to her rightful owner.

After giving the dolly a hug, Katie handed it to her mother and rested her hands on her hips. "Miss Belle, do you remember your promise?"

"How could I forget?" I winked at Katie. "Missy will have the most beautiful pink dress with bows and ribbons." I patted Katie on the head.

"Wow, Jules. I can hardly recognize my daughter."

I turned to Astrid and said, "Katie is an absolute delight. She had me in stitches the entire time." I rubbed my right butt cheek that was still throbbing from where Katie used it—once—like a human pincushion.

Close to noon time, I found Hazel's antique pearl and rhinestone tiara beside the coffee maker. I must have accidentally put it there when I brewed a cup of coffee this morning. I looked at my watch. Hazel was due any minute now to pick up her wedding gown. I grabbed the headdress and rushed over to place the tiara in the garment bag where I had left it hanging on the office door.

No bag. Just an empty door hook.

"Oh, no!" I cried to no one in particular. Trying not to panic, I searched the office for the gown. No luck.

"Zoë, can you come in here right away?" I called over the intercom.

I could hear Zoë's clicking heels on the marble floor as she walked over at a snail's pace to join me. "What do you need, Jules?"

"Have you seen Hazel's gown?" My words came out like rapid-fire.

"Who?"

"Hazel Nutt!" I eyed Zoë as though she were from another planet.

Zoë was still looking at me with a blank expression on her face.

"Oh, for crying out loud. You know, Hazel Nutt, the hand model." I threw up my arms in frustration.

"Oh, sure, Hazel. With the small mole on her neck." Zoë slapped her forehead.

"Yes, yes, that's her. Now, please tell me you've seen her gown."

"Nope. Sorry. Do you want me to check the workroom?"

"I suppose. But I know I hung it up in here this morning."

The entire staff turned the store inside out trying to find the missing dress while I sat at my desk, cradling my face in my hands and wondering how I was going to tell Hazel I had lost her wedding dress.

Zoë's booming voice over the intercom broke my concentration. "Jules, Nathaniel's calling, line one."

I picked up the phone. "Hel-looo," I said, just shy of sobbing.

"Jules, is that you?" Nathaniel asked.

"Uh-huh. What's going on?"

"Can I come into work late tomorrow? Haden just called and said that he's coming home tonight."

"I though he's performing in Boca Raton all week."

"As luck would have it, his next three performance at the

Little Palm Family Theater were canceled due to flooding, and we were hoping to go antiquing in the morning."

"Whatever," I said, blowing my nose.

"I mean, we don't have to go. It's just that we haven't seen each other for a while and could use some alone time."

"That's fine. Just take the day off. Who cares anyway?"

"Hey, I care. Is everything okay? Sounds like you're crying?"

"Yup." I sniffled.

"What's wrong?"

"Hazel Nutt's dress is missing."

"What?"

"We've looked everywhere."

"Did you check the Weeping closet?"

"Yeah. It wasn't there, either. It just disappeared—into thin air."

"Oh, my God!" he yelped.

"Nat, what is it?" I asked, regaining some calmness.

"Was it in a garment bag hanging on the office door?" he asked, sounding panicked.

"Yes, it was. Do you know where it is?"

"I do. It's on the run…the run…"

"What does that even mean?" I snapped. "Nat, calm down and breathe."

He paused and took a breath. "The dress…is about…to be worn out…on the runway."

"You've got to be kidding me! How's that possible?"

"Oh, Jules. I'm *so* sorry. The dress was in the same kind of garment bag as the fashion show gowns. It looked too large to fit on the rack, and I assumed it was the final gown."

Now I took a deep breath. "Listen to me very carefully. You must bring me Hazel's gown immediately."

"Don't worry. I'm headed for the dressing room as we speak."

"Please hurry. Hazel will be here any minute." I felt the sweat dripping down my back.

"Hey, stop that model!" Nathaniel yelled out, and the phone went dead.

"Nat? Nathaniel? Dammit!" I slammed down the receiver and dashed out the office door, wanting to find Zoë and tell her the news before Hazel arrived.

"Looks like someone's in a big hurry to get somewhere?"

I turned around to see who was speaking, and came face-to-face with none other than Hazel Nutt.

Hazel's long thick brunette hair looked tousled, her eyebrows unruly, and her brocade jacket was unbuttoned, revealing a simple tank underneath. She was holding a cigarette in her left hand and a can of pop in her right.

I looked at her in horror. "Hazel," was all I managed to say.

She took one last puff of her cigarette before approaching me. I watched as she slid the lipstick stained cigarette down the opening of the pop can. Hazel pressed her lips together, rubbing off any trace of remaining lipstick. "I'm here to pick up my gown."

I eyeballed the large front window of the showroom, envisioning Nathaniel pulling up in a taxi cab with the gown. Unfortunately, he was nowhere to be seen, and I needed to stall until he returned.

"May I?" I asked, taking the pop can from Hazel's hand and slowly walking over to the garbage receptacle next to the design table. My heart was pounding as I threw away the can.

"Why don't we have a seat?"

Hazel sat down in the chair next to me.

"Before I get your dress, would you like to get a drink with me? I'm parched, and there's a great new concept coffee shop nearby that serves oxygen-infused coffee."

"No, thanks," she said, with little expression.

I looked at my watch as inconspicuously as possible. "Well, can I get you a cup of tea or something else to drink?" I asked, trying to smile.

"I'm not thirsty," she said, sounding aggravated.

For the next ten minutes, I tried making small talk by asking questions about the minuscule details of Hazel's wedding, still trying to stall for time. My time ran out when I asked the question, "Have you considered having your dog in the wedding? We could go over to your house right now, and I could measure Petunia for a dress."

Hazel looked at me. "Look, I just walked ten blocks because I couldn't flag down a taxi, and I'm tired. I would like to get my dress and go home."

"Um, well, the gown's not quite ready," I said grimly.

"Are you serious? It's one eighteen." She held up her wrist to show her watch.

"I'm sorry for the delay, but it will just be a few more minutes," I said as calmly as I could, but my fidgeting, nose twitching, and eye shiftiness weren't helping my defense.

"Oh, will it?" she said, glaring at me.

"If you'd rather not wait, I could have the dress delivered to your home."

"You must take me for a fool?" Hazel said, raising an eyebrow.

"Of course not," I replied, looking puzzled.

"Juliana, stop with the bullshitting."

I could feel my face turning a dark shade of crimson. I dreaded what she'd say next.

"On my walk over here, my mother called to tell me that she just saw a wedding gown identical to mine, traipsing down the runway of a charity fashion show at the Fairmont Hotel."

"Well, that's quite a coincidence," I said, avoiding her eyes.

"You and I both know it was no coincidence. My one-of-a-kind wedding gown was based upon my mother's original dress design. You don't think that my mother wouldn't recognize her own bridal gown?"

I shrugged my shoulders.

"Of course, she would," barked Hazel. "Now, tell me, how could you use my gown in a fashion show without asking for my permission?"

I was about to make a full confession when Nathaniel came rushing into the shop yelling, "I've got it! I've got Hazel's dress!"

I gave him a nasty look. What timing he had. "Give me that," I said, grabbing the garment bag from him. Nathaniel stood there for a moment and gave me an apologetic smile.

I tried to say, "Please, help me," but only a whimper escaped my lips. He took that as a sign to leave and exited the room.

I laid the garment bag housing Hazel's wedding gown on the table and sat down.

"Juliana, I'm going to ask you one more time, and I expect an honest answer. Was that my gown in the fashion show today?" Hazel asked, pointing to the nylon bag.

"I'm very sorry." My shoulders slumped as I lowered my head.

"I knew it!" Hazel's face contorted with anger.

"If you would only allow me to explain…"

She interrupted me mid-sentence. "What's to explain? You purposefully used my gown in a show today."

"Please," I begged. "You're wrong."

"I'm never wrong," Hazel spat, crossing her arms in front of her chest.

"I swear to you that it was an accident. Nathaniel…"

Hazel interrupted me in mid-sentence. "So you're telling me that my Cinderella ball gown magically ran out of the shop without you noticing?"

"Well, sort of."

"Juliana, I don't know what type of unscrupulous business you're running here, but I'm going to tear you to pieces," she said, with a smug grin.

I looked at Hazel in disbelief. What a horrible thing for her to say after I'd spent an inordinate amount of time designing her dress. And if that wasn't enough, I referred her to the best wedding vendors, spell-checked her invitation and called in a favor to The Season's Hotel catering director, asking him to secure the Grand Ballroom for the wedding.

But she wasn't finished. The insults kept pouring out of her mouth. After ten more minutes, my head was spinning.

"I can't believe this is happening," she cried. "You've ruined my wedding day, so I'm going to ruin your life." Hazel thought for a moment and added, "First, I'm going to bad-mouth you around town, and then I'm going to sue you for everything you've got."

She had taken a quick breath before she screamed at full volume, "But for the time being, I demand a refund."

I wanted to run out of my store and never come back. Maybe I could design gowns for WeddingGirls Direct? Not only would I quadruple my sales by selling a boatload of gowns for discount prices, but also I would *never* have to work with another bride again.

Unfortunately, Zoë interrupted my bridal fantasy by coming over to the table. "Your mother's calling on line two."

"Please," I begged. "Tell her I'll call her back."

"Sure, will do." And Zoë was gone.

An honest mistake could not only cost me my reputation, but it could ruin my family name. And there was nothing I could do about it. "I'll be right back with your check, Hazel," I said, defeated.

"Well, that takes care of the expense, but how do I get a new gown two days before the wedding?"

"You can have the gown. It's in perfect condition."

"After some emaciated model wore it? I think not." I could tell from the look in her eye; Hazel was about to launch into another tirade when Zoë ran up to me.

"Excuse me, Jules," Zoë interrupted.

"Go away!" Hazel barked.

I shot Zoë a look that said, *Not now—not ever*, but she

didn't get the cue.

"Jules, listen to me," she said slowly, as though she were speaking in code. "You have an important phone call on line two."

"Tell Mother I'll call her back."

"It's not your mom this time," Zoë wailed.

I stood up and took Zoë by the elbow and led her towards the corner of the showroom.

"Please, Jules. Autumn from *Brides* magazine is on the phone; she needs to speak to you about the finale gown."

"You mean, *my* gown," corrected Hazel, who was now standing behind us, eavesdropping on our conversation. "Go ahead, Juliana. Why don't you answer the phone? I would love to hear what she has to say."

"Fine," I said. "Zoë, do me a favor and draft a refund check for Hazel while I take this call."

I walked back over to the table, followed by Hazel, and picked up the portable receiver. "Uh, hello?" I said, meekly.

"Jules, darling, it's Autumn from *Brides*," said the bubbly voice on the other end of the line.

I took a deep breath. "Hello, Autumn."

"Sweetheart, I wanted to be the first to congratulate you on your exquisite finale gown," she chirped. "People were raving about it all afternoon. You've truly outdone yourself this time."

"Well, thank you, Autumn. I appreciate the call," I said unenthusiastically.

"Wait!" Autumn said. "Don't hang up on me just yet. I'm calling with life-altering news; you're going to owe me big-time after I tell you what I did for you."

"What is it?" Hazel's wild eyes were burning a hole in me.

"I e-mailed some pictures of the gown I took at the show to the New York fashion editor, and she flipped over the dress. She wants to use it for the cover of the May issue."

"The cover?" I squeaked. "Wow, Autumn. That would be

a dream come true." I could feel the tears beginning to well in my eyes.

"So I need you to pack up that fabulous gown and overnight it to the New York office, ASAP."

"I can't," I said.

"Awww, come on. Hello! We're talking the cover."

I felt faint. "Listen, Autumn, the gown belongs to a customer, who happens to be here right now. And frankly, I'm not sure she'll agree."

"Agree to what?" Hazel demanded.

I held up my finger signaling for her to wait a moment. In the meantime, Zoë had returned with the check and placed it on the design table.

"Jules, I don't think you are hearing what I'm trying to say," Autumn said. "The cover of *Brides* will be such a boost for your career."

"Oh, believe me, I know."

"Let me talk to the bride," Autumn insisted.

"What? I don't think that's a good idea."

"Juliana, please put her on the phone."

"Hazel," I held out the phone receiver. "Autumn from *Brides* magazine would like to speak to you." I had a sick feeling that Hazel was about to tear me to pieces.

Hazel grabbed the phone and turned her back to me. "Hello, this is Hazel Nutt."

I always wondered why Hazel never changed her name. After all, I snipped off the last three letters of my last name, Belleski, since I wanted my name associated with wedding bells, not sleigh bells.

I continued listening in on her side of the conversation.

"Yes, uh-huh…absolutely not…no way… Oh? I see. The Grand Ball Room at the Four Seasons Hotel. Three hundred and fifty guests? Oh, really?" Hazel was laughing now. "Well, you probably heard my name around town. I'm a well-known Chicago model."

By the look on her face, she didn't like Autumn's

response. "No? That's surprising. I bet if you saw my work, it would strike a chord."

I inwardly groaned as she named some obscure companies that she'd worked for in the past. Then Hazel screamed. "Yes, I would love to! Oh, my fiancé won't mind at all; he'll be thrilled... I, too, am very excited about the opportunity... I agree, Juliana's the best in the business... I'll be sure to pass along the compliment. Bye for now." Hazel ended the call and spun around to give me a big bear hug.

"What just happened?" I asked, pulling away.

"I'm going to be on the cover of *Brides* wearing my wedding gown!" she said, giving me another big hug.

Thanks to the runway gown fiasco, Hazel Nutt's dream had just come true. She had successfully upgraded her status in the modeling field from an above-average hand-and-foot model to a cover girl.

"That's unbelievable," I said, amazed.

"That's not all; the magazine is going to write an article about my wedding. I'll be the talk of the town."

Better you than me, I thought to myself. "Well, I'm glad everything worked out," I said. "I mean, everything did work out, didn't it?"

"Darling, of course, it did," Hazel purred. "Autumn will be calling you this afternoon to follow up. Thanks to Autumn's gracious offer, I may not have to go through the trouble of suing you, after all."

"Wait a minute," I moved closer the table and tapped on the refund check. "I just remembered, the dress no longer belongs to you. It belongs to me," I said in the sweetest voice possible. I slid the check in her direction.

"Oh, stop." Hazel picked up the check and ripped it into shreds. "Let's forget this ever happened, shall we?"

I looked at her skeptically.

"Seriously, it was just a little misunderstanding." She laughed nervously. "Let's kiss and makeup. What do you say we go get a cup of that delicious oxygen coffee?"

I was emotionally exhausted from the dress altercation but grateful for the outcome. Inadvertently, Hazel had taught me an important lesson today: the customer isn't always right, but the customer is always the customer. If I were going to survive my career as a bridal gown designer, I couldn't allow customers like Hazel to push me around.

Even though my nerves felt shattered, I accepted the truce and took her up on her offer that would, hopefully, ensure future harmony. One thing was for sure; I wasn't going to drink a drop of any oxygenated hazelnut coffee. I already had more than my fill of highly reactive Hazel Nutt crap for one day.

CHAPTER 13

Dinner, polka, and the chicken dance, that was how my parents chose to celebrate their 40th anniversary at the Polka Palace. They certainly had their pick of places since Chicago had the largest Polish population outside of Warsaw.

The restaurant smelled like warm butter, grilled onions, and potatoes. I felt as though I had gained ten pounds just by breathing in the succulent aromas when I walked through the doors of the famous establishment.

"Madam Belleski!" shouted Peter, the maître d', as Rocco, Jack, and I walked into the banquet hall festooned with traditional decorations. As we stood under an enormous statue of the Polish eagle hanging majestically over our heads, Peter ran over to greet us. "Welcome. It's so great to see you again," he said, kissing my hand.

"We're thrilled to be here," I said.

"This can't be your little boy!" Peter looked at Jack. "Jack, you're getting so big. What are you now, like sixteen?"

"No," Jack said, laughing. "I'm five." He flashed all five fingers on his right hand. "And a half," he quickly added, struggling to bend his left index finger and add it to the tally.

"Unbelievable," Peter said. "I could have sworn you were growing a mustache."

Jack ran his finger under his nose and doubled over with a full belly laugh.

Rocco cleared his throat.

"Oh, where are my manners?" I said. "This is my, uh, boy, my friend, Rocco Delgado."

"Hi, I'm Juliana's boyfriend, Rocco." He shot me a look as he shook hands with Peter.

"Rocco," Peter said, rolling the "R" in his name. "Is that a Polish name?"

"No, Italian."

"I see. Do you speak Polish?"

Rocco tugged on his ear. "Sorry, I can't hear you, the music is crazy loud."

"No," I answered for him over the sound of the *um-pa-pa, um-pa-pa*. Peter and I continued to speak in Polish for another minute. Rocco pretended to listen, but he wasn't amused.

After we had stopped with our Polish banter, Peter said, "Now, let me show you to the private Old Warsaw room your parents selected for the party. It's newly redecorated. You're going to love it!"

Rocco tried taking Jack's hand, but Jack slipped his hand out of his grasp. Rocco grabbed it again.

"Ouch, you're squeezing too hard," Jacked yelped.

"Well, if you'd stop fidgeting…" Rocco started.

"Here, Jack," I said, a little anxious. "Take my hand. Your grandparents are waiting."

Rocco looked at me and shook his head.

As we walked to the back of the restaurant, Rocco kept tugging at the knot of his tie. "Why did you make me wear this stupid thing?"

"You look very nice," I said. "You should wear a tie more often."

"And you should go to a Sox game more often," he countered.

"Fine. Ditch the tie."

Rocco pulled off his tie and crammed it into his sports coat pocket.

"Sveetheart!" Mom exclaimed as she waved us over.

"Enjoy the party," said Peter, as he slipped back to the front of the restaurant.

The room did, in fact, look like Old Town Market Place. A mermaid stood in the center of the room, armed with a sword and shield. Photographs of the Royal Castle, Sigismund's Column, and 18th-century houses, shops, and restaurants filled the walls, with a huge Polish flag covering one entire area. Dad would have decorated my entire childhood home like the Polka Palace if Mom had let him.

Growing up as a Belleski meant understanding our roots, the Polish culture, and traditions. Weekdays might have been all about the wedding dress, but the weekends were all about the sauerkraut. Speaking of which, huge bowls of sauerkraut, picrogi, kielbasa, pickled cucumbers, bigos, pork, potatoes, and beets covered the buffet table from end to end. I was getting hungrier by the minute.

"Hurry up, Jules," Mom said, as she flagged us over to the table. Your father is about to give his speech."

We rushed through the room, giving friends and family quick hugs and introductions. Rocco shook hands with some of the guests as we weaved through the crowd. We'd barely said hello to Mom before Dad starting clinking his glass.

"Good evening, my friends and family," Dad said, in a much heavier accent than Mom. "Thank you for being here to celebrate Bianca and my 40th wedding anniversary." Dad took Mother's hand and gave it a gentle kiss.

Everyone let out a collective cheer in response.

"For a young couple with only twenty dollars to our name and not knowing a word of English when we arrived in America, we did all right."

More clapping.

"You could say we are living the American dream. Not

only that, but we have a loving family. We have a beautiful daughter," Dad said, smiling and pointing at me.

I returned the smile.

"An amazing grandson," he said and saluted Jack. Jack saluted back at his grandpa.

"And hopefully, a new son-in-law!" Dad pointed to Rocco.

I felt like the woeful coyote bulldozed, shot, and exploded all at once after the roadrunner had beeped, beeped away. I turned to Jack, who looked as horrified as I felt. Then I looked at Rocco, who was beaming. He held up my hand like he'd just won a prize boxing match.

"Oh my God! Juliana, are you getting married?" Mom squealed.

The room went silent.

"Mom, please," I said under my breath. "We're not getting married. Please let Dad continue with his speech."

"What has it been, like three years you have been dating?" interjected Aunt Audrey. Now I remembered why I disliked her so much—whether I was drunk or sober.

"No, Aunt Audrey," I said. "It's been just over one year."

"Still you're no young chicken anymore," my aunt said. "You don't want to wait too long. And I'm probably not going to be around much longer. Maybe you can get it right this time."

"Thank you. I'll keep all that in mind. Now, Dad, don't you have a speech to give?" I turned my attention to my father.

"Yes, where was I?" Dad said.

"Your anniversary, remember?" I prodded.

"Oh, yes. Bianca, my dear. Can you please join me?" Dad said, helping Mom to her feet. "I have something special that I want to give you." He reached into his jacket pocket and pulled out a vintage necklace.

Mom covered her mouth with both hands. "Is that what I think it is?"

Dad smiled at her. "Yes, they are Mama's pearls."

I remembered my father telling me on many occasions that this was the only keepsake he had from his mother because everything else was taken away from his family during World War II. "Would you like to wear them now?" he asked.

"Would I?" Mom turned around and lifted her hair to expose her neck.

Dad put the necklace around her neck, making sure the diamond clasp was secure. Mom held the necklace as she turned around and gave Dad a big hug.

"It looks beautiful on you," Dad said. "I wanted to give it to you years ago, but Mama told me I had to wait until our 40th wedding anniversary, just to make sure that you were a keeper."

The crowd loved this, but the laughter died when Mother's smile faded.

"Keeper?" Mom asked. "She should be happy I kept *you* around."

"Oh, Bianca," Dad said. "Why do you always have to be so serious? Can't you take a joke?"

"Mama was not joking. I was never good enough for her precious son."

"What are you saying? She adored you. She just didn't like your cooking."

"What? What was wrong with my cooking?"

By now the crowd was getting into it too, some taking Mom's side, others talking about my grandmother's cooking.

I stood up and held up my glass. "Excuse me," I yelled over their bickering. I clinked my glass so hard I worried it might shatter. "Excuse me! I would like to propose a toast to my parents."

That got everyone to quiet down, including Mom and Dad. For as long as I could remember, my parents put me in the middle of their arguments. Being an only child, I felt a lot of pressure to help fix their problems and became quite good at the role of mediator in the family. But after what Dad just did to me with Rocco, I desperately didn't want the peacekeeping job any longer.

"Thank goodness you both stayed together and created an incredible life for our family," I said. "It took tremendous hard work and love, but you did what most people only aspire to." I paused and took a deep breath. "Someday, I hope to find what you both have." I took a short pause. "Please…let's all raise our glass to my loving parents and wish them another forty happy and healthy years."

Cheers echoed through the room as I turned to the white-bearded bandleader. "Hey, do you boys know the "Beer Barrel Polka"?"

"Does the Pope speak Polish?" the bandleader said.

"Yes!" everyone said in unison.

"Then hit it, fellows!"

As the music started playing, everyone began clapping and dancing. After a few minutes, Aunt Audrey came hobbling over to me. She had a way of invading my space by standing too close whenever we saw each other.

"You know, you could pick up the phone and call me some time," she said, peering over her reading glasses.

Before I could answer, I heard Dad calling out to me. "Juliana, look what your son is doing." I had to hand it to Dad; he had a way of rescuing me from bad situations, at least those not of his making. I looked toward the stage, where Jack stood with one of the smaller accordions strapped onto his thin frame, playing right along with the band. After he had finished playing, everyone gave Jack a standing ovation. I ran up and hugged him.

"That was incredible," I said. "I didn't know you could play the accordion."

"It's like playing the piano sideways," Jack said, breaking out of the hug and laughing as he did so. Even as a baby, Jack had an ear for music and enjoyed playing various instruments. Tatiana had been teaching him piano, and apparently accordion—the instrument she played in the Miss Minsk contest. I'd have to cut her a little more slack.

Rocco sauntered over and joined us. He patted Jack on the back, and then with a big grin on his face, said, "Gotta hand it to you, Jackie Boy. You're talented."

"Thank you," Jack said, his face registering disbelief.

"No, I mean it, Kid. Keep playing that violin. You're going to be a famous musician someday."

Jack smiled. "I'm thirsty. I could sure use a kiddy cocktail." When he walked towards his grandparents, that left Rocco and I standing on the dance floor.

"Have you ever danced the Polka before?" I asked.

"No, can't say that I have."

"Well, come on. Let me show you how to do it." I grabbed him by the hand and put my arm around his shoulder.

To my surprise, Rocco proved to be an exceptional polka dancer. From the corner of my eye, I could see Jack watching our every move. After a few minutes, Jack ran onto the dance floor to join in. Rocco scooped him up in his arm, held him in a dance pose, and spun him around as they galloped around the room. Jack was giggling so hard; he seemed to be enjoying Rocco's company.

Eventually, I joined in again, and then Mom broke in to take her turn on the dance floor. As the music stopped, we all needed to catch our breath. Rocco brought over some Kompot, a Polish fruity drink and handed Mom a cup. "Beautiful necklace, Mrs. Belleski."

"Thank you, Rocco," she said.

"But it looks like the clasp is open," Rocco pointed out to her.

She tried closing it again, but the clasp kept popping open.

"This is awful," Mom cried out and took off the pearl necklace.

I looked around the room.

"Juliana, who are you looking for?" Mom asked, looking concerned.

"I wanted to find Dad and tell him about the necklace," I said.

"Let's not tell your father about this right now. It will only upset him."

"Hey, I know this great guy Ronnie, he owns a small jeweler shop. I can take it to him tomorrow, if you want," Rocco offered.

"That would be great, Rocco. My husband would kill me if I ever lost his mother's pearls." Mom handed him the necklace.

Rocco slipped the pearls in his pocket. "Hey, don't sweat it. I'll take good care of it for you."

"Thanks for your help," I said, giving Rocco a peck on the cheek.

Mom looked relieved. "Come and dance with Glammy, Jack," she said. The gesture was subtle yet unmistakable. Mom was giving Rocco and me some time to dance alone.

The music turned slow, and Rocco and I stood still on the dance floor. "May I have this dance, Kumquat?"

I frowned.

"I mean...Juliana," he quickly added.

That's better. "Yes."

"It's been a good night, right?" he said.

"Yes, it has."

"It's good to see you relax and enjoy yourself."

I nodded.

"It *could be* like this all the time."

I swayed in his arms, feeling the heaviness of the food lift with every step of the dance. "I don't think I could eat meat and pirogies every night."

"You know what I mean."

"Rocco, please. Not here. Not right now, okay?"

"At some point you need to dance or get off the stage, Jules."

The tempo changed, and the band began playing the chicken dance. The guests cheered and filled the dance floor again.

"Can we please talk about this some other time?" I asked. "For tonight, I'd like to keep on dancing."

Rocco nodded and spun me around. Everyone seemed to be having the proverbial barrel of fun. Even I was doing a good job of keeping the blues on the run. Then I felt a tap on my shoulder.

"Are you Juliana Belle?" a voice asked.

I spun around to face the man and smiled. "Yes, I am."

He handed me an envelope and said, "You've been served."

CHAPTER 14

Beads of sweat were beginning to form on Kizzie Winkelmann's forehead, and her body was trembling from standing still too long on the pedestal in front of the mirror. While I continued pinning different areas of the bodice, I was utterly frustrated by how poorly the wedding gown was still fitting her waify frame.

Kizzie had been on an extreme, 800-calorie, pre-wedding diet. Three months before the wedding, she had successfully lost a total of 120 pounds. From there, we began the actual production of the dress. Unexpectedly, Kizzie continued losing weight.

For the last month, I constantly had to remake portions of the gown to fit her shrinking body. Today was no different, and I was afraid that I might need to remake the dress entirely.

I began vigilantly pinning the left side of the bodice, but every time I released the fabric to reach for another pin, the dress would slide down her bony frame. My guess was that Kizzie weighed under 100 pounds now, and I was concerned. I noticed her protruding collarbone, vacant-looking eyes, dull complexion, and thinning black hair—and her strapless bra that was holding on for dear life to breasts no larger than two baby-size yarmulkes.

"Okay," I said, my patience just about gone, "let's try

pinning the back seams of the bustier and see what happens."

Kizzie placed her hand on her stomach. "If it helps, I'll try sucking in my gut," Kizzie said, without taking her eyes off her reflection.

"I would appreciate it if you wouldn't," I said.

I know I sounded aggravated. Usually, I had endless patience for fittings, but I couldn't stop thinking about being served legal papers from William last week. It will take months, no, make that years before I will fully forgive Tatiana for telling William that I was at the Polish Palace celebrating my parents' anniversary when he called to talk to Jack that night. She unknowingly led William's court paper serving crony right to me.

In the legal documents, it stated Jack was living in an unhealthy environment and he needed more parental interaction. Not only did he request extensive visitations, but he also wanted Jack to live with him and his new wife, Vanessa, in a shared-custody arrangement. The thought made me sick, and my plans to fight him were just getting warmed up.

After hearing about Scarlett's bang up job of getting Penelope's charges dropped after Penelope banged up the entire Gold Coast room of The Drake Hotel, I felt good about my decision to hire Scarlett, hoping she'd help me win my upcoming court battle.

"Sorry, I was only trying to help," Kizzie said but sounded sad.

"I'm the one who's sorry. I didn't mean to be short with you." Anyone could plainly see the girl was weak and so rail thin she was practically transparent. I wondered what she thought when she looked at herself in the mirror.

I heard my share of insecure comments from not only my heavy-set clientele but from virtually all of my clients. I've never heard any client say how much she loved her stomach, upper back, or arms. The self-deprecating comments usually began when I measured the bride for the dress. During the dreaded process, which could last up to ten minutes, most clients uttered excuses for their appearance and confessed they needed to lose weight. It broke my heart to hear their hurtful, self-disparaging comments that no woman should ever hear coming out of someone's mouth, especially her own.

I thought they all looked beautiful just as they were. If only my clients would believe that I was logging a page full of measurements to ensure their newly designed gown fit like a glove—and not judging their self-proclaimed flaws—the troublesome experience would instantly become pleasurable.

Afterward, when a client asked to see the measurement sheet, I always refused to show it. I've learned it doesn't matter if there are such a thing as the perfect set of measurements scribbled across the page; I haven't met a client who would be satisfied with even those numbers.

So, it was my mission to make these lovely, intelligent women, who were carrying around these massive insecurities, feel beautiful on the day of their special event. I especially wished that for Kizzie.

Once again, I regarded her stationary torso. "I would rather you breathe normally."

Kizzie looked at me skeptically. "Then, maybe I should slip on my Spanx."

Usually, my clients use every form of miracle bondage available on the market to look two sizes smaller. Today that wasn't necessary.

"No girdles for you. You could use something with a little padding."

"No way," she shook her head. "I worked too hard to remove all of the padding."

"I hear you, Kizzie. Now, can you please breathe out?"

"I am!" she exclaimed.

I was frustrated. It was late in the afternoon, and I was angry with myself for not insisting on a halter-gowned design instead of a strapless gown that was all the rage these days.

"Hi, Mom," Kizzie waved, trying to control her shaking hands.

Kizzie's mother, Mitzi, had just come into the store carrying a take-out bag from the bakery down the street. "You should have seen the line. I nearly got into a fight over the last bear claw. But I got it," she said, proudly holding up the bag. "Jules, you want a piece of rugelach?"

"Boy, does that sound good," said Kizzie, chiming in.

"I wasn't asking you, Kizzie. I was speaking to Juliana."

Kizzie lowered her head in shame.

"No, thank you," I said.

"Are you sure?" Mitzi asked. "You're looking kind of skinny these days."

I was rather taken aback by the comment, but replied, "Yes, positive."

"Suit yourself." Mitzi shrugged her shoulders and added, "Mind if I eat at the table?"

"Well, the table's covered with fabrics, and…"

"Don't worry, there's plenty of room," she said, pushing aside a roll of white silk fabric. With a thump, she placed the large bakery bag and an uncovered, paper coffee cup on the table.

"Great," I answered, trying not to think about the possibility of Mitzi spilling coffee on treasured fabrics I'd spent years collecting.

"You know, there was a time when I could eat four bear claws and never gain a pound," Mitzi chuckled.

I looked at Mitzi and thought the bear claws must have finally made their dent because she bore a slight resemblance to the famous "Chubby little cubby all stuffed with fluff." For a heavyset woman, she wore bright, tightly fitted clothing inappropriately, with her long, black mass of corkscrew hair surrounding her heavily made up face. I could tell this was a woman who didn't want to blend into the background.

"So, I was watching this extreme-weight-loss reality show set on a deserted island last week," Mitzi said between bites.

"Oh, yeah!" Kizzie exclaimed. "I saw the same show. That was the one where a group of people ate only plants and dirt."

I nodded. "'Survivor?'"

"Yes, that's the one!" Kizzie said.

"Kizzie, can you please stand still?" I begged.

"Sorry."

"I don't think the premise of the show is about dieting. It's more about wilderness survival," I added.

"I don't know about that," she said, as she teetered on the edge of the pedestal. "But you should have seen how much weight these contestants were losing weekly. If I could, I would totally sign up for the next season."

I had the sudden urge to grab the huge pastry from Mitzi's tight claws and force it down Kizzie's bony throat. But I told myself to stay out of this family drama. It was obvious that Mitzi wanted her daughter to be the thinnest bride in her synagogue, some weird transference that was proportional to Mitzi's growing heft.

As I examined the hem of the dress, I was disappointed to see that the front looked uneven. I knew that as long as Kizzie fidgeted, this dress was never going to fit properly. My mind was so preoccupied with worries about the fitting; I jumped when my Russian seamstress, Svetlana, was suddenly by my side.

"Excuse me, Juliana," she said in her thick accent.

I began to teeter on my four-inch black stiletto boots. After regaining my balance, I smoothed out my houndstooth skirt. "Uh, what, Svetlana?"

"Vat do you want me to do vith these?" She held up a pair of black satin tuxedo pants.

"How should I know?" I was out of sorts today. I tried never to speak to my staff that way.

"Cause you're the boss, not Olga. Olga, she say I work on these pants. So, I told Olga to…"

I raised my hand just in time to stop Svetlana from spouting out nasty cuss words in Russian. Svetlana, and her not-so-identical-twin sister, Olga, fought nonstop. Svetlana had been upset to hear that everyone in her huge family agreed that Olga was the better-looking twin. More importantly, she was also the better cook. Personally, I couldn't tell the two plump Russians apart all the time. They both had short, curly hairdos and brown eyes. The only way I could tell who's who was that Svetlana had sprouted a light, prickly mustache. I supposed that was why Olga was considered the knockout in the family.

I tried to stare a hole through Svetlana's head and whispered, "Later…much. Got it?"

She shrugged her shoulders. "Yeah. Okay. But if pants not ready on time, then you put blame on Olga, not me. *Do svidaniya!*" She turned on her heels and headed back to the workroom.

I'd lost my focus, and I needed a moment to figure out where I had left off in the fitting. Halfway through re-pinning the bottom, I realized that Kizzie's swaying was becoming more pronounced.

"Kizzie, please," I begged. "You have to stand still."

"Yes, darling," Mitzi said. "It's great practice for when you get married by Rabbi Shimmel in the synagogue on Sunday." She turned to me and added, "Jewish weddings tend to be a little on the long side if you know what I mean."

I nodded and continued with the fitting. As I stood up, I noticed how arresting the contrast between Kizzie's pasty skin and her straight, black shoulder-length hair was. She looked as white as her satin gown.

"Oh my God," I said, as I reached for Mitzi's coffee.

"What's the matter?" Mitzi asked with a full mouth.

I ignored Mitzi and grabbed the cup. "Kizzie, have a sip of coffee. It will make you feel better."

As Kizzie reached for the cup, she went limp. Slowly, her body floated to the floor. I couldn't believe my eyes as she lay on her back, motionless on the floor. My heart raced as I quickly put down the coffee and knelt beside Kizzie. Gently, I placed my hand on her chest. A chill went through my body. I could feel each bone beneath my fingers. Thankfully, I also could feel her shallow breathing.

I turned to Mitzi sitting at the table. She hadn't said a word.

I leaned forward, staring straight into her eyes. "Kizzie, wake up. Wake up!" I begged.

I grabbed a bridal magazine and began fanning her with it. Next, I took a ring-bearer pillow from the display case and carefully placed it under Kizzie's head. As I continued to fan her face, I tried to remember what I had learned years ago in a CPR class I had taken at my local American Red Cross office.

My hand shook as I placed it on the center of Kizzie's chest. I was about to begin the compressions when Mitzi said in a relaxed voice, "Jules, that's not going to help."

I turned to Mitzi still sitting at the table. "I don't know what else to do."

"Hold on," said Mitzi, looking annoyed as she polished off her pastry.

I shook my head. I expected her to be surprised, maybe even emotional, but never hungry. Who could eat at a time like this?

"Don't look so worried, Jules," said Mitzi, brushing away some crumbs from her jacket. "She just fainted. It happens all the time." Mitzi walked over to her daughter, moving slower than an African Pancake Tortoise. She groaned as she lowered herself to the floor, one knee at a time. Once in place, she unhurriedly removed a black strand of hair stuck to Kizzie's cheek.

Mitzi's snail-paced speed infuriated me. "Hey," I shouted to the workroom, "I need someone to help me!"

Moments later, Nathaniel came racing into the shop, followed by Zoë. I motioned with my hand for them to join me. Soon other staff members gathered behind me. I could hear their whispers in the background, but I was trying to focus on Kizzie.

Meanwhile, Mitzi slipped her hand into her side jacket pocket and began rooting around for something. She pulled out an object the size of a lipstick case, yanked off the cap, and began waving the tiny silver tube back and forth under Kizzie's nose.

Kizzie didn't move an inch.

"That's it," I announced. "Nathaniel, call 9-1-1!"

As he rushed to the nearest telephone, Mitzi gestured for him to stop. "Hang up that phone. Do you hear me? No one's calling the paramedics."

Nathaniel obliged.

Once she made sure that the phone was back in its cradle, she said, "It's okay. I know what I'm doing." Everyone listened as Mitzi spoke to Kizzie. "Wake up, Kizzie. Jules needs to finish your fitting."

"Wait, hold on one second," I said, interrupting Mitzi. "I'll do no such thing."

Mitzi ignored me and continued talking to her daughter. "Kizzie. You're being a bad girl."

Stay calm, Jules, I kept saying to myself.

As Mitzi scolded Kizzie, I motioned for one of the older Polish seamstress, Elizabeth, to join us. Even though Elizabeth had lived in the States longer than any of the other seamstresses, she spoke very poor English. And, I didn't want Mitzi to know what it was I had in mind when I asked Elizabeth, in Polish, to go to my office, call the paramedics, and bring me a box of pins.

Mitzi watched Elizabeth rush to my office. "Where's she going?" she asked, glancing at me suspiciously.

"She's bringing more pins," I explained. "We need them for the fitting."

Mitzi pulled out the tube again and held it under Kizzie's nostrils. Her head began to roll back and forth slowly on the miniature pillow. My heart was pounding in my chest as I held my breath and watched Kizzie begin to move her fingers.

"Very good. Now, sit up," Mitzi prompted.

Kizzie shook her head.

"Oh, you're not going to get up?" asked Mitzi.

Kizzie shook her head again.

"So be it. Jules will just have to pin the bottom of the dress while you're lying there. But don't blame me if the dress turns out to be lopsided."

Elizabeth returned with the box of pins.

Mitzi turned to me. "Okay, Juliana. Time to get to work."

I just stood there, glaring at Mitzi and staring at poor Kizzie stretched out on the floor.

"Now!" demanded Mitzi, her temper running hot.

Elizabeth and I traded glances. I took a few pins from the open box Elizabeth was holding and gave her a knowing look. Elizabeth nodded her head slightly. I assumed that meant the ambulance was on its way, so I had to kill some time. I turned to Mitzi. "Perhaps Kizzie could come back tomorrow when she's feeling better?"

"That's impossible! The wedding's Sunday, and it's already Friday afternoon. How do you expect to finish the gown in time?"

Hmm. She had a good point. The dress wasn't close to finished; the bodice needed taking in, and the skirt and train required hemming. And yet I've always managed to get the dress to the synagogue on time, and I swore to myself that I would find a way to finish Kizzie's gown.

I turned to Elizabeth, hoping she would understand me if I enunciated every word. "Can you stay and work on the dress tonight?"

"Tonight? No!"

"Please, Elizabeth!" I begged, tears welling in my eyes.

Elizabeth eyed me for a moment before she let out a heavy sigh. "Okay, I stay."

"Not good enough," Mitzi said. "Elizabeth needs to finish the gown by sunset tonight."

"Wait! Why sunset?" I asked.

"Because tonight is the beginning of Shabbat."

Elizabeth looked at me, confused. I was confused myself. "I'll explain later," I told her in Polish.

"I am assuming that neither one of you are Jewish," Mitzi said, her tone imperious.

We shook our heads no. "Well, Shabbat is our way of embracing the sacredness of time. No one's allowed to work on Kizzie's dress from sunset tonight to nightfall on Saturday night."

"Wait just one minute," I said, then caught myself. I was about to fly off the handle at Mitzi. Instead, I tried to remain calm and allowed Mitzi to finish the story.

"Because our religion demands all Jews to rest, Kizzie cannot take part in another fitting until Shabbat ends."

Kizzie needed more than rest. Food for starters, I thought as I looked down at Kizzie. *Keep it together, Jules, for Kizzie's sake.*

"Look, Mitzi, there shouldn't be any issues. Elizabeth is a devout Catholic; I'm Catholic, and so is Zoë—I think," I said, shooting Zoë a look.

"Sure," Zoë responded unconvincingly, raising her shoulders in the universal sign of "whatever."

"Can't you understand what I'm trying to say? It doesn't matter," Mitzi replied. "I don't care if Elizabeth is a Buddhist or practices Scientology. She would still be a Scientologist working on a Jew's dress. Neither Jew nor non-Jew will work on the dress after dusk, and that's final. Now finish the fitting before the damn sun sets."

Mitzi was running the show now, and she'd left me with no other choice. "Fine, I'll do it."

"I knew you'd see it my way."

I looked at Mitzi. "First, I need Kizzie's permission."

"So hurry up and ask her," Mitzi prompted.

Really? Was Mitzi seriously calling my bluff? I took a deep breath and leaned in closer. "Kizzie, do you give us permission to continue the fitting?"

To my surprise, Kizzie opened her eyes a sliver and gave me a faint smile. "Sure, Jules. That's fine," she managed to say before she shut her eyes again. I was flabbergasted.

"See, I told you so," beamed Mitzi. "Do I know my daughter, or what?"

The whole scene made my stomach churn, but what could I do? To the seamstresses I said, "Let's go, girls. Grab a ruler and a handful of pins and try to make this quick."

The workers rushed over and formed a circle around Kizzie.

"Start pinning!" I ordered.

Like a room full of ravens, everyone pounced on different sections of the dress. As I worked on the bottom of the train, which I'd extricated from underneath Kizzie's body, I fell back into my thoughts, replaying the afternoon's events in my head. Had I made the right decision? Considered all options? Kizzie had been in and out of consciousness now for nearly twelve minutes, and I was terrified.

In the past, I've had some shaky, heart-pounding brides suffer their way through a long fitting. For the faint of heart, I tried to keep crackers and some orange juice on hand, which usually did the trick to stop their symptoms. In Kizzie's case, I was fearful for her life and hoped I hadn't made a terrible mistake that might haunt me for the rest of mine.

I began to envision a fluorescent-yellow taped body outline drawn on the floor and felt a panic attack coming on. I took a couple of deep breaths and tried to speak calmly. "We need to roll Kizzie over and finish pinning the back," I said. "On the count of three. One, two, three."

As we rolled Kizzie over, I heard an ambulance siren.

"I thought I said no ambulance!" Mitzi sounded perturbed. No one spoke a word as they continued to pin.

"Are you mostly finished?" Mitzi growled.

I gave the dress one final check and looked to each seamstress for her final approval. Apprehensively, I watched as they one by one nodded their heads.

"Well," Mitzi asked, anxiously.

"We're done," I announced. All in the room cheered.

"Thank Gawd," Mitzi exclaimed. "Get her out of that dress, now!"

The seamstresses took their places. "Nathaniel, you hold her up, and we'll pull," I ordered. We heaved and hauled, but the dress wouldn't budge. After several seconds of jerking, yanking and pulling, we managed to remove the figure-hugging gown from Kizzie's body.

Miraculously, moments before two young paramedics walked through the door, Kizzie, dressed only in her push-up bra, pantyhose, and pumps, stood up and ambled over to the table. She reached inside the bakery bag and pulled out a handful of rugelach. To our amazement, she began to devour the pastries.

"Kizzie, when was the last time you ate?" I asked.

Kizzie spoke with her mouth full, "I'm not sure, but I remember having had some prune juice this morning."

I felt the lump in my throat growing bigger and bigger and, all of a sudden, I burst into tears. I was sobbing so hard I could barely catch my breath.

"We got an emergency call from one of your employees that someone here needs our help," said the shorter paramedic.

Still crying, I pulled a sheet of fabric off the table like a magician and threw it over Kizzie's shoulders. Unable to speak, I pointed to Kizzie. Kizzie pointed to Mitzi, and Mitzi pointed to me. Looking confused, the other paramedic rushed over to me and started to slide a blood-pressure cuff around my arm.

"I'm not the one who needs help. She does," I said, pointing again to Kizzie.

"You leave my daughter alone," Mitzi screamed. "I'll have you fired!"

"All right!" said the taller paramedic. "That's enough. Could someone please explain what's going on here?"

"I'll tell you what's going on," I started. "The young lady over there collapsed during her fitting."

The shorter man rushed over to Kizzie's side and tried to examine her. Mitzi moved quickly, standing between him and her daughter.

The tall paramedic asked me, "What caused her to faint?"

"I don't know," I said. "It all happened so quickly. But I think she's starving herself before her wedding."

"Juliana, let me handle this," Mitzi cut me off. "You've done enough damage for one day."

Furious with Mitzi, I walked over to the worktable and listened for the next fifteen minutes as Mitzi squared off against the paramedics. There was no way I was getting in the middle of that scuffle. Besides, I had more important things on my mind. Like canceling dinner plans with Rocco for the second time this week, as well as avoiding Mitzi's phone calls for the remainder of Shabbat while furiously working side by side with Elizabeth to finish Kizzie's wedding gown.

The paramedics insisted on taking Kizzie to the hospital for a full exam, despite Mitzi's protests, and in the end, Kizzie's dress made it to the synagogue on time. However, weeks after the wedding, I became increasingly concerned about my actions. I prayed there was something a nice, Catholic girl could do to repent for disrupting a family's Shabbat (even if the family technically didn't know about it).

I decided to visit Rabbi Shimmel from the synagogue across the street. He had a long, unruly gray beard and dawned a yarmulke atop his almost-bald head. He wore black pants and a black waistcoat with a white button-down shirt. His demeanor was intense as he stared at me through his rimless reading glasses. I felt intimidated as I sat in front of him, but I tried to focus on his kind, gentle eyes as I explained the reason for my visit.

He was quiet for what seemed like forever before saying, "You knowingly sewed Kizzie's gown after dusk for which there is no forgiveness."

"Nothing?" I said, feeling nervous.

He shook his head vehemently.

"Not even a little something?" I prodded.

The Rabbi looked deep in thought.

We agreed on a custom-made silk scarf and a donation to the synagogue's preschool. He also gave me a book about Judaism and a long lecture about the sacredness of Shabbat. He explained, though, that as long as I didn't sew any more gowns for my Jewish clients during Shabbat, I probably wouldn't be going to hell anytime soon.

As I walked home, I still felt some concern about the 50/50 chances of going to hell. So, I changed course and visited Holy Name Cathedral for a second opinion. After I had left the confessional booth, I felt somewhat better.

On my way to my apartment, I couldn't stop thinking about Kizzie. I felt sad for the growing number of women, including myself, who had so many insecurities about their body image. Things had to change. I thought that I might be able to play a small role, and God willing, change the Rabbi's odds. After all, brides were always asking me my opinion on everything bridal: the best wedding planners, florists, eyelash extensions, bridesmaids' gifts, etcetera. From now on, I added a healthy-eating plan to the list.

The next day, I started telling every bride who came to Belle's that if she wanted her dress to fit properly on her wedding day, she couldn't fast the week before the nuptials. Also, on the day of the wedding, the bride should enjoy the delicious food that she carefully selected at their food-and-wine tasting appointment.

As for dessert, it was imperative for every bride to have her cake and eat it, too!

CHAPTER 15

Lately, my dark roots have looked nightmarish. Not even pulling my hair back into a sleek ponytail hid the two-tone mess. All things considered, I decided to do something that I had never done before: I spontaneously booked a hair appointment in the middle of a workday for a much-needed highlight.

As I sat under the futuristic-looking hairdryer dome at Purr Salon, waiting for my foil-wrapped hair to process, I took a sip of hot chocolate and looked around the packed salon. I saw women holding court in their revolving salon chairs while their stylists fawned over them. I felt as if I was on another planet.

These women spoke rapidly, words gushing out in torrents. *Who are these tickled-pink pampered women?* I thought to myself. They were so at ease as if they didn't have a care in the world. I, on the other hand, was just given my latest court date assignment. William's attorney had appeared before the judge three times now, asking for another extension. How many more times was I going to have to rearrange my work schedule because William had to travel on vacation and was unable to keep his commitment?

Between the warm air blowing from the dryer and hot drink in my hand, I dozed off. A few minutes later, I was startled awake by pounding on the acrylic dome, causing me to spill hot chocolate all over my lap.

"OHMYGOD, Jules!" Zoë exclaimed. She grabbed the towel from around my neck and tried wiping away the chocolate running down my legs.

I couldn't look down with my head wedged inside the dryer. "Turn off the dryer! You're causing a scene," I said, trying to keep my voice down.

Zoë held her finger to her pursed lips and made a "shhh" sign to me as she lifted the hood. Some of the foils got caught in the frame. I felt a sharp pain and pulled the hood back down.

"You have to use the knobs on the side of the dryer!"

"I'm trying!" Zoë turned the knob in every direction. It took a couple of seconds for the air to stop blowing before the hairdryer finally shut off, and I could safely extract my head.

"Ouch," I said, trying to untangle the foils.

Once I finished separating them, I pulled on Zoë's chiffon-patterned skirt, encouraging her to take a seat next to me on the plastic-covered couch. "What's wrong with you?" I hissed in a loud whisper.

"I'm sorry, Jules. I wasn't thinking."

"Please tell me that there's still some hair remaining on my head."

"Yes, you still have hair," Zoë said, practically in tears now.

"That's a relief," I said, patting her knee. "Now, what's going on?"

"We need you back at the shop. The maid-of-horror from the Brenner wedding is freaking out, big time."

"Why?"

"The gown doesn't fit."

"How bad is it?" I asked, hoping it wasn't too awful.

"Pretty bad. Honestly, it's terrible. It doesn't fit her at all."

"That's impossible."

"No. It's possible. I can't close the zipper; the skirt is way too tight, and the back is so loose that the fabric's draping like crazy."

I rolled my eyes, frustrated with the situation.

"Come on, let's go," she said. "The client's waiting for you."

I'd never dared step foot in the door of my shop in jeans or a hoody. "Well, I certainly can't go looking like this," I said, blowing away a piece of foil that was flapping in front of my right eye.

"But you have to," Zoë said in a panic. "She's threatening to come over here and go ballistic if you don't."

"Why did you tell her that I was here?" I asked, biting my nails. "You could have told her anything—I was getting my driver's license renewed, or I was at the dentist or Bible study class."

"When did you start going to Bible study lessons?"

"Oh Zoë, that's not the point! I don't want any more scenes today!" The minute I said it, I regretted losing my temper with her, because the last thing I needed was a crying receptionist.

She slapped her hands over her eyes, fighting back tears.

"Don't cry, okay?" I said. "Everything will work out just fine. It always does."

I got up, tied the belt of the black polyester smock tightly around my waist, and headed towards the door. The hot chocolate made my thighs uncomfortably sticky as I walked, but I ignored it. I pushed back the foil mess on my head with the back of my index finger and made my way through the hair salon.

"Melissa, please tell Kimberly that I had to go to the shop for a moment," I called out to my hairdresser's assistant on my way out.

"Hey, wait a minute. Jules, you're still processing!" Melissa yelled after me.

"Oh, don't worry. I'll be back in plenty of time."

I hurried out the salon door and ran down the corridor towards the shop.

"Dammit, I knew this was going to be a problem," I told Zoë. "Do you remember what I said when we got Connie's paperwork?"

"Yeah, you've never seen measurements like these in your lifetime."

"And?" I prodded.

"Um…you said that she must look like a big-breasted wood sprite."

"That's right. Was I close?"

"Nowhere near," Zoë said with a heavy sigh.

We arrived at the shop moments later. Before I opened the door, I peeked through the glass door and got my first glimpse of Connie Foster. She scowled, as she posed in front of the mirror in her maid-of-honor dress. Zoë was correct. Connie was no big-breasted, wood sprite—she was a flat-chested, incredibly tall and muscular, athletic-looking woman with boring beige, shoulder-length hair that looked like brittle straw. Her body language alone told me that I needed more than a pair of scissors and a few pins to get out of this mess.

Over the years, I found that out-of-town bridesmaids were the most difficult type of client because they were usually only available for one fitting. Depending on the style, I always recommended at least three fittings to ensure a perfect fit. If a gown was still fitting poorly close to the wedding date, it became a nerve-wracking experience—something I tried to avoid at all costs.

When I finally received Connie's paperwork last month, the measurements didn't make any sense to me. So, I called her.

Her response to every one of my questions was a resounding, "I dunno." I ran out of ideas and asked Connie if I could speak with the person who took the measurements.

I'll never forget Connie's tone of voice. "Absolutely not!

She's a professional seamstress and would be offended by your line of questioning," she barked at me. "The worksheet is an exact blueprint of my body."

And then she added, "Listen, I'm a very busy woman, and I'm going to hang up on you now." Click.

I tried calling her many times after our conversation to schedule her only appointment, but she never returned any of my phone calls. I breathed a sigh of relief when the wedding planner called last week to make that appointment for her.

"Jules, everything will be fine," Zoë said, parroting my earlier comment to her.

I took a deep breath, raised my head up high, and walked into my fate.

"Hello, you must be Connie," I said, extending my right hand. "I'm Juliana Belle."

"Hi," she said, giving me a weak little handshake. "What happened to you?" she snickered.

"Um, I had a little accident."

She shook her head with disdain.

"It's chocolate," I added, a bit too defensively, as I tried rubbing off the brown streaks.

"Maybe the spa next door offers a Swiss Shower treatment," she said, dripping with sarcasm. "You could certainly use one."

I tightened the belt on my smock. "It's not a spa; it's a hair salon." Suddenly, I felt an overwhelming amount of guilt for taking time off to have my hair done. But I had a feeling that this woman would feast on any morsel of guilt I exhibited, so I tried to stay calm and be lighthearted.

"No matter how busy we may be, we still need to find time to get our hair done. Right?" I joked nervously.

"I wouldn't know. I cut my hair."

Well, at least that explained the whole uneven-sloping-bangs look.

"Well, hello, ladies," Rocco said, rolling in through the

front door. He stopped in his tracks when he saw me in my robe and hair full of aluminum foil.

"Is this a new look you're rocking, Kumquat?" he said to me.

I laughed. "Yes, it's the latest bridal runway craze for spring? Do you like it?"

"I love it! It makes you look edgy."

"Well, hello," Connie cut in. "Who is this big, strapping, handsome man?"

I looked around the store.

"Umm, hello, Jules." Rocco grimaced. "She's talking about me, Babe."

"Oh, of course," I said. "Rocco Delgado, meet Connie Foster."

"Pleasure to make your acquaintance."

"Pleasure's all mine." Connie grinned from ear to ear.

"What brings you in, Rocco?" I asked.

"If memory serves me right, I thought you had a two o'clock. I wanted to see if you had time for a quick lunch before your appointment."

"Juliana can't make it today," Connie spoke for me. "You see, I had a sudden change in plans. The manicurist at the Peninsula Hotel had a two o'clock opening. So, I took it." She glanced at my hands. "You should consider having a manicure when you go back to the spa."

I wanted to scream at the top of my lungs; *It's not a spa!* But I kept it together and managed to ignore her comment.

"The dress was supposed to be ready today. Who knew that it wasn't going to fit—at all!" Connie said.

"Well, I think it looks hot," Rocco said.

"You think I look hot?" Connie turned toward the mirror.

"Definitely," Rocco said.

"Well, maybe there's hope after all."

"Good." I felt relieved. As much as I hated having Rocco (or anyone!) seeing me like this, it didn't seem to faze him at all. Plus, Rocco was helping the situation. "Do you like the style of the dress?" I asked.

"I don't know. It's not terrible," Rocco added.

What a resounding endorsement, I thought.

"Yes," Connie said, raising her shoulders then turning her back toward the mirror. "It's ordinary, but it will do."

A dozen snappy comebacks sprang to my lips, but they died there. I had to admit, Connie was right; the dress fit terribly. If I didn't know any better, I would have sworn that Olga sewed the dress in the dark while drinking a whole bottle of Sibirskaya vodka. Not only did the skirt length baffle me, but the neckline was so high that she could practically pull it up over her nose and mouth like a scarf.

"And, look here," she said, "who would pick such a ridiculous style? The draping is so low that you can see my butt-crack."

I clenched my jaw. How could I tell Connie that the design didn't call for any draping and that my pattern maker, Phu, must have done shots with Olga?

"Honestly," said Connie. "I expected more from Catherine. She usually has such great taste."

"Catherine didn't design the bridesmaids' dresses; Andrew did," I said.

Connie was speechless.

Andrew Brenner, the father of the bride, was charming and outgoing unlike his wife, Judy, who was quiet and reserved. Their personalities could not have been more opposite. Andrew was fifty years old when he sold his successful interior design business and retired to help plan his only daughter, Catherine's, wedding. Judy ran a private-equity company and had to travel weekly. She was delighted when Andrew offered to organize the extravagant affair.

Andrew worked endlessly to pull together an underwater wedding fantasy at The Shedd Aquarium. Imagine: 20 cooks, 300 waiters, a 100-member building crew,

10,000-square-feet of aqua carpet, 4,000 pieces of china, and 10,000 flowers. Because the heavily adorned wedding gown was so massive; the dress was expected to arrive at the hotel in a separate car.

When the time came to choose the bridesmaids' dresses, Catherine couldn't make up her mind. She asked Andrew and me to design the most exquisite gowns that any bridesmaid would be delighted to wear. Even though the gowns looked similar at first glance, each gown was slightly different. The same gold iridescent silk organza embellished with embroidery was on the skirts, but each bodice matched the individual bridesmaid's personality and figure.

As for the maid-of-honor, well, her gown's design was even more spectacular. I specifically remembered telling Andrew that I couldn't wait to see the maid-of-honor's reaction. Needless to say, this dress wasn't anywhere close to what I expected.

"Now I understand everything," Connie said, trying to look wounded. "Why would Andrew give me any thought? After all, I'm just a glorified bridesmaid."

"That's not true. I know for a fact Andrew wanted to design a unique dress for you."

"Really?" Her tone softened. "Well, if that's true, I'd like to see his reaction after I tell him about my horrific first fitting." Connie continued to insult my design until my hairdresser, Kimberly, interrupted her.

"Jules, you *have* to come to the salon and have your hair washed immediately. If I don't get you out of those foils, Marilyn Monroe is going to look like a washed-out brunette next to you."

I recognized the panic in her voice.

Connie parted her lips and ran her tongue over her teeth. "Please, don't let me stop you from your precious spa time," she rasped.

I felt nauseous.

"I have an idea," Rocco said. "Why don't I drive Connie

to her manicure appointment, and Jules, you can get your hair fixed."

"Really? You would do that for me?" I asked.

"It would be my pleasure, Babe."

"Thank you," I said feeling incredibly grateful to Rocco. "Would that be all right with you, Connie?"

She grinned from ear to ear. "That would be fine."

Well, I guess, it was back to the old drawing board for me. Though, perhaps, it wasn't so much a drawing board as a sketchpad.

"Zoë, please have Olga measure Connie for a new dress." I looked at Connie, who wore a malicious grin. As our eyes locked together, I felt a cold chill creep up my spine. I forfeited the staring contest and turned to my hairdresser. "Let's go, Kimberly."

"And let's go, Rocco," said Connie, grabbing him by the arm. "You can walk me to the dressing room."

After taking a few steps, she stopped and looked back at me. "Oh, and by the way, I will overlook today's inconvenience by having you paying for my manicure."

I nodded and dropped my head in defeat.

Connie laughed like a super villain. "You know what? I like you. I have a feeling we're going to become the best of friends by the time the bridesmaids' luncheon rolls around, won't we?"

"Of course we will," I promised. "Can't wait."

The tables for the Bridesmaids' luncheon were set exquisitely at The Standard Club, a prestigious, nationally recognized private club that caters to the Chicago business elite and fashionable society. I found my seat, but I didn't have much of an appetite for the lobster tail that Andrew had specially flown in from Maine. I was still stewing over how much money Connie had cost me yesterday.

She must have caught me looking at her from across the table and asked, "Is there something you want to say to me, Juliana?"

There was plenty that I wanted to say, but I decided to keep my mouth shut. "You're manicure looks nice."

Shooting me a wicked smile, Connie put down her napkin and raised her wine glass. I felt uneasy sitting across from her, listening to her complain about how overcooked the lobster was. Quietly, I nibbled away at my sourdough roll and couldn't wait for the luncheon to end.

"Sir," Connie said as she waved over a waiter. "Can you please bring my girlfriend some hot chocolate," she said, pointing to me. "Juliana, I know how much you loooove hot chocolate. Try not to spill any this time."

I just looked at her for a moment. "How nice of you to remember." Frustration set in as I ran my fingernails through my much shorter hairstyle. Regrettably, I waited too long to have the foils removed, and the bleach had played havoc with my hair. But I didn't mind the new edgy, long platinum bob cut.

I tried to avoid any more conversation with Connie and chatted with the other bridesmaids. After a while, I excused myself from the table and set out to organize the bridesmaids' gifts in the other room.

I walked through the door of the bar and took a seat at one of the tables. I've been to a lot of weddings in my career, but I had never seen such exquisite bridesmaids gifts before. Not only did Andrew pay for the dresses, but he had custom gift bags made for each bridesmaid that matched the pink satin garment bags hanging nearby on the chrome rolling-rack. Each gift bag contained personalized makeup, toiletries, satin shoes, a lace purse, and a crystal hair clip. The best gift of all was the delicate gold ring with the bridesmaid's name engraved in a small diamond heart.

Andrew also paid for the bridesmaids' airfare and transportation, hotel suites, spa treatments, hair blowouts and updos, makeup artist, and the gourmet bridesmaids' luncheon. Today, these lucky ladies were going to squeal with delight when they see their custom-made gown and matching gifts.

I thought of all those unfortunate bridesmaids who were asked to pay for their heinous polyester dresses and Greyhound bus tickets. They would feel envious over Connie's dress. I wouldn't put it past Connie to mistaken Andrew's kindness and generosity for a gratuitous display of wealth and affectation.

Speak of the devil. As I was busy retying a pink satin bow on one of the bags, I heard Connie's voice coming from the wine-tasting room. A large stone-and-glass-fireplace separated the two rooms, so I peered through the flames and spotted Connie talking on her cell phone.

"I agree," Connie said as she admired her nails. "It will be an amazing start to the wedding weekend." Silence, then Connie spoke again. "True, but he deserves it." She paused and sniffed a little. "You don't understand; he ruined my life. And now I'm going to ruin his."

I was intrigued by the conversation.

"Wrong again. He deserves it." Connie paused. "Why? Because, he needs to know how a broken heart feels."

I could see Connie shaking her head.

"I don't know; I'm still waiting for the perfect opportunity."

I was about to walk away when I heard her say, "I can't wait to see the expression on Judy's face when I tell everyone that her husband's a complete liar."

Andrew's not a liar!

"I know for a fact that their twenty years of marriage are a sham. I'm telling you—he's gay."

"No!" I let out a gasp and immediately covered my mouth.

"Hold on," Connie said. "I think I heard someone."

I quickly crouched behind the fireplace and held my breath. Silence. I began to worry until I heard her say,

"Nope. False alarm," followed by a short pause to be sure.

My brain was spinning, and her words brought tears to my eyes.

"It sounds like he's staying quiet until after the wedding's over." There was another lull in the conversation. Ha! That's a joke. No, you're totally wrong. It's not about Catherine's special day, at all. Andrew doesn't want to ruin *his* special day after all his extensive wedding planning." Pause, then Connie continued, "Yeah, I'll let you know. I'm thinking right after his speech."

"Oh my God," I mouthed.

"Okay, I gotta go," said Connie. "Wish me luck."

The shock of her words made me unable to move. Eventually, I managed to poke my head out to see if the coast was clear.

After I had taken my seat at the table, I didn't know how I was going to keep the tears from flowing.

Andrew walked over and placed his hand on my shoulder just as I was about to pour sugar in my tea. I practically dumped the entire bowl of sugar into my cup.

"Take it easy, Jules. I didn't mean to startle you."

I stared at Andrew as though he were a stranger.

"Hey, Jules. It's me, Andrew," he said with a grin. "Is everything okay? You seem preoccupied."

"Oh, no. I'm fine," I said, picking up the teacup and taking a sip. The sugary brew made my teeth ache.

Andrew glanced at the mound of sugar floating in my drink. "Okay?" he asked again.

I nodded though he didn't look convinced.

"Good. By the way, was the crystal purse delivered to Catherine's room today?"

I put down the cup. "Yes. I believe it was."

"Hmm, that's strange. She hasn't said anything." He looked perplexed.

"Maybe it just slipped her mind."

"You're probably right."

"I'll call the concierge later to check to give you piece of mind."

He smiled the warmest smile imaginable as he looked over at his daughter and added, "That's a good idea. I just want to make Catherine happy."

It warmed my heart to see the loving way that Andrew looked at his daughter.

Catherine must have sensed her dad's attention because she looked our way and smiled, causing Andrew's face to light up.

Catherine was a living, breathing doll. Her dewy makeup was perfect, showcased by her chestnut brown hair pulled back with a black satin headband.

"That's all I want—to see my Catherine happy," Andrew said again, looking off into the distance.

"Are *you* all right?" I asked.

"Oh, yes. I'm fine," he said, wiping a tear from the corner of his eye. "My little girl's getting married tomorrow, and everything is going to change forever."

"Change is good," I said. "Catherine loves you very much. She'll always be Daddy's girl."

"Thank you, Jules," Andrew said, patting my shoulder. "I needed to hear that."

"I'm being honest. I've spent a lot of time with both you and Catherine over these last few months, and I can tell how much Catherine respects you, how she hangs on your every word."

Andrew nodded in agreement. "Well, then I'd better pull myself together and find my notes for the speech." He fished around in an inside pocket and pulled out some index cards.

That's when I noticed Connie getting up from her table.

"Wait!" I said, standing up. "It's not like Catherine to not mention the purse. I'm going to call the concierge right now."

He looked at his watch. "Can't it wait?"

"Please," I said, a little too anxiously. "It will only take a minute."

I walked away without waiting for a response from Andrew and followed Connie out of the dining room and into the bathroom. As she stepped into the handicapped stall, I called after her, "Connie! Wait!" Before she could close the door behind her, I pushed my way inside.

"Hey, what are you doing in here?"

I quickly slid the lock closed and leaned up against the door.

"Get the hell out!" she shouted at me.

"I need to talk to you."

"About what?"

"I know what you're up to."

Connie's face went ashen. "I—I don't know what you're talking about."

"I heard your nauseating phone conversation earlier. You're beyond contempt." My voice was like a bullwhip.

Connie came face-to-face with me and looked me in the eyes. "Stay out of it, Juliana. It's none of your business."

"Listen to me!"

"I'm not going to listen to the hired help." She fought to keep her voice steady.

I hesitated for only a second before telling her exactly what I thought of her. "You're nothing but a bully. You're also a two-faced, cunning, certifiable liar…"

"How dare you?"

"I'm not finished yet. You're a rude, miserable person without any manners."

"Your words bore me. Can you just shut up already and get back to work."

"I'm warning you, don't go through with your plan. Or else—"

"Are you threatening me?" she asked, with more than a hint of melodrama. "Juliana, you're a nobody. And nobody cares what you have to say." She pushed my shoulders.

"A nobody?" You'd better watch out. Cause you're talking to the guardian of the dress, Lady!" I said and pushed back harder.

One thing was for sure. I sucked, sucked, sucked at the intimidation game.

Connie looked at me as if I was crazy. "What in the world are you talking about?"

As I struggled to find the right words, I became more enraged by the second. Before I could stop myself, I grabbed a fistful of her hair and pulled it with all of my might.

"Let go!" she screamed.

I tightened my grip.

"You little guardian of the underpants! You think you're going to stop me by pulling my hair?" She slammed me hard against the stall door, causing me to let go of her hair.

"It's *dress*, not underpants!" I screamed at the top of my lungs. I realized I was completely out of control, but I didn't care. I might not have known it right then and there, but I was about to release years of pent up frustration towards Bridezillas, William, Tatiana, and even Rocco. So, as soon as I regained my balance, I went after her lopsided bangs with a vengeance.

Meanwhile, someone came rushing into the bathroom and knocked on the door. "Hey, is everything okay?"

We stopped fighting and stood perfectly still, staring at the door.

"My…life suh-uh-ucks…" Connie burst into tears.

"Lady, you think your life sucks, try working in a bathroom for half your life," the woman replied.

I managed to recover my composure. "We're good. Everything's fine in here."

"Okay, just don't make a mess."

I listened for the sound of her footsteps retreating and heard the creaking door open and close again.

Connie plopped down on the toilet seat.

"You must hate Andrew."

"No. I'm in love with Andrew," she said through her tears.

"Really? You're in *love* with Andrew?"

"Yes."

"Connie, I'm sick of your lies. Do whatever you want," I said, waving my hands in disgust. "I'm leaving."

"Don't leave," Connie begged, grabbing me by the hand. "I'm not lying this time. I can explain everything."

I turned around and faced her. "I'm listening."

Connie took a deep breath. "Growing up, I spent a lot of time with Catherine. I would eat dinner at her home practically every night, and her family invited me to join them on their vacations. All those times we traveled, I never saw Catherine's parents in the same room together." Connie wiped her eyes with her hands. "They lived separate lives. Andrew was the one who took us to riding class, shopping at the mall, and to the movie theater. He was kind and considerate and acted like he loved me. So, it started as an innocent teenage crush, but my feelings for him grew, and by my senior year in college, I was deeply in love with him. I obsessed over the idea of taking Judy's place and becoming the loving wife that I thought he deserved." She closed her eyes for a moment, then opened them again. "I knew it was wrong, but I couldn't help myself."

She was quiet a moment and grabbed the end of the toilet paper roll, practically pulling all of the remaining tissue out of the dispenser. After she'd blown her nose for what seemed like a long minute, clearing out her sinuses once and for all, she continued. "These thoughts were taking over my mind, and I became painfully depressed. After graduation, I decided to separate myself from Catherine and try to forget about Andrew. When Catherine called me a few months later to ask me to be her maid-of-honor, I wanted to cry."

Nope, I was wrong—those must be some pretty blocked sinuses. Again, Connie blew her nose like a foghorn before she continued.

"I didn't want to be in the wedding because I still had strong feelings towards Andrew. I couldn't say no to my best friend. So here I am." She looked down at the floor.

"So, you accepted your best friend's invitation to be her maid-of-honor, only to hurt her in the end."

"Of course not."

I just stared at her, waiting.

"I had planned on putting my feelings aside and being there for Catherine, but when I checked into my hotel room, I found the most beautiful crystal purse sitting in the foyer. A note attached read: *To my beautiful girl. You mean the world to me. In case you still have any doubts, I will always love you.* The stationery belonged to Andrew."

"But...that purse wasn't..."

"Please let me finish," Connie said, interrupting me mid-sentence. "I read the note over and over again. I couldn't believe it, Andrew loved me. I needed to tell him that I loved him, too. But with the busy week leading up to the wedding, I had trouble finding a moment to talk to him in private. Later, I remembered that Catherine and Judy had reservations at the spa that afternoon. They love going to the spa practically as much as you do."

Really!

"That's when I decided I'd go to Andrew's hotel room. My heart was pounding as I stood at the door to his suite. I was about to knock when I noticed the door was open. So, I went inside. That's when I heard two men fighting. A man, whose voice I didn't recognize, was yelling at Andrew. He was saying things like, 'This has gone on for too many years now. When are you going to tell your wife?' I assumed that Andrew must have told him about being in love with me. But then Andrew told him, 'I can't do it before the wedding. I refuse to ruin the most important day of my daughter's life. I swear I'll tell her on Monday.' The other guy sounded relieved, and the room went quiet. I decided to wait thirty more seconds before going inside. My heart raced as I walked around the corner and then my heart sank. I couldn't believe my eyes. They were embracing."

It was sad hearing Connie talk about Andrew's secret with such contempt in her voice.

Connie continued, "I was so confused and backed away unnoticed. Then I ran back to my room and cried for hours. After staying up all night, staring at the purse, I wondered what kind of sick game Andrew was playing. By this point, my feelings were so hurt I decided two could play at the same game."

"Connie, listen to me. The bellman made a mistake."

"What are you talking about?" she asked.

"The purse was a gift from Andrew to Catherine. The bellman delivered it to your room accidentally."

"So you're saying that he doesn't love me?"

"I'm sure that he cares a great deal about you. But he doesn't love you the way you want him to."

"Oh my God. What am I supposed to do now?"

"Move on," I said.

"How?"

"Get some help. See a doctor."

"Why, do you think I'm crazy?"

I stood there studying her disturbing facial expressions. "I… I don't know what to say." I opened the stall door to leave.

"Close the door, Juliana."

Something in Connie's voice sent out a warning signal. I started to leave when she pleaded, "Stay."

I closed the metal door. "What do you want from me, Connie?"

"Answer the question!" Slowly, Connie's eyes filled with tears. "Do you think I'm crazy?"

She didn't bother to wipe the tears away when she threw her arms around my neck. I could feel her monster tears soak through my silk blouse.

"Please, don't cry."

"Oh God, I'm ashamed. When Andrew finds out, he'll hate me forever. And, believe it or not, I love Catherine like a sister. So, now I'm going to lose her, too."

"No one is going to hate you."

Connie thought for a moment. "I suppose you're going to tell them all about our bathroom brawl."

"I wasn't planning on it."

"Why wouldn't you? Especially after the way I treated you these last two days?"

"Because the Brenners deserve to have their dream wedding."

"I... I don't know what to say."

I cocked my head at her. "Then don't say anything—to anybody."

"I promise. Not a word."

"Good. Come on, I'll help you clean up," I said, unlocking the stall door.

Connie and I spent the next few minutes brushing out her matted hair and reapplying her makeup. Once Connie looked presentable, she turned to me and said, "I'm sorry I gave you such a hard time about the dress."

"Let's just forget about it, okay?"

"I can't. I need to tell you something."

I was afraid to ask. "What is it?"

"The reason my dress didn't fit was because I sent you my Aunt Gertie's measurements."

The first thought that popped into my mind was that Aunt Gertie was a hideous-looking woman. "Why?"

"Because I thought if the dress didn't fit, I wouldn't have to be in the wedding."

"Oh, Connie, you have no idea what you put my employees through. My pattern maker, Phu, almost quit. And Zoë's been popping Xanax ever since your last appointment."

"I've made a terrible mess of things. Haven't I?" Connie said, shaking her head.

I nodded in agreement.

"But I'm going to make things right starting today. First, I'm going to give Catherine back her purse and be the supportive maid-of-honor that she deserves. Next, I'm going to have lunch sent to your staff next week with my sincerest apologies."

"Thank you. I'm sure that will make them very happy."

"Would you ever consider forgiving me?"

"Possibly," I said, grinning. Today was a game changer. Not only did I get to the bottom of Connie's dress dilemma, but it felt good to stand up for myself.

Connie gave me a big smile. "I want you to know that I love the new dress you made for me."

"Well, that's a relief. Let's hope that Aunt Gertie feels the same way." I raised an eyebrow. "She's very lucky to have a generous niece buy her a matching dress."

Connie gave me a knowing look and unzipped her purse. "Oh, she most certainly will," said Connie. "Now, do you prefer cash or credit?"

CHAPTER 16

While I was checking for extra toilet paper and hand soap in the hotel suite bathroom, determined brides-to-be lined up single file in the hallway leading to the InterContinental Presidential Suite, anxiously awaiting the start of my two-day, yearly blowout sample sale. They were grumbling about the line, but they were the lucky ones. Half an hour after the doors opened, a portion of Michigan Avenue experienced a power outage that trapped dozens in the elevators.

Darkness didn't stop the brides who'd hired personal trainers to get them whipped into shape before their wedding. They had no problem climbing the generator-lit stairwells to the twentieth floor, joining the early birds to shop till they drop.

The light creeping in through the windows illuminated the many fine antiques displayed in the Presidential Suite. As the temperatures climbed into the high eighties, the air felt hot and sticky, unseasonably warm for April. The humidity was making my hair frizz out of control. Out of desperation, I tried using the only thing I could find—Static Guard—as hairspray, but I still couldn't manage to tame the frizzy mess.

While brides fluttered about the suite, fanning themselves with pink sample sale fliers and trying on dresses, I waited impatiently for Zoë's return from the coffee shop. Once Zoë arrived carrying a tray of ginger-macadamia breakfast rolls, she told me about the huge lines forming in the lobby. As brides on a budget arrived from all over Illinois and neighboring states, the hotel was forced to section off the main entrance to the lobby and create a velvet rope barricade leading to the stairwell. Zoë also mentioned that the fire marshal had the unenviable task of telling impatient brides they had to wait for the next group to be escorted up to the suite by security guards.

Lately, my entire office at the shop was overflowing with wedding gowns. Every time I walked in, I had to make my way through the fog-like tulle and ended up with ostrich feathers stuck to my lipgloss. A little reminder that it was sample sale time again. And I needed to empty the nest.

The suite I'd selected this year for my annual liquidation sale included three large connecting rooms that now overflowed with racks of gowns, mounds of petticoats and enough tiaras to crown pageant winners across the country. I quickly learned that an event like this catered to a very different clientele than I was used to.

I watched in astonishment as piranha-like women ransacked the room, searching for bargains and snapping at anyone who got in their way. Immodest women stopped, dropped and rolled off their summer dresses in the middle of the aisles, bunny-hopping their way in and out of dress after dress. I hated hearing the sickening sound of materials ripping as brides forced their big booties into sample-size dresses. I grew weary of their outrageous demands and constant griping about the prices being too high.

Who did these women think I was? Someone at the local swap shop who could be haggled by the old, "I don't need, want or like it, so, if you want the sale, you'd better give me a much better price" tactic?

No, dammit, I was Juliana Belle, a well-known Gold Coast designer who used her talent and skills to create a complicated work of art. But in all honesty, I didn't feel that way today, and maybe they had picked up on that. I was trying hard not to take their intentional criticism personally. If I did, I would have taken all my beautiful gowns back to my lovely air-conditioned shop and charged full price again.

The rest of the morning dragged on for what felt like an eternity. By noon, the lights had come back on, but the air conditioning was still not repaired, with the carpet moist from the humidity. And the room began to smell stale. *Hang in there, Jules. Just four more hours to go,* I chanted to myself.

I needed to lighten up. Mother was right. I was turning into a sourpuss. These women weren't piranhas. They were bouncing bunnies running around the lettuce patch, happily chatting away and sharing their endless wedding details. Maybe I was envious. Maybe I'd been dealt a bad hand. Rocco was a good guy and maybe if I married him, William would back off because I, too, would have a family. And I wouldn't feel like a phony any longer. I could join the ranks of all of these women and plan my dream wedding, too. That made me feel better.

I was about to turn down a bride who was angling to work for me in exchange for her gown when I heard a familiar voice.

"Well, hello, Juliana Belle."

Slowly, I turned around to see a woman who looked remarkably like my bride, Penelope. She sashayed over to where I was standing.

"Hello, gorgeous!" she chirped, giving me a hug that practically took out all of the air from my lungs.

"Penelope, I *almost* didn't recognize you," I managed to say as I got my breath back.

"I probably look different without the handcuffs," she said, holding up her wrists.

We both laughed.

Miraculously, Penelope had transformed from a

champagne blonde socialite to a shoulder-grazing auburn-haired beauty in relaxed jeans and a white t-shirt.

"What are you doing here?" I asked.

"While I was having a double latte at Starbucks nearby, I noticed your pink sale flyer on one of the tables. I felt like it was a sign from the fashion heavens. So, I grabbed the flyer and came rushing over." She took a deep breath and flashed a lovely, yet unassuming, pear-shaped diamond ring. "I'm in for another wild ride!"

Penelope was about to join the ranks of second-time brides—the latest trend in the bridal industry for all the Millennials getting remarried. And most salespeople at upscale bridal stores were behind the times. It was no secret they could be snobbish, if not outright rude as they pressured brides to purchase a gown on the day of their appointment, not deigning to extend themselves beyond what was formally required to make the sale. But what they didn't seem to understand was this latest trend meant the brides were out in full force planning bigger, better weddings. More than likely, a first-time bride would be making the bridal rounds again, so if a retailer wanted to make the cut the second or third time around, they needed to leave a lasting, good first impression.

"Congratulations! I am so delighted for you," I said, giving her a big hug.

She grinned. "Me, too. I couldn't be happier."

I looked around and noticed that my sales associates were all helping brides, and nobody was in need of my immediate attention, including the bride that had been haggling over the price. I decided to find out more about the upcoming nuptials. "Come, sit down and tell me everything," I said.

"Okay, but I don't have much time."

"So, give me the abbreviated version," I said, walking her over to the floral couch. "Who's the lucky man?"

She plopped down next to me. "His name is Ross, and he is ridiculously hot. Come to think of it, you've probably met

him. He was the hunky arresting officer at my wedding."
She tapped vigorously on her heart, apparently remembering
only the good part of that awful day.

"Really? I do remember him."

"Yes. It was so romantic—well, not the arresting part;
that totally sucked. I mean, what happened later. After he
had taken my mug shot and fingerprints, he brought me an
extra blanket and pillow for my cell. Sweet, right?"

I smiled in response.

"After his shift ended, he had to work overtime. And
here's the romantic part: I was ready to pass out from
hunger, so he snuck in some candy and a can of soda."

"How romantic."

"I know attacking Tad was a slightly hysterical move.
But if I hadn't, I never would've met my soulmate. We've
been dating for eight months, and Ross proposed to me last
Wednesday."

I thought, *slightly?* Instead I said, "That's wonderful.
Have you set a date?"

"Well, we want to get married, like, yesterday," she said,
giggling.

"That's pretty quick."

"It's crazy, I know. But he's The One, so why wait?"

"Well, there is the matter of…"

"Don't worry," Penelope interrupted me mid-sentence.
"Your attorney friend, Scarlett's got my back. She's been
great, by the way."

"I'm glad to hear it. I think she's an amazing lawyer."

"And I hear she's got a knack for dress design."

"She's talented in many ways."

"That's why I don't make any more rash decisions without
consulting with her first," Penelope said. "So with Scarlett's
blessing, we've set the date for a week from today," she
announced. "We're getting married in the Bahamas, with
only our closest friends and family members present. See,
everything is moving at lightning speed."

"And she doesn't consider that to be a rash decision?"

"She does, but there's a romantic side to her that she risks letting you see from time-to-time."

"Wow, we'd better get to work then," I said. "What do you have in mind?"

"I know for a fact that we both want to be barefoot and breezy. At first, I was thinking of the dress you designed for the cover of *Bride's Magazine*, but it might be too formal."

"Oh, that dress," I said, cringing at the thought of the run-away, runway bridal gown for Hazel Nutt. "I agree. You need something light and flowing for a beach setting. Come to think of it, I have a very special gown in mind that I think you'll love."

"Sounds great. I'm excited."

Zoë was standing behind us, pretending to be folding bridal gloves, but I guessed she was there so she wouldn't miss a bit of the latest gossip. I stood up and whispered something in her ear.

"Of course," she said. "Be right back."

I took my seat again on the couch.

"How's the little fella?" Penelope asked. "What is he, like six now?"

"Yes, can you believe it? Jack's an absolute sweetheart," I said, beaming. "Thanks for asking."

"Is there a man in your life?" asked Penelope.

Butterflies started swarming in my stomach. "Sort of."

"That's fantastic news!" Penelope said, patting me on the knee.

"Thanks."

"What's his name?"

"Rocco Delgado."

"Roccoooo Delaahhhago? Hmmm?" she said in a sexy voice. "How long have the two of you been dating?"

"I don't know if you'd call it dating, but I've known Rocco for about a year and a half."

"So why didn't you ever mention him during our appointments?"

"You never asked."

"Okay, well, that's fair. Are you guys serious?"

I shrugged my shoulders. "Define what you mean by 'serious'?"

"Are you going to get married? Have a fairy tale wedding and wear a beautiful gown. That sort thing."

I could feel my face turning red. "Oh, I don't know about that. It's different the second time around."

"Not for me. I can hardly wait to get my dress."

I could feel my shoulders tightening. "Then I'd better get my act together," I said, trying to change the subject.

"Where did you meet Rocco?"

Guess it didn't work.

"At Delgado's on Randolph. He owns the market," I said, biting my lip.

"I love that place. They have the best Puerto Rican passion fruit."

"I know! Right?"

Zoë returned carrying the wedding gown and my cell phone. "Excuse me, Jules," Zoë interrupted, "Rocco's calling."

"Speak of the devil," Penelope said, grinning wide. "Go ahead, take the call."

"Thanks." I smiled at Penelope.

Zoë handed me the cell phone and held up the dress. While Penelope studied the wedding gown, I answered the call.

"Hi, Rocco," I said, trying my best to sound perky.

"Hey, Babe. How's it going?"

"As good as can be expected for selling wedding gowns on a hot day without AC."

"Well, I know something that will cheer you up."

"What's that?" I asked.

"The bank decided not to foreclose on my condo."

"That's terrific news!"

"Yeah, I'm looking at the letter now. It's official. We need to celebrate."

"Definitely," I said.

"So, what time do you think the sale will be over?"

"Oh, I don't know. Maybe never."

He laughed. "Why?"

"I'm still waiting for the overnight security guard to arrive. The last time I talked to him, he was on a coffee break. I haven't heard from him since." I covered the receiver and whispered, "Sorry, Penelope."

She smiled and mouthed, "It's okay."

"Rocco, I hope you don't mind, but I'm going to go straight home whenever he gets here."

"But what about our date?" asked Rocco.

"Can I have a raincheck? I'm exhausted."

"Come on. Just lock the damn door and come over."

"There's no way I'm going to leave the gowns unattended."

"Jeez, Jules. Can't you get one of the hotel's staff to stay until the security guard gets there?"

He sounded angry, and I looked at Penelope before I forced a smile. Penelope returned the half-hearted expression. I walked to the corner of the room.

"Rocco, my gowns cost thousands of dollars. Not to mention, the tiaras, bridal jewelry, petticoats, and accessories. I'm sorry, I just can't leave whenever I want to."

"All right. I give." He paused for a moment. "As long as you're making the sales, I'll keep my mouth shut, stay home and watch the Bulls-Celtics game. I've got some money riding on it."

"I'm certainly trying to make sales, and in fact, I need to get back to it."

"OK, that's good news. I mean about the sales. Your little Rocco needs a Red Lambo."

I stared at the phone receiver, confused. I never knew he wanted a Lamborghini.

"Hello?" he said. "Jules, are you there?"

"Yeah. I'm here," I sighed. "Hey, would you mind dropping by my apartment and checking on Jack for me?"

"I don't think that's such a good idea," he said, shrugging off the request.

"Why not? I'm sure he'd love the company."

"He probably won't want to see me."

"I thought you guys were getting along better after my parents' anniversary party."

"We were, up 'til I told him that he danced like a girl."

I shook my head, disappointed. "Why would you say such a thing?"

"I was joking."

"Jack is six years old. He doesn't understand sarcasm."

"Well, he'd better get used to it because I can't change who I am."

Really? "Well, you at least need to apologize to him."

"Fine. I'll give it a few more days, and then I'll talk to him. But not today." I looked up and noticed Penelope fighting in her seat.

"Thank you. Gotta go," I said. "I'm with a client."

"Sure, call me after the game."

I hung up and turned to Penelope. "Sorry, that was Rocco."

"He sounds...nice?" she said but didn't seem convinced.

"Penelope," I paused for a moment. "Tell the truth, are you scared to get married again?"

"Sometimes, but I try not to let fear guide my life. I've done the hard work and let go of my past. I'm finally ready for my fairy tale ending."

"You give snake-bit girls like me hope." I laughed.

"Don't give up, Juliana."

"I'll try not to," I said, thinking back to a heartbroken Scarlet. If she could let her snake bite heal, maybe I could, too.

Scarlett Smith became engaged last month and decided to wear her mother's lace wedding gown. She asked me to sell the dress at the sample sale. After hearing Penelope carry on about Scarlett, I had the brilliant idea of showing Penelope Scarlett's dress. It didn't take Penelope long to fall in love with the wedding gown—an enchanting blush-tone organza mermaid-style dress with tiny flower clusters trailing down the back. From the moment I saw Penelope's expression when Zoë showed her the dress, I knew that I had made the perfect love connection.

Between Scarlett's amazing turn of heart and Penelope's exciting news, I began to rethink my situation. Maybe it was time for me to let the hurt go and get on with my life—and love.

Once Penelope left, only one bride remained in the suite. Thank heavens this day was almost over. I forced myself to concentrate on her, but after half an hour of hearing sob stories while she tried to negotiate a better price, I was seriously considering lynching myself with the nearest wire hanger.

But then, I noticed Rocco among the bridal gowns. There he was holding up two large brown take-out bags from Gino's East.

"Rocco!" I called out.

As he sauntered over, the waiting bride caught my eye. *Oh, why not?* I thought. I needed to get this blessed day over. "Sold!" I said, agreeing to her last negotiating price and grabbing the dress. I then hustled it over to the credit card machine. The happy bride followed close behind.

Rocco walked up and gave me a quick kiss on the cheek. "Well, I remembered that I hate to eat alone," he said, holding up one of the bags, "so I figured I'd drop by."

"Awww, that's so nice," I said, my voice trailing off as I wrote the invoice.

"But I'm telling you," he said, "it was a long hall to get up here?"

I looked up from the invoice and noticed beads of sweat on his forehead.

"There's bottled water in the bar," I replied, handing the bride the invoice.

She smiled and gave me a credit card without saying a word. No doubt she knew she was getting the deal of the century and was afraid to say anything that might make me notice I was practically giving it away.

"Sorry, Rocco, but no sympathy from me," I said to him as he guzzled water. "You have no idea what kind of a day I've had. Try being stuck up here with no electricity half the day, and then no AC for the rest of the day with a million women having hot flashes. See how you like it." I looked at my client. "No offense."

"None taken," she said, nodding in agreement.

I suspected I could have called her a redheaded-barracuda, and she wouldn't have taken offense as long as I'd take her credit card for this amazing bargain.

"Add that to Jack's endless calls asking when I'd be coming home."

"Yeah, well, I'm missing the Bulls-Celtics game."

I held up my finger telling Rocco to hold that thought while I finished the credit card transaction.

"How much?" he asked, whispering in my ear.

"None of your business," I laughed.

Before Rocco could come up with a snide retort, the credit card went through. It took only five seconds for the bride to grab her gown, wish me well, and leave me alone with Rocco. He then continued to tell me what a sacrifice he was making by bringing me dinner when a scrawny-looking security guard arrived at the suite.

"Well, it's about time!" I said, exasperated.

"Sorry, ma'am," he said, shrugging his shoulders. "Crazy day."

"Tell me about it," Rocco and I said in unison.

Rocco looked at the short, lanky man. "That's the security

guard?" he said, with a smirk.

"Rocco, please," I said, and looked apologetically at the man.

"Don't worry, ma'am," the man said. "Your gowns are safe with me."

"Thank you," I said, and then turned to Rocco. "Ready to go?"

"Hey, wait a minute. What do you want me to do with all this food? I paid good money for it," he protested.

"You can enjoy it at home in front of your big screen TV."

"*What?* You're not coming back with me?"

"I told you; I'm going home to see Jack."

"Well, that's just great," he barked.

"Why don't we talk about it downstairs," I said, signaling with my eyes that I did not want to have this conversation in front of a stranger.

"Ma'am," said the security guard, "I'm afraid to tell you that there's a long line for the elevators. It's going to take you a while to get down."

"Great," I said, throwing up my arms in the air. "Can I ask, how did you get up here so fast?"

"Well, I came up on the freight elevator," said the guard. "I can give you the key if you promise to leave it with the bellman downstairs."

"Sure," I said, feeling a great sense of relief. I took the key from him, grabbed my oversized purse, and walked towards the door. "Good night. See you in the morning— nine o'clock sharp." I grabbed Rocco's arm and added, "Let's get out of here."

"This is utter bullshit," Rocco said under his breath, but I heard him. Then he grabbed the bags of food and breezed past me. I gave the security guard one last wave before he closed the door behind me before I ran down the hallway, trying to catch up to Rocco. We eyed each other unhappily as we stepped into the freight elevator and slowly began our descent.

Suddenly, the lights flickered.

I felt my toes lift slightly off the ground before slamming back down. I bounced into the padded wall as the elevator screeched to a halt. The lights shut off, and the elevator car went dark.

After a moment, a faint red blinking emergency light came on. What are the odds? Two power outages in one day?

I felt a wave of panic come over me. "No!" I whined, kicking the metal grate elevator door. "We're stuck."

"Don't panic," Rocco's voice remained calm and steady. "There has to be an emergency switch here somewhere."

I could see the red outline of Rocco's shadow as he searched for a panic button. Seconds later, an alarm bell shrilled, and my stomach jumped into my throat.

"Found it!" Rocco yelled. "Come on. Somebody answer!"

After ten minutes, we were both relieved to hear a muffled voice come over the loudspeaker. "Hello?"

"Yeah, hi," Rocco replied. "You've got two people stuck in the service elevator."

"What?" the voice said. "Can you speak up? I'm having trouble hearing you."

"We are stuck in the service elevator!" Rocco shouted, enunciating every word.

"We're aware of that, sir, and we'll do everything possible to get you out."

"That's great," I chimed in. "When do you think that will be?"

"We're not certain. It all depends on when the power's restored."

"Listen, I've got to get home."

"I understand that, ma'am. But there's not much we can do right now. We've got people stuck in the main elevators, not counting the garage elevators. So for the time being, please be patient."

"Patient?" I turned to Rocco. "He wants me to be patient?

I've been *more* than patient this entire time William's attorney has been pushing the court date out further and further. Now, I have my first court appearance on Monday and have to prepare a boat load of documents this weekend. Now, I'm going to have to pull an all-nighter." I stopped ranting.

Silence.

"Hello!" I screamed, looking up at the ceiling. "Hello, anybody up there?" I began pounding on the door. "Somebody, get me out of here. Now!"

"Jules, what are you doing?" Rocco asked. "No one can hear you."

I finally lost it and began pushing every floor button as tears rolled down my face. Then I slid my fingernails in between the metal frames and tried to pry the doors open. This move always seemed to work in the movies, but all it did was break my fingernails. The door remained closed. After my meltdown, I rested my cheek against the cold metal.

Rocco walked over to me and took my hand, trying to ease me away from the door. He enveloped me in his large, strong hands and said, "It's going to be okay. I'm sure the power company has a crew working on this right now. Relax, Jules. They'll get to us eventually."

I nodded meekly and whimpered, "I promised Jack I'd be home before he went to bed. I wanted to tuck him in." I felt a pang in my heart, thinking how much I missed Jack. It had been a long week, and I had worked late every night. "Wait, I've got my cell phone. I can call him."

I pulled away from Rocco and sank to the floor. I grabbed my purse and began fumbling around, searching for the phone. I kept finding last week's Happy Meal toys and other nonessentials, so I finally dumped all of the contents onto the floor and grabbed the silver cell phone.

I speed-dialed my home number and pressed the send key, but all I heard was the annoying busy signal telling me

I had no service.

"Jules, give it a break already. No wonder Jack is such a mama's boy. You smother the poor kid."

"*Give it a break?* I can *never* give it a break. You have no idea what it's like being a single parent." I stared at Rocco as I felt a sinking feeling in my heart. I could see the hurt expression in his eyes, and felt bad losing my cool. But I hadn't seen Jack much all week, and that was just something Rocco didn't, maybe couldn't, understand.

Rocco shook his head and stepped aside. He couldn't go far, though.

I walked over to join him. "Rocco, I... I'm sorry," I said.

His eyes softened a little.

"I'm such a jerk," I admitted.

"Hey, I completely get it. I know it's not easy being a working mom."

"It's not. But that's still no excuse for my behavior." I smiled for the first time.

"It's okay. Let's just forget this ever happened."

I nodded in agreement. I looked down at my pathetic nails and hands, and we both started laughing. After that, the tension began to wash away quickly.

"For what it's worth, I was looking forward to this evening," I said. "It seems that whenever we have a special night planned, something gets in the way."

"I think it's still possible," Rocco said, pulling open one of the paper bags.

We sat down on the floor of the service elevator, ate pizza and proceeded to have a good time sharing stories and laughing. I set aside all my fears about marrying this guy, and just enjoyed having him as a good friend.

"Come here," he said, patting the floor.

I slid over and sat next to him.

"I'm sorry again about my behavior earlier," I said.

"Don't worry about it. We were both cranky," he said, giving me a little nudge.

"You know, I'm amazed how well this evening ended after all."

"Me, too, Jules." He turned to face me. "I was planning on doing this during dinner tonight, but this feels like the perfect time. There's something I want to tell you."

"What is it?" I said, smiling.

"How about instead of telling you, I'll just show you," he said, flashing a nervous grin.

I watched him reach into his front jean pocket and pull out the teeniest plastic baggie, the size of a disposable pill pouch, and open the seal. He shook the pouch upside down until a ring fell into the palm of his hand. "What do you say, Jules?"

My smile fizzled.

Okay, I'll be the first to admit that working in the bridal business, I was starting to think that all marriage proposals were beginning to sound insipidly generic, but I never expected to be given a ring wrapped in a plastic baggie inside a service elevator. After realizing that my mouth was still hanging half open, I covered it, attempting to curb my shocked expression.

"What's wrong?" he asked, placing his hand on my shoulder. "I thought you'd be happy."

"I… I… I'm speechless," I said, incredulously, as I continued to stare at the ring.

"You don't like it?"

"No, it's lovely. Really."

"You're sure not acting like it."

"It just seems so sudden, and you're having financial problems, and…" I said, tears welling up.

"Maybe you'll feel better wearing it when I tell you the great news." He slipped the ring on my finger and took a deep breath. "I've been making money to pay off my unpaid mortgage payments."

"That's great news."

"Now we can have a fresh start."

"And Jack?" I added, looking down at my finger.

"Of course, Jack, too."

I half-nodded in agreement. "How did you get the mortgage payment?"

"Playing craps at the Riverboat Casino."

"What?" I said, my voice rising. "You could have lost all your money!"

"But I didn't lose; I won."

"Then you're lucky because the house always wins there."

"Well, the house didn't win this time." He laughed. "You might say I won my house!"

"I wish you'd talked to me about this first, Rocco." I began to remove the ring.

"Slow down, Jules," Rocco said, grabbing my hand. "I wanted to talk to you in person, but you've canceled on me the last three times we were supposed to get together. When we finally met for lunch last week, you seemed preoccupied with work, and I didn't want to worry you. Besides, I don't have to ask for your permission. I'm not Jack."

I let that one go, working on the bigger problem facing me. I had to pick my battles after all. "It worries me that you think gambling is the easy way out."

"Relax, Babe. I know what I'm doing. Craps are my go-to game. I never lose."

"Yeah, right."

"Maybe once or twice, but having a winner's mentality doesn't allow me to focus on those times."

I had to look at the positives. "Wouldn't it be a smarter and safer bet to focus more on your business? It's such a great fruit market; you could open up another location."

"Seriously Jules, who are you kidding. I'm not going to hit the jackpot by selling Croatian cantaloupes."

"My business started out small, and look how much it's grown."

He shrugged. "Must be nice to be handed a family business on a silver platter."

"Hey! I've had something to do with the store's success."

Rocco put his arm around my shoulder. "Sorry, Kumquat. That was a cheap shot. I know how hard you work. Forgive me?"

"Fine."

"Hey, if my gambling bothers you so much, I promise to stop after we get married."

"I don't believe you."

"Promise." Rocco held up his hand in the Scout's honor three-finger salute. "Listen, Babe. I've got an even better idea. Let's elope. You've been all stressed out lately, why add any more hassles? Fuck the wedding. Let's just go to Vegas and get married!"

"What? You can't be serious. First of all, I didn't give you an answer yet. And second of all, how could I tell Jack that he's not going to be in the wedding? It would break his little heart."

"Why would Jack be in the wedding?" Rocco asked.

I stared at him. "Why wouldn't he be?"

"Because a wedding is about a man and his wife."

"It's man *and* wife. Not *his* wife. He doesn't own her. And I can't get married without my family present and Jack by my side."

Just then, the lights came on, and the elevator shaft jolted into motion. We were going down. Finally.

CHAPTER 17

I grabbed my phone from the kitchen counter and flipped it open. Thank heavens it wasn't Rocco. After last night, I needed some time to let his freight-elevator proposal sink in. "Hello?" I said, breathing hard.

"Hello, may I speak to Juliana Belle?" a female voice asked.

"Speaking."

"Juliana, this is Darlene Cook, the concierge at the Four Seasons calling."

"Hi, Darlene, how are you?"

"I'm well, thank you. I'm sorry to be calling you on such short notice, but I need to ask you a favor."

"Sure, what is it?" I asked.

"I know it's Sunday, but I have a special request from one of our hotel guests, Crystal Shandelier. She'd like to visit your business today. Would you be willing to make an exception and open the store for her?"

Would I ever! Even though I felt tired from the sample sale, I didn't care. Pop legend, Crystal Shandelier was coming to my shop.

Teen pop queen, Mavis Hildegard, AKA Crystal Shandelier, became an overnight sensation during the 1980s pop scene. Mom and I loved going to her concerts whenever she was in town. We could barely control our excitement while we sat in the front row, dressed in everything Crystal at Mother's insistence: feather boas, huge chandelier earrings, rhinestone bracelets, and hoodies covered in crystals. Every year, we anxiously awaited to see Crystal perform on a stage surrounded by thousands of twinkling lights.

During her last concert, we counted 56 costume changes for Crystal and her dancers. After performing her finale, Crystal announced that she had inked a two-year deal to perform her own Las Vegas show at Caesar's Palace. These days, she was living in Vegas and rehearsing for the upcoming show. I wondered what she was doing in Chicago. I guess I'd soon find out.

"Darlene, it would be my pleasure," I replied.

Over the years, I had formed great relationships with the hotel concierges throughout the Gold Coast and never declined their requests.

"Wonderful! I'll inform Miss Shandelier. I know she'll be thrilled. Can you please hold for a moment?"

"Sure." I waited on the line for Darlene to return.

"She can be there in forty minutes," Darlene announced. "Does that work?"

I looked down at my wrinkled pajamas and ran my fingers through my greasy hair. "Can we make it an hour?" I asked.

"No. Unfortunately, she's running on a tight schedule today."

"Of course. Please tell Miss Shandelier I look forward to seeing her in forty-five minutes."

"Fabulous! Thank you so much, Juliana."

I dressed quickly, hoping not to wake anyone. As I pulled open my top vanity drawer searching for a hairbrush, Rocco's engagement ring rolled out. I sighed and stopped what I was doing and stared at the ring before slamming the drawer shut. I could hear the ring make a dinging sound when it hit the back of the drawer.

"Oh, whatever," I said to myself. I'd deal with Rocco later. All that mattered now was that Crystal Shandelier was coming to my bridal shop from the wedding capital of the world. Just the thought of it gave me butterflies.

My phone rang again. *Mom.* "You'll never believe what just happened?" I said, as I grabbed a hairbrush from the middle drawer and began brushing my hair. "Crystal Shandelier's on her way to the store, as we speak!"

I found it telling that I didn't share with her about Rocco's proposal yesterday but instead chose to tell about my new celebrity client.

"Oh my God. I *love* Crystal Shandelier!" Mom squealed.

"I know. Isn't it thrilling?"

"I'll say. I just saw her picture in *Enquirer Magazine*. She lost all her baby fat and looked gorgeous. Supposedly, she's taking some miracle 'fountain-of-youth, anti-aging growth hormone' that's only available in Denmark. Would I like to get my hands on some of those pills."

"Please, Mom. Don't get any ideas. Let's stick to FDA-approved."

"Fine. Whatever you say, Juliana."

Wow. That was easier than usual. She probably didn't mean a word of it.

"Why is she coming to the store?"

"I don't know." I shrugged.

"Maybe she wants you to design her wardrobe for her Vegas show?"

"Wouldn't that be an incredible coup?" I said. My mind immediately began thinking of styles. "I could make her a jaw-dropping gown dotted with thousands of hand-placed Swarovski crystals with matching show-stopping rhinestone corsets and tiny ruffled skirts for her backup dancers!"

"Yes! And don't forget the feathers," Mom said, cracking us both up.

"I wonder what she's like," I said.

"I'm sure she's fabulous. You have to get me her autograph."

"I don't know. That could be awkward."

"I'm sure people ask her all of the time. Oh, and don't forget to get one for your Aunt Audrey."

My answer to Mom was, "I'll try," but I mouthed the words *never ever* to myself.

"I heard that, Juliana Bell!" Mom announced.

How does she do that? She must be psychic; I thought to myself.

"Also, get me the name of her plastic surgeon."

"Mom, I can't do that."

"Okay, then just the name of the hormone pills. Please," she begged. "You'll ask her if you love me."

"Oh, I think I hear Jack in the other room. I want to give him a hug before I leave. Gotta go. Love you."

"Love you, too."

I put on the bare minimum of makeup and twisted my hair into a knot. A couple of minutes later, dressed and ready to go to the shop, I was once again in search for my keys. Just as I was about to yell out to Jack to give me back my keys, the doorbell rang. I heard Jack open the door.

"Boże drogi." Hmm, that was odd. Jack was saying "Oh, God" to someone in Polish.

"English, Jack," scolded Rocco.

Boże drogi! My stomach heaved. What was *he* doing here? I completely forgot that Rocco was coming over this morning. And to make the morning even crazier, Tatiana was walking around, ranting in Russian, probably something about her latest boyfriend or a missed modeling opportunity.

"For crying out loud, does anyone around here speak English? If so, Kid, is your mom ready?" Rocco sounded grumpy.

Great, I had to break another date, and Rocco was already in a bad mood. I grabbed my work tote and ran out the bedroom door. As I exited, my purse strap caught on the door handle and jerked my body back inside. After I had managed to unhook the strap from the handle, I tripped over the corner of the area rug. Thrashed and whipped, I somehow managed to join the boys at the front door. Rocco was holding a small crate in his arms.

"Well, good morning, boys." I hugged Rocco and kissed Jack's head. "I didn't hear you get up this morning," I said to Jack.

"Yeah," Jack said. "I've been up for a while looking for my Lego submarine."

I ignored that comment. I'd stashed his submarine in my closet until I could find time to fix it. Luckily, Rocco jumped in.

"Wow, I see you finally got rid of all the wedding gowns. I can see your apartment for once. You must have made a killing. I should charge you for these." He held up the crate, but caught my look and quickly added, "Just kidding. For you, Babe." He handed me the crate of Fujian Lychee. "Fresh off the truck."

"Thanks, Rocco," I said, but I was thinking about how late I was for my appointment.

"Sure. I know how much you love them," he said, glancing at my bare ring finger as I took the box from him.

Instinctively, I curled my fingers around the crate to hide my finger. During the car ride home after the stalled elevator ride last night, Rocco gave up his crazy idea of eloping. When I told him I wasn't ready to give him my answer, he said to keep the ring and told me to think about it some more. He seemed genuine when he told me he didn't want me to feel any pressure. When I was ready, he told me, just wear the ring, and we would take it from there. I guess I couldn't blame the guy for checking my ring finger today, but it was too soon for him to be getting antsy.

I turned to Jack and said, "Look what we just got." I opened the box and showed Jack the bumpy but succulent fruit. "Remind Tatiana to give you some for lunch."

"Why do you have your work bag?" asked Jack.

"You got somewhere to be?" Rocco asked. "I thought we

were going to brunch and a matinee."

I bit my lip. I had to tackle these problems one at a time. "Jack, please put this crate in the refrigerator. Mommy has to go to work. But I'll be back in a few hours. Love you." I gave Jack a kiss on the cheek.

"Love you, too." He turned to leave, balancing the small crate.

"Hey, not so fast," I said. "Before you go, I need my keys."

He smiled. "They're in my side pocket."

I pulled out the keys and gave him a playful pat on his behind. Now for Rocco.

"Jules, what's going on here?" he asked.

I looked at my watch. Not much time to explain. "Umm, I owe you big time for this, Rocco, but I'm designing a dress for Crystal Shandelier in like, five minutes."

"You're making a dress for a light fixture?"

I had to laugh. "No, the singer. You know, Crystal Shandelier." I grabbed my purse from the front table.

He grimaced. "Never heard of him or her."

"Well, *she's* a big star, and I couldn't say no. Do you know what this could mean for business?"

"No, I don't."

"It would give the business a tremendous boost if Crystal Shandelier hired me as her costume designer for her new Vegas show." I felt a surge of excitement and gave Rocco a huge smile.

He frowned at me, instantly crushing my joy.

Feeling deflated, I said, "I know this sucks, but you might recall I had to go to Melody's wedding alone when you received that shipment of rotten bananas." He didn't say anything to that—just looked sad. I handed him the tickets and kissed him on the cheek. "You could still go."

He refused the tickets. "Really, Jules? I'm not going to a movie alone."

"Why? People do it all the time."

"Complete losers. I'll just hang here for a while and make Jack watch the Sox game with me."

"That's a nice thought, but I'm not sure he'll want to."

"Stop protecting him. It won't kill the kid to watch a ballgame."

I certainly didn't want to get sucked into that conversation right now. "Fine. Then I leave it up to you to decide."

"Okay, then," Rocco answered, shaking his head.

"Oh, by the way, do you have my mom's necklace? She was asking about it."

"No, it's still out for repair. Ronnie said it might be a while cause it's an old necklace, and it needs a special part for the clasp."

"Well, thanks again for doing that for my mom. See you later." I adjusted the strap on my purse and rushed out.

As I closed the door, I could hear him muttering, "Thank you for your permission to go to the movies alone. Between Jack and that store…"

I was practically running as I hurried toward the shop. As I was closing in, my phone rang. I pulled out the phone and flipped it open. Rocco. I snapped it shut.

Because of his call, I wasn't paying attention to the traffic light until a taxi driver laid on his horn. I waved apologetically and backed up to the curb. As I waited for a green light, I saw a white stretch limousine pull up in front of my store. I watched the driver open the passenger door. An extraordinarily beautiful woman stepped out of the limousine. She had her long cherry red hair artfully crimped and wore a stunning black leather outfit. Another woman climbed out the other side of the car holding a handful of rhinestone leashes attached to five well-behaved, Maltese dogs.

And Mother.

I blinked my eyes, shook my head, but she was still there. Just a few feet from the limo, Mom wore a white feather boa around her neck with the ends flapping in the wind. She waved a record album in the air. "Crystal!" she shouted. "Please! Please, autograph this for me."

Thanks to Jack hiding my keys and Rocco's standoff, Crystal had arrived before me. I hoped that didn't cost me my Vegas show gig.

I looked both ways for cars and crossed the street. As much as I wanted to intercept Mom, I knew I had to get to the shop if I wanted to be there to greet Crystal.

I made a sharp left turn and ran towards the back of the building towards the secret entrance to the store. I took the freight elevator to the mezzanine level, feeling relieved first to arrive. I ran around turning on the lights and stereo and grabbing anything that was lying out of place, throwing it into a fitting room. When I returned to the front door, I was surprised not to see anyone. Mom was probably pumping Crystal for information about where she went to have her nostrils waxed. Just the thought of it made me cringe.

Ah, then the elevator dinged. The doors opened, and the largest, angriest-looking bodyguard I've ever seen emerged from the elevator. This guy would make the Fur Coat Bandit I'd encountered a few years ago look more like a chipmunk. He removed his black sunglasses.

"How you doin'?" he said in a deep voice. "I'm Sam. One of Miss Shandelier's bodyguards." Sam was six-foot-six and weighed at least three hundred pounds. His head was so big that his ear receiver looked like a nugget of corn inside his ear.

"Nice to meet you, Sam." I shook his hand; his strong grip took my breath away. "I'm Juliana Belle," I said, barely able to get the words out.

"Miss Shandelier should be up shortly. In the meantime, can you show me the workspace where she will be sitting?"

"I usually work with clients at that table over there," I said, pointing to the worktable.

"No, that's not going to work."

"Why?"

"She would prefer to meet with you in a more private location, preferably somewhere without any windows."

"Really?"

"She doesn't want the paparazzi taking pictures of her through the front windows."

"Ummm… Well, the only area that doesn't have windows is the workroom in back."

"Perfect."

"It's not very glamorous."

"She doesn't care about that. As long as there's a big enough space for a food table."

"What do you mean? Like a buffet?" I asked.

"Yes."

"The room's pretty small. I guess we could use one of the cutting tables."

"That'll be fine." He pushed a button on the ear receiver and said, "There's a table in the workroom. Gather everyone and come up. Oh, and don't forget the pee-pee pads."

It was hilarious hearing a man his size say 'pee-pee pads.' I had to stop myself from laughing. "Where is Miss Shandelier now?"

"She's in the manager's office," said Sam. "She'll be up shortly."

"Why is she in his office?"

"We needed to get her inside the nearest enclosed area to get her away from a super fan."

My heart skipped a beat. *Mother!*

"Not a big deal. It happens all the time."

"We'll, I'm glad she's okay," I said.

"She seems to manage well through all the nonsense."

Maybe she can give me some pointers.

He paused and listened to further instructions. "It looks like we're about ready," he continued. "But before Miss Shandelier can come upstairs, her manager will need to ask you to sign a non-disclosure form agreeing not to talk about anything that you'll be discussing at today's meeting. Do you have a problem with that?"

"Not at all."

"Then I'll be seeing you shortly. In the meantime, my partner's doing a final sweep of the building. The rest of the staff is on their way up. Oh, I almost forgot. Don't shake hands with Miss Shandelier. She's a total germaphobe. And try not to stare at her. She doesn't like that very much. Do you have any questions for me?"

"No. I don't think so."

"Great. Thank you for your time." He put on his sunglasses and vanished down the hallway.

While I reviewed the non-discloser contract, the entourage shuffled through the showroom and up the stairs to the workroom. When Crystal Shandelier arrived, the first thing she did was pull off her red wig. A mass of beautiful platinum hair tumbled past her shoulders. She swung her hair back-and-forth and brushed it out with her fingers. "Ahhhh, that's much better," she said, handing the bushy wig to her stylist.

I stood frozen, staring at the celebrity before me.

She tucked a luxurious blonde tress behind her ear. "Hi, I'm Crystal Shandelier. Thank you so much for agreeing to meet with me."

"Hello," I said, extending my hand before I remembered what Sam told me. I quickly slipped my hands into my pockets. "Such a pleasure to meet you," I said, flashing a huge smile at Crystal.

"Thanks. I'm looking forward to working with you," she said in the silken voice of a seasoned crooner.

"Miss Shandelier, would you like to follow me upstairs?" I asked.

"Please, call me Crystal."

"Right this way, Crystal." I directed her to the stairwell leading up to the workroom. I was afraid she would have trouble walking up the steps in her metal zig-zag heeled boot, but she climbed the steps like a pro.

As I walked with Crystal into the workroom, her dogs ran up to us. The perfectly groomed pups had their hair fastened with bows that matched their collars and painted nails.

I was so busy admiring the dogs that I didn't notice the magnificently set worktable. An elaborate flower arrangement surrounded two huge candelabras on a lavender damask tablecloth. A sumptuous spread of food and beverages covered the table: a medley of fresh fruit, a tower of sandwiches, platters of sushi, cheese boards and a selection of fine wines and spirits.

I looked around the room and was surprised to see the so-called pee-pee pads were ten-foot squares of grass sod. Waterford Crystal bowls filled with water sat on crocheted placemats, and pâté-like dog food filled silver platters.

We needed somewhere to sit. I was about to get some wood chairs for us to sit on when two assistants came rushing over, pushing leather rolling chairs and dragging a small table. Crystal and I settled into the seats.

"I'm sorry it took so long for me to get upstairs," said Crystal. "Things got a little out of control outside."

I held my breath, afraid of what she was going to say next.

"I'm usually happy to sign autographs, but I'm trying to keep things low-key during this trip to Chicago. No one knows I'm in town. Except for, apparently, this crazy fan who came running after me this morning."

"How awful," I said, looking down. For the first time, I was glad not to be sharing eye contact with this superstar.

"When Sam tried stopping her, the elderly woman pushed right past him, all three hundred pounds of him. I've got to hand it to her. The woman had moxie."

"I'm sure she meant no harm. But enough about her. What brings you in today?"

An assistant dressed in a studded leather jacket and ripped jeans brought over a steaming cup of tea on a saucer. She blew on the tea and handed it to the chanteuse.

"Thanks, Love," Crystal said, taking the tea from her.

The assistant smiled brightly. She stopped smiling when she looked at me and said, "Feel free to help yourself to something to drink," then walked away without waiting for me to respond. I wondered where Nathaniel was when I needed him to fawn over me? Oh, right. That wasn't part of his job description.

Crystal took a sip of tea. "I heard about your shop from my boyfriend's sister, Piper Livingston. You designed her wedding gown and the entire bridal party's attire."

"Of course. She's an absolute doll. We had such a great time working together. I remember how she would bring her adorable little Yorkie to all of her fittings."

"Sounds like Piper, all right. She raved about you, as well. She was delighted with her entire experience and sends her regards."

I nodded and smiled. "Thank you. Please give her my best."

"She mentioned that you're extremely professional and discreet when it comes to your celebrity clientele. That's what I need. Someone to keep my secret."

"I can assure you that your secret's safe with me."

"I'm getting married."

"Congratulations," I said. "That's fantastic news!"

"After hearing Piper rave about your shop, I couldn't wait to come over and see it for myself."

"I'm so happy you're here."

"Me, too. I figured that no one would ever guess that I would be coming in here to shop."

"Oh, right."

"You see, we haven't told anyone about our engagement. We want to keep things very private."

"Mum's the word." I had stopped myself before I made that stupid zipper-lip motion with my hand.

"That's great because I would like you to make five beautiful dresses for my wedding."

"Really? Five dresses!" I said, taking it all in.

Crystal nodded her head.

I've heard of brides changing into a fun, flirty dress or a sophisticated evening gown sans veil for the reception, but five seemed dramatic. So Crystal! To me, that was even better news than my Vegas show prediction.

"That's a fabulous idea. Let's see?" My brain started doing the math. "You'd probably need to change gowns every half hour. And we could make the dresses progressively sexier. So you could finish off the night wearing an amazing going-away outfit that's…"

"That's not exactly what I was shooting for," Crystal said, interrupting me in mid-sentence. She paused for a moment. "I need five fabulous dresses for my doggies."

It had taken a moment before reality hit. The most influential woman in Vegas just asked me to design dresses for her dogs.

Crystal continued, "I see my dogs as an extension of me. I want them to look chic and fabulous for my wedding. And Piper says that you're just the person to do it."

Well, as the saying goes: every dog has his day. I just wasn't expecting it to be today, at Belle's Bridal. I managed to smile, but inside I didn't know how to feel. Rejected, insulted, inadequate? So, I decided to go with, "I'm flattered."

Crystal paused a moment before saying, "Oh my God, I just realized that you probably thought that I was here to buy my wedding gown."

"Oh no, not at all," I stammered, trying to hide the truth. "It's just most future brides…and, I happen to own a bridal shop…and, um, you said you were getting married…so, I just assumed…"

"Of course you did. I'm terribly sorry; that was very inconsiderate of me. I should have clarified that I already have a wedding gown. I popped into a shop and bought the dress on a whim the day after my fiancé had proposed. If only I'd known about your lovely store earlier, I would have bought my gown here."

"Please, don't give it a second thought. Fortunately, my design talents far exceed designing just wedding gowns. As a matter of fact, it can get monotonous at times. I'd be delighted to design your dogs' dream dresses."

Crystal's expression brightened. I turned to the tail-wagging, yapping group of happy pups and said to myself, *Okay, I can do this. Just pretend you're designing dresses for a group of chatty bridesmaids.*

To tell the truth, this might not be so difficult after all. I patted my knees to call the dogs over. "Hey, puppies," I said excitedly. "Now, who likes tulle?"

I've learned you can't assume anything in life. As much as I would have loved to design Crystal's wedding gown, I really couldn't fault her for buying her gown elsewhere. Perhaps it's kismet that leads the bride into that one bridal shop where the stars align, and her dress miraculously appears before her. It's like finding the right man. When the time's right, you'll know it in your heart that you've found "The Dress."

I reminded myself that I needed to feel grateful for my miniature Maltese clients. After all, my customers came in all shapes, sizes and breeds. I put my pride aside and unleashed my creative subconscious.

That afternoon, I designed five fabulous, frilly dresses the Juliana Belle way. Sparkling, elegant, flowy, and puppy perfect!

CHAPTER 18

My heart skipped a beat when the bearded coachman, wearing a black top hat and suit, shook the reigns. "Giddy up, boy," he said, and then made a clicking sound with his tongue.

The horse responded with a head thrust and a jerking motion, and we were off. The elegant 19th-century chariot painted in Brewster Green and Black, with elaborate gold-plated hardware and a collapsible hood folded up like an accordion, started to pick up speed. My dad brushed away a loose tendril of hair that had fallen across my face. I smiled lovingly at him and took a deep breath of the perfumed spring air. Two bumblebees performed figure eights in the air for us as regal swans floated around a small pond as though it was just an average day.

After the carriage had passed by the rose garden, I ran my fingers over the red velvet tufted seat and listened to the large wheels churning beneath, grinding and crushing the gravel. Slowly, the carriage angled its way down a meandering forest path, and I could see the majestic wrought-iron gates up ahead.

As we rode through the enchanted gardens, I heard the faint sounds of César Franck's "Panis Angelicus" playing in the distance.

My featherweight organza ball gown gently floated up

each time the carriage shifted its weight, revealing the lightest shade of "something blue" tulle peeking out from beneath the skirt.

When we arrived at the wrought iron gates emblazoned with the French Chateau's ornate crest, I turned to Dad and smiled. With his thumb and index finger, he pinched the inner corners of his eyes to keep the tears from falling and forced a smile. I felt grateful having him by my side and thought he looked extra handsome in his shawl-collared tuxedo.

The huge iron gates opened. Slowly, we drove through the stone arch entrance and up the tree-lined driveway leading to the stately manor house. When the carriage came to a halt, Dad clasped my hand between his two large, callused hands and spoke softly, "It's time."

I kept my eyes on Dad.

"Jules, it's time," he repeated. But this time he spoke in a much softer, almost more feminine voice.

"It's time. Come on. Jules! Wake up."

"Dad?" I asked, stretching out my arms on the beige, velvet sofa in my office.

"No, Jules."

I opened my eyes and squinted at the black, spiky hair jutting out at me. "Ahh!" I cried out. A shudder of fear went through my body.

"Take it easy. It's just me—Zoë."

I looked at her in shock and then gave her a funny look. "Wow. I must have dozed off."

"You've got to get up. Your lunch appointment is here." Zoë grabbed my purse and jacket from the chair in my office and handed them to me. "Hurry up and put on your coat. Victoria's waiting in the showroom."

I came rumbling to life. "I can't believe I fell asleep," I said, wiping the drool from the corner of my mouth. I usually didn't fall asleep in the middle of a workday, but I was feeling incredibly tired lately. For the last few weeks,

I've jolted up in bed, my heart racing, unable to catch my breath. Too much on my mind is all I could figure.

I still hadn't put the ring on, and Rocco was getting impatient. I'd been holding on to my secret and hadn't shared Rocco's proposal with a soul.

I didn't want to get my parents involved, so I decided to talk to my most savvy friend, Victoria, whom I greatly respected.

Victoria Wakefield, a former acclaimed English barrister, who became the first African-American woman on the cover of The Guardian for winning a huge child custody settlement, had recently moved to Chicago when her husband's international trading company relocated his London office to local LaSalle Street. Victoria seemed perfectly happy to place her career on hold so she could enjoy raising her three children. In my eyes, she had the perfect marriage and family, and I knew she'd give me sound advice.

Victoria and I sat down for lunch at the restaurant, located adjacent to the world's largest Ralph Lauren Polo Shop on Michigan Avenue—*the* place to see and be seen. We sat at the most coveted table near the fireplace in the front room bar. As I drank my tea, I couldn't help but notice Victoria staring at my shaky hands.

"Jules, darling," she asked curiously. "Are you feeling sick?"

"No," I said, "why do you ask?"

"You seem nervous."

An awkward silence had occurred before I finally said, "I need your advice on something important."

"Of course."

"Rocco asked me to marry him a few weeks back," I blurted before I lost the nerve.

"Congratulations are in order, then."

"Not just yet. I haven't given him an answer yet."

"Oh." She looked up in surprise. "Why not?"

"I need time to think through the pros and cons."

"And you need a month to do that? That must be some specific list."

"It is," I said. "I can't make the same mistake twice. If he loves me, he's just going to have to be patient and wait for the day that I'm one hundred percent ready to put on the ring."

"Is it a nice ring, at least?"

"Yes. It's lovely. Do you want to see it?"

"Of course, I want to see it!"

Slowly, I unzipped the side pocket of my black leather bag and took my time feeling around for the ring in the purse's pocket. I found it mixed in with some loose change; I plucked it out and threw the coins back into my wallet. I handed Victoria the ring.

"For God's sake," she chortled, "it looks minuscule compared to the rock William gave you. I need a jeweler's loupe just to see the diamond." She took out her reading glasses to look closer.

"Victoria, stop being a snob."

She carefully examined the ring and glanced at me in astonishment. "This looks to me like a quarter of a karat."

"So what? I have small hands."

"Oh, wait a minute. That's not a diamond—it's cubic zirconia."

"I, uhh, what?" I asked.

"Darling, if there's one thing I know, it's diamonds." She flicked her fingers in the air. Except for the thumbs, she wore a ring on each finger of both hands. I just stared down at the stone, at a loss for words.

Victoria took another long look at the ring and slammed her hand on the table. "Bloody hell!" To my surprise, she was no longer speaking the Queen's English. "Trust me when I tell you, it's fake!"

"I don't care," I said. "Why does it matter?"

"Because it does. He should've at least manned up and

told you." She handed me back the ring. "Now I'm getting the picture why you don't know if you should marry this man or not. You shouldn't! This guy's a fake, just like the ring."

"You think his intentions aren't genuine?" I asked, surprised.

"Dear Heart, he's not just a fake, he's a fuckwit. You need to tell him to bugger off!"

I couldn't look at her as I slipped the ring back inside my purse pocket.

"This is nuts, Jules. You're not seeing him for the guy he really is. You did the same thing with William. You made a ton of excuses for him and believed his lies. And you're okay with that a second time?" she asked, trying to look me in the eye as I fumbled around in my purse.

"I could care less," I said. "I have bigger things to consider than the diamond."

"I don't mean the diamond—which is a zirconia—I mean the man."

I met her eyes. "All I want is a simple ring, a simple man, and a simple life."

"You deserve better than that."

I bit my lip, trying to stave off another round of tears. But I had to admit; this time they were tears of relief. For years, I've neglected to acknowledge my fear of being disappointed by someone I loved. With Victoria's help, I was beginning to believe that I might be able to overcome this fear.

"Darling, forgive me if I'm harsh. All I'm trying to say is that you can't lower the bar anymore when it's already lying on the ground."

Little did Victoria know, but I felt I'd already buried the bar *below* ground level. To save face, I said, "William wants to share custody of Jack, and he's taking me to court."

"You're kidding me?" Victoria said, stunned.

"I wish I were, but I'm not. The worst part is that he's

dragging his heels. I've lost track of how many times William's attorney has asked the judge for an extension. If William can't make it to his own court hearing, how will he ever take care of Jack?"

"Obviously, he'll do a lousy job."

"Exactly. And I don't want to put Jack through that. I have a better chance of fighting him as a married woman than a single working mom."

"Oh, come on, Jules. That's a bunch of malarkey, and you know it."

"It's not. I also want Jack to have a family. Possibly a brother or a sister."

"Fine. Have a family someday, but find the right guy first." She put down her elbow firmly on the table, resting her chin on her fist, and looked deeply into my eyes. "You don't want Jack to have a deceiver for a male role model, again. Do you? A con artist who buys zircons and passes them off as diamonds?"

"Oh, you're being ridiculous now," I said. It was hard to admit I'd screwed up an entire year of my life with a con artist. In my defense, I said, "He runs a fruit market."

"Darling, your ears must be full of bridal tulle because you're not listening to a word I've said." It was clear Victoria was getting frustrated.

"Go on, I'm listening."

"Well, little Miss-Fix-It, you simply cannot rescue every injured bird, runaway cat, and stray asshole. Don't settle for mediocrity because if you think small, your life *will be* small."

I nodded.

"Look, Jules. Divorce happens. Yes, you were a hopeless romantic who didn't see the warning signs in your marriage. That's water under London Bridge. For the time being, you have to figure out why you're afraid to unleash your emotions and allow yourself the chance at happiness. Continue to be that hopeless romantic, just remember to pay close attention to the flashing yellow warning light next time, and you'll be fine."

Victoria left me feeling unsettled. I realized that I'd been seeing that yellow flashing light for some time now. Everything had changed so dramatically since my divorce became final. My days were fast-paced and more hectic than ever. Instead of taking the time to find that perfect combination of a soul mate and best friend, I panicked and settled on the man who gave me free produce.

All girls dream of their perfect wedding, and I was no different. After all, I was immersed in that story every day. I recalled the dream I had about the carriage and top hat before my lunch with Victoria. Even though this would be my second wedding, I still wanted to feel as though there was time for something special to happen in my life. Oh, I didn't really expect to ride off with my Prince Charming into the sunset, but I did want to feel the excitement of true and deep love. I wanted to meet someone who was worth spending the rest of my life with, but I was beginning to doubt that dream would ever come to pass.

"Whew!" I said, looking at my friend. "I guess I missed a gaping pothole."

CHAPTER 19

The morning was already stressful with William coming to visit Jack, but what I had to say to Rocco couldn't wait. I took the day off from work and planned to talk to Rocco while Jack was having lunch with his father. Unfortunately, Jack was still here when the doorbell rang. And, as usual, he got to the door before me. He swung open the door, and his smile quickly faded. "Oh, hi," Jack said unenthusiastically. "I thought you were my dad."

"Nice, Jack, really nice way to greet someone," Rocco said.

"Welcome, Rocco," Jack said sarcastically, moving his little arm in an exaggerated butler-like motion before walking away. We both stood there in silence until Jack had disappeared around the corner.

Rocco shook his head and handed me a box of coconuts.

"Thanks," I said, thinking about how much Jack hated coconuts.

"What was so important that it couldn't wait?" he asked.

"Well, I..."

"You won't believe the kind of day I've been having," Rocco said, interrupting me. "I've been dealing with diseased pears all morning, and I'm totally worn out. I've been yelling at my supplier, and then he's..."

"Rocco."

"...been yelling at the distributer..."

"Rocco."

"And he's telling the guy everything's fine. In the meantime, I'm looking at crates and crates of fucked up pears that look like dried out granny tits."

"Rocco!" I yelled, wondering if he'd ever hear me.

"Sorry Jules, I mean breasts."

"I'm trying to talk to you, and all you care about are your stupid dried out pears."

"Rocco, you can't use potty language in the house," Jack said from the hallway.

"Jack, please go to your room and shut the door," I begged. "We have some grownup business we need to discuss."

"So, is today the day that Jackie Boy finds out that I'm going to be his new daddy?" Rocco said, trying to grab me into an embrace.

"Shh," I pulled away and held my finger up to my lips, shaking my head no.

Rocco held up his hands in front of him.

"Jack, do you hear me?" I called out.

Silence.

I hoped he hadn't heard Rocco's last remark.

"Relax Jules, he's not there. He's probably sewing a quilt in his bedroom." Rocco chuckled at his wit.

"Is that supposed to be funny?" I said.

"Wow, tough crowd. Has everyone around here lost their sense of humor?"

"I'm in no mood to laugh. I just got a call from your friend, Ronnie. How could you not tell us that his "small jewelry store" was a pawn shop?"

"That son-of-a-bitch! He promised he wouldn't call you. Listen, Jules. Don't believe a word he said about selling your grandma's pearls."

"What! You *sold* my grandmother's necklace?"

"Wait. What? That wasn't what Ronny called you about?"

"No. I had trouble understanding anything he was

telling me—things about a fire at your warehouse and your gambling at the racetrack. But he never mentioned anything about Grandma's necklace?"

"No, no, none of that's true. And you know I like to play the ponies."

"Then why don't you answer the question? Did you *sell* my grandmother's pearls?" I enunciated every word.

"Okay, technically speaking, I did."

I gasped in horror.

"It was only meant to be temporary. I knew I'd have the money sooner rather than later."

"Where's the necklace now?"

"Relax, Jules. I have it right here." Rocco took the necklace from his pocket and dangled it in front of my face.

"Stop telling me to relax," I said and grabbed the necklace from him. "I want you to leave right now and take this with you." I handed Rocco the engagement ring.

"I can't believe this is happening. Why are you doing this, Jules?" he asked.

When I just stood there, holding the pearls up as evidence, his face turned so red I thought he was going to explode.

"Oh, then. Fuck you, Jules," he finally said. "I'm sick of you and your indecision and that smart aleck son of yours. And that ring? You can keep it. It's worthless. It's a Smirnovski crystal, or something like that."

"Oooh, you can say anything to me, but leave my son out of it." I picked up a coconut and threw it at him. I started throwing one coconut after the other at Rocco. "And Jack hates coconuts, and I'm not that wild about them," I added with my next throw.

"You're insane," Rocco said, as he tried to dodge the coconut missiles. "Those are Argentinian green coconuts, you heartless wench. The finest coconuts in the world." Rocco began picking up all the coconuts.

I stopped, looking down incredulously at the coconut in my hand. I caught my breath and said, "I'm sorry. I don't know what came over me."

I picked up some of the coconut pieces. Pools of coconut water covered the floor. We put the unbroken coconuts back safely inside the crate, our tempers no longer flaring.

"What does this remind you of?" Rocco asked.

"The kumquats."

"Yeah. That was a good day for me. Too bad that you didn't feel the same way about me as I feel about you."

"I'm sorry, Rocco. I tried to make it work, but we just want different things."

"Speak for yourself, Babe. I saw this going somewhere."

"Again, I'm sorry," I said.

"Yeah. Whatever."

"You're a good guy. But I can't be married to someone that I can't trust."

"So you're calling me I'm a liar. Is that right, Jules?" Rocco was getting angry all over again.

"I guess I am," I finally admitted.

"I'll tell you what, I'm so sick and tired of you acting like you're so much better than me. With your she-she clothing boutique and your fancy weddings. I'm out of here." Rocco stormed out the door.

"Rocco, wait. I don't want you to leave this way. Can't we part as friends?" I asked, holding the door open.

"Are you kidding me? That's all we've been so far— friends," he said and trudged down the hallway. "I was hoping that if we got engaged we could take our relationship to the next level. I guess I was wrong." Rocco continued to rant as he made his way toward the elevator and out of my life. "Why don't you see a movie by yourself? I'm going to the racetrack." He pushed the elevator door button and stepped into the waiting elevator.

"Rocco, please listen…"

I heard the elevator ding and the doors close. I stood with

my forehead resting on the cold metal elevator door for a minute. And that's when it came to me—what great relief it was to have Rocco finally out of my life.

I ran back into the apartment and closed the door behind me, and then to Jack's room to tell him the news that he never had to see Rocco again. But when I opened the door to his room, he wasn't there. I checked under the bed, and then I ran around the entire apartment. No Jack. William could show up any minute, and Jack was missing.

The doorbell rang.

Oh my god, if that was William, he could sue me for sole custody—and win!

Instead, I found Jack standing at the door, holding hands with a stranger.

I grabbed Jack and started crying. "Are you okay? You had me so worried."

"I'm sorry, Mommy. I heard you talking to Rocco. Please don't marry Rocco."

"Mommy's not marrying anyone." I remembered the stranger and looked up to thank him. But then Jack started screaming.

"He *is* coming back!" Jack said. "He left all his coconuts on the counter. He's coming back; I know it…"

"No, honey, he's never coming back." I held Jack and calmed him down, assuring him we were a team. Just me and Jack. He finally stopped sniffling.

"Mommy, this is my new friend, Leo. He's got a cat and a fish tank."

"Hi, I'm Leo Hughes," said the tall, nice-looking man.

"Juliana Belle. Nice to meet you," I said.

"I'm your new neighbor from across the hall. I just had the pleasure of meeting your son on the rooftop of the building. We had a nice conversation sitting on the bench talking about geckos, cats, and you. You've got a great kid there."

I nodded and returned his smile. "Thank you."

"Mommy, can Leo have dinner with us tonight?"

"I'm sure Mr. Hughes is very busy moving in," I said to Jack.

"Please, Mommy. Leo can tell you all about how he makes these huge arms for robots and has them do all these cool tricks."

Leo laughed. "I'm afraid they're not the kind of robots that Jack's probably thinking about. I'm a robotics technician and develop computer programs that control the robots and direct them to perform tasks."

"Sounds fascinating. I'd love to hear more about your work, Mr. Hughes. Would you care to join us for dinner?" I asked. "Jack has a date with his father for lunch, but we're here all evening. We're just having pizza, so I totally understand if…"

"Please, it's Leo," he said. "And actually, my kitchen's a disaster. I would love to join you for dinner."

"Yes!" Jack cheered and gave Leo a big high-five.

Then my phone rang.

"Oh, excuse me, I need to take this. Jack, why don't you show Mr. Hughes your room?" I grabbed the phone. "Hello? William? Where are you? Jack's been waiting." I didn't mention to William that he seemed to have forgotten all about his lunch date.

"I won't be coming, Julianna. I'm sorry," William told me. "Apparently I've just failed at marriage number two, and I won't be moving to Chicago and asking for joint custody, after all."

I didn't know what to say.

After a brief silence, William continued, talking about being a bad father to Jack, how I was a wonderful mother, and so on. The conversation dragged on in that vein for a while, William doing a pretty believable *mea culpa*. And at last I got an apology out of him for also being a lousy husband. I took it all in but wasn't particularly upset. I was so over him.

But Jack? I hoped my little guy wouldn't take it too hard that his father was once again walking away from him.

I hung up and sat quietly by the phone for a while. I could hear Jack chattering away, with the occasional "Really?" or "How about that!" coming from Leo.

I got up and walked down the hallway to Jack's room. He and Leo were playing the game of Life. I stood by the door and listened.

Our new neighbor looked perfectly content propped up against an enormous stuffed lion across from Jack, who was lying on the floor on his stomach, his legs happily kicking in the air.

I finally took a moment to regard Jack's friend. Leo was ruggedly handsome, with short black hair, and an angular bone structure. I'd guess he was in his early to mid-forties. He scratched at the dark stubble on his jaw, while apparently deliberating his next move.

"My daughters constantly fight over who will be the blue car," he said, laughing and shaking his head. "The eight-year-old always ends up with the car, and the ten-year-old insists she was pretending to want the blue car only for the purpose of tricking her sister out of the yellow one," he explained with a twinkle in his eyes. "So, what do they do next?"

Jack shook his head.

"Simple, they start fighting over the yellow car." Leo made a funny face that made Jack laugh.

I kept watching our new neighbor, and I guessed there was nothing simple about him. I'd finally come to realize that I no longer wanted a simple life, either. I wanted a life that mattered. One with all the ups and downs of being together with someone worth spending my life with every day. For now, that was Jack, but I could still dream.

CHAPTER 20

"Happy Anniversary!" Leo said as he stood in the doorway of my bedroom holding a tray and smiling.

"Oh my gosh. What time is it?" I asked, stretching out in bed.

"Eight o'clock."

I sprang up and looked at the alarm clock. "Why didn't my alarm clock go off at six like it always does?"

"Because I turned it off," Leo said.

I heard giggling in the background.

"We didn't want you getting up before the food arrived." Leo walked into the room followed by Jack, and his petite daughters, Ivy and Sadie. The kids were marching in a straight line behind him, each holding a single yellow rose.

Leo placed the tray on my lap and tucked a napkin into my pajama top.

"We've been cooking all morning in our apartment," announced Sadie. Sadie was Jack's age, same curly blonde hair and blue eyes and just a bundle of energy.

"I decorated the cookies," Ivy interjected shyly, pointing to the stack of heart-shaped sugar cookies neatly arranged on a plate. Ivy was two years older than Sadie, with thick, chestnut hair similar to a horse's mane, and hazel eyes as big as saucers. She was the quieter more methodical sister, but she became quite animated and chatty at times, like when she played with dolls. She also loved everything girly. Since Jack was losing interest in visiting the shop and would rather spend time with Leo, I enjoyed bringing Ivy to the store with me on Saturdays, where she spent the entire day designing sparkly outfits for her dolls and playing dress up.

"Jack, I can't believe it's been three months since you've invited Leo over for dinner."

"You're welcome," Jack said, coming closer and giving me my morning hug, still holding on to the rose.

"Is that for me?" I asked.

Each child slipped one rose into the small glass vase of the tray.

"The kids were up early this morning picking roses from the rooftop garden for you," Leo said.

"Thank you so much." I smiled at each one of them. "Now come over here all of you and give me a hug."

The kids jumped into bed with me, almost knocking over the tray. Thankfully, they decided to go with paper plates. While I chowed down on the peanut butter and jelly sandwich filled with crushed potato chips that Jack made for me, the kids engaged in a pillow fight. As I crunched away, I looked into Leo's gorgeous eyes and wondered if I was still asleep and dreaming. I got a quick wake-up call when I took a neck roll to the side of my head, and realized this was no dream. Leo and I had been dating now for three blissful months.

"Okay, everyone let's clean up the mess and let Juliana get ready for work. She has a big day ahead of her.

Leo wasn't kidding. Today was going to be my biggest wedding adventure, yet!

The noise coming from the propeller of the single-engine Cessna plane made it impossible to hear anything the pilot was saying to Billy, the barrel-chested, bearded co-pilot. I wished I could read lips because nothing about their expressions made me feel at ease, especially their body size. Combined, they must have weighed a total of 500 pounds. Could this plane carry the weight of these two huge, muscular men plus passengers?

I looked around the tiny, four-seater plane and ran my fingers across the name "Mile High" stitched on the back of the gray leather seat in front of me. I've never been to Longmont, Colorado, and wondered what could be so special about this town that my client, Jessica Blossom, picked it for her wedding destination. A quick glance out the window, and I had my answer—its proximity to the Rocky Mountain National Park. Being an avid outdoorswoman, this was Jessica's number one destination to visit on her ultimate adventure bucket list. And her fiancé, Brett Bunion, was about to make that wish come true.

I leaned forward and tapped Brett's shoulder for the third time in two minutes, interrupting the conversation he was having with his bride-to-be. He stopped talking to Jessica and turned around to face me. "What's up, Juliana Belle? Not feelin' well?" he said, his brown eyes staring a hole in my head.

I ignored his snide remark and yelled, "How long has the pilot been flying this kind of aircraft?"

He plugged his ear with his index finger and wiggled it around. "I have no idea," he replied, looking annoyed as he turned his attention back towards Jessica.

"There's nothing to worry about, ma'am," yelled Billy, who was listening in on our conversation. "Hound Dog's a former Air Force pilot. When Special Forces need a ride, they call the Houndster." He nodded approvingly at his boss. "After he retired, he opened The Mile High Sky Diving Center and hires retired military skydivers, like me, as tandem instructors." Billy smiled and added, his Southern drawl oozing, "So no need to be shakin' in your shoes, Lil' Lady. Everything's gonna be just fine."

Ever since we'd left the Longmont Aviation Airport, my left leg was trembling. You'd think *I* was the one jumping out of the airplane. The truth was, I wasn't crazy about small aircrafts, especially ones that didn't have a tray table (or bathroom!). I dug my nails deeper into the gray leather seat, trying to stop myself from shaking.

"Billy's right," the pilot added, speaking into his mike. "There's nothing to worry about." He poked Billy with his elbow as he asked me, "By the way? Did you design both of your outfits?"

"Yes, I did."

"I'm impressed. Those are some nice fancy pants you've got on there. Right, Billy?"

Billy nodded in agreement.

The cabin temperature was uncomfortably warm. I fumbled with the plastic eyeball air vent above my seat and aimed the blowing air on my forehead. It was warm and stale. "Billy, do you think you could please ask Captain Hound Dog to open a window?"

Billy just shook his head and laughed. "Sorry, Fancy-Pants, no can do."

Not only was I having a stressful flight, but I was none too pleased about wearing a navy gabardine tailored pantsuit with white tennis shoes (though spray-painting the soles Christian-Louboutin red helped somewhat) to a wedding, per Jessica's request. I guess it could've been worse. I could've been wearing an Evel Knievel jumpsuit like the one I'd designed for Jessica.

I gave up on the air vent and focused my attention on my glowing bride. Jessica looked amazing in the skintight white satin spandex jumper covered with thousands of Swarovski crystals. Her bright red locks looked like flames escaping from the matching crystal-covered helmet. I was glad I went with the extra packet of crystals; it truly made all the difference. In the end, you always have to stick to your glue guns.

My temperamental seamstress, Natasha, wanted to ring my neck every time I came into the workroom and asked her to glue on more crystals. She said I was slowly trying to kill her with the toxic glue fumes. That was a nice thought, but she was my most talented worker, and I couldn't afford to kill her off, just yet.

"Hey, Jess?" said Brett. "Are you going to do a bat hang from the edge of the wing today?"

"What's a bat hang?" I asked nervously.

"It's when a skydiver hangs upside down from the leading edge of a wing," Jessica explained.

"Sounds frightening!" I shivered at the thought.

"Oh, it's not that bad," Brett said, smirking. I wasn't sure what Jessica saw in this guy, but fortunately, that problem wasn't part of my job description.

"Maybe not for you, Mr. Hotshot," Jessica said, laughing. "It's still way too advanced of a move for me."

"Come on. You can do it, Jess," Brett prodded her on.

"Are you kidding me? I've done only a handful of solo jumps. I prefer a quick hop & pop."

"Yeah, baby!" said Brett. "And that's why it's called the Mile-High Sky Diving Club."

Jessica giggled. "Jules, don't listen to him. A hop & pop is a jump made from a lower altitude." Jessica gave Brett a playful shove.

I didn't have time to react to Brett's attempt at a crude joke because the plane went into a sudden drop in altitude, and I immediately tightened my seatbelt. I stopped listening to their conversation and began counting the minutes until these two lovebirds took their leap of faith together into matrimony, and the pilot would make a safe landing. Then, I could get out off of this godforsaken plane and join the happy windblown couple on the drop zone for the ceremony.

In the meantime, I tried to breathe deeply, but that just filled me with more of the hot air blowing from the vent. I tried to calm down by telling myself, "Whatever you do, don't look down." Of course, I looked and caught another glimpse of the Rocky Mountain range.

"Hey everyone. This is your Captain Hound Dog speaking—Woof, Woof!" he announced in a deep, husky voice. "It's a beeeauuutiful day in Longmont, Colorado. The temperature's a comfortable 71° Fahrenheit. If you look over to your left-hand side, you can see the spectacular Rocky Mountains. In about fifteen more minutes, we'll be approaching the 10,000-foot mark over Long Peak. So, it's time for everyone to get on their parachutes."

I watched Billy help Jessica and Brett with their equipment.

"Are you partnering with Billy?" I asked Jessica.

"Aww, these lovebirds don't need me. They're skydiving together," Billy said before Jessica could answer me. "I'm pairing up with you, Fancy-Pants. Here you go," and with a quick flick of his finger, he unlatched my seatbelt and handed me a helmet and a pair of goggles.

"Very funny," I said.

"It's no joke, Little Lady."

My eyes darted to Jessica and then to Brett.

"Surprise Jules," Jessica said nervously, raising up her hands.

I was too stunned to speak.

"Okay, now, no time to waste. Let's get on your equipment. I've got our parachute all ready."

"That's enough," I said. "I don't know where you're hiding the candid camera, but the joke's over."

"This is no joke, Jules," said Brett.

My heart was racing, and I felt a sudden urge to go to the bathroom. That's right, no bathrooms. Note to self: I'm only flying commercial from now on.

Jessica chimed in. "I knew if I had asked you to go skydiving with us for our wedding, you wouldn't have agreed to be my maid-of-honor," Jessica shouted over the noise of the engine and my pounding heart. "And I need you here with me, Jules. I miss Sammy Jo terribly."

"I know, Jessica. And after the pilot lands this plane, with me safely inside it, I promise I'll be by your side for the entire ceremony."

"Jules, it's Long Peak mountain. Think about it. It's a peak. There's no place for the pilot to land," Brett said.

"OK, I get that," I said. Brett was really beginning to annoy me now. "But…this isn't happening."

"Hey, back off, Brett," Billy barked. "You said she would totally go along with the surprise. You call this a surprise? Well, I call it a goddamn trick."

"I swear, that was never our intention," Jessica said as she began to cry.

"Hey, what's going on back there?" shouted Hound Dog. "We're minutes away from the jump site."

I listened intently, trying to hear the conversation going on between Billy and the pilot.

"Everything's fine, Boss. Just need another minute," yelled Billy, wiping the sweat from his brow. "The bridesmaid didn't know that she would be diving today."

"Dammit, Billy. Why wasn't I informed? I can fucking lose my license, and we can both be out of a job," the pilot said. "I take that back, one of us will positively be out of a job by the time I land this plane, and it ain't me."

"But Captain, I had no idea!" Billy raised his arm in frustration. When Jessica and Brett booked the wedding package, they asked if I would be willing to help surprise the bridesmaid. They promised me that she would be a great sport."

Great, now they think I'm a fancy-pants-wearing poor sport!

"Please, tell me that she signed a permission form and received the briefing." Hound Dog sounded concerned.

"Well, not exactly. When I chose her to be my volunteer during the lesson, she had no idea that I was secretly instructing her on the procedures. Brilliant, right?"

"You're quite the genius," the captain said. "But was she paying attention during the other parts?"

Billy nodded. "Pretty much. I only noticed her texting for the last part of the briefing section."

"First of all, I'm not the bridesmaid; I'm the maid-of-honor. Second of all, my son Jack needed help with his math homework," my voice was rising and speeding up with each word as if I'd taken a deep breath from a helium-filled balloon. "And third of all, I found it rather odd that you would need a volunteer to show these guys how to use the equipment properly, considering they are seasoned skydivers, but what do I know? I'm only the bridesmaid. I mean, maid-of-honor!"

"Ma'am, don't get me wrong, I appreciate the fact that you want your son to get good grades in school, but the free fall is a pretty important part of the lesson, wouldn't you say, Billy?"

"But, I followed all of the guidelines and took her through the entire briefing session like all of our other students."

"Are you out of your fucking mind?" Hound Dog yelled.

I continued listening to their arguing and felt duped. Finally, Hound Dog asked the important question, "Yeah, and what about the signature form?"

"I have it right here," Billy said, pulling a sheet of paper from the inside of his jacket pocket. He handed me the permission sheet of paper and a pen. "You can use my back to sign it." He turned around and spread his enormous back muscles like a roll-top desk opening up.

"I'm not signing that!" I said, pushing Billy away.

"That's it. I'm turning this plane around!" said Hound Dog.

"No!" cried Jessica. "Brett, you have to do something."

"Please, Jules," Brett begged. "I know that I can act like a jerk at times, and I'm sorry for that. But this means the world to Jessica. If you can't do it for her, then do it for her sister."

I wasn't sure what Sammy Jo had to do with me jumping out of a plane, but I appreciated Brett's apology.

Jessica grabbed my hand. "Honest, Jules. I know that I'm asking for a lot, but in my mind I saw this whole scenario playing out."

"It's okay, Jessica. I believe you," I said, giving her a hug.

"I'm so unhappy with this situation," the pilot said, not sounding as chipper as the Houndster had a few minutes ago. "Juliana, we're almost to our destination. You don't need to do this. You can ride back with me and wait for everyone at the manifest."

"Otherwise, you have to put this on right now," Billy added, holding up the harness. "Like I said, don't worry, we're going in tandem."

I looked at Billy, then at the harness.

"Oh, that's what you meant by 'tandem,'" I whimpered. I beseechingly turned toward Jessica, hoping reason would prevail, but all I saw was her sad, puppy-dog eyes. She looked so worried and disappointed.

As a bridal dress designer, I often formed close relationships with my customers. Many brides have even asked me to be in their wedding party, and I'll admit I was flattered by their offers. But I made it a rule to decline because otherwise I'd be in a wedding practically every weekend of my life. Jessica was the exception.

When she came into Belle's Bridal a few months ago to purchase her wedding outfit, she told me that she and her fiancé loved to skydive. They thought it would be great fun to dive to the wedding spot. Jessica's sister, also an avid skydiver, was her maid-of-honor. Tragedy struck a few weeks before the wedding when her sister died in a car accident. Jessica was devastated and didn't think she could go through with the wedding.

I gave Jessica a lot of moral support during her bridal jumpsuit fittings, and when she asked me if I would be her maid-of-honor, I agreed. But she never mentioned anything about me skydiving alongside her, holding her bouquet.

Billy offered some soothing instructions (though, believe me, they weren't helping). Then he began hurriedly strapping me into our parachute and slipping on a helmet.

"Get this off of me!" I said, whipping off the helmet. "There's no way I'm jumping. I want off this plane. Right now!"

"That's the plan," he said, patting me gently on the back once he'd successfully strapped on the helmet again. "Looks good. You look like a pro."

I gave him a wan smile.

"All joking aside, I admire your courage for even considering jumping out of a plane. That's pretty fucking cool."

Funny, how a little flattery can make all the difference. I took a deep breath and said, "Okay, let's do this."

"What about a release form? She can't jump without a release form," the pilot yelled.

"Please, Jules! Just sign the form," Jessica begged.

Billy quickly turned his back to me again. I scribbled my name on the paper and handed it to Billy.

"YES!" cried Jessica.

I felt dizzy with so much adrenaline racing through my body, and somewhat excited. I could do this, dammit! How bad could it be?

Billy opened the hatch. My knees buckled. Then I thought of Leo, and my heart sank all the way down to my feet. Leo had already lost his wife to a freak skiing accident; he would be so upset if he knew that I was about to jump out of an airplane.

Why hadn't I told Leo that I loved him last night after he told me that he was in love with me. Even though I fell in love with Leo from the moment our eyes met months ago, I still didn't have the nerve to share my feelings with him. Now I was afraid that I might never get the chance to do so.

I desperately needed to call Leo before I jumped to tell him that I loved him with all my heart.

I started reaching for my cell phone to call Leo when Billy grabbed my hand and said, "There's no time for that. You can make all the phone calls you want once your feet are touching land." Billy continued buckling my harness, as I continued to unbuckle it.

I looked out the window. "No, I'm sorry. I've changed my mind. I just can't do this," I said, my voice quaking.

He pulled out a small silver flask from his back pocket and handed it to me. "Have a sip," he said. "It will help calm your nerves. Come on, it's getting late, and I promise you, I'll take care of you all the way down."

My hands shook as I unscrewed the cap and took a large swig of whiskey. I started coughing as Billy picked me up like a rag doll and pushed me towards the large exit hatch.

Jessica and Brett gave each other one final kiss in the open doorway of the plane. With big smiles on their faces, they jumped out of the plane in tandem, free-falling to the ground below.

I watched as the sunlight reflected off of Jessica's jumpsuit like a match had lit her on fire. I had to squint from the brightness of the reflection. My throat was still burning from the whiskey, and I could feel the tears welling in my eyes.

Billy shuffled me towards the opening of the hatch and yelled out some instructions that I could not comprehend. Since I gave up drinking after my moonshine debacle, my head began spinning from the alcohol. As I stood by the open door, I used my fingers as a comb to brush the strands of blonde hair out of my eyes. Of all the days to wear my hair blown out. Why hadn't I pulled it back into my usual wrapped ponytail? I brushed away a few more strands, leaned into Billy like he was a La-Z-Boy recliner, and shut my eyes tight. It was time.

The next thing I knew, I was gliding through the air with

an enormous Mutant Ninja Turtle strapped to me like a backpack. I held on tight to the fresh flower bouquet pressed against my chest as it blew to bits on our descent—like a flower girl strewing rose petals. Better the bouquet than me.

I was always known to go the distance for my brides, but this was ridiculous, even by my standards. My face flattened out like a pancake from the tremendous amount of force, and the air pressure felt like my nose was going to break off. I couldn't describe the sensation, but it was a combination of nausea and utter and complete freedom.

Eventually, though, the fall began to feel meditative. This out-of-body experience inspired me to write a poem mid-dive.

> *Swirls of cotton-candy clouds bewitching me to*
> *pluck their fluffy spun sugar, daring me to eat it.*

I stopped there because I couldn't come up with a word that rhymed with "eat it." Besides, who would ever read it? Oh, wait. That rhymes perfectly! After twenty more seconds of pontification, I decided to layoff the whiskey-inspired poetry at 10,000 feet and focuses on the moment.

The beauty of the mountains below drew me toward them (not to mention the role gravity was playing!). Snow-capped mountains cradled the deep, dark green of untouched valleys, lakes, and natural forests. I was beginning to become one with the Universe.

Then I threw up all over myself. Thanks to gravity and blowback, Billy got a dosing too.

Today was not at all how I had envisioned my life as a bridal dress designer.

We landed remarkably smoothly, and I didn't get crushed by behemoth Billy. In fact, he was as agile as a ball-room dancer, dancing us to an upright position across the plateau. Once he unhitched our harness, and I took a few deep breaths, I realized that I was safe. Finally. And that I was standing in one of the most serene places I had ever seen. Simply breathtaking.

Once we slipped off our gear, we walked over to the drop zone specially selected for the ceremony. Exquisite natural rock formations and lush greenery surrounded the area. I looked around.

"What're you looking for, Fancy-Pants?" Billy asked, wiping some remaining vomit of my cheek.

"The minister."

"Well, you're looking at him."

I began laughing, uncontrollably.

"Hey, what's so funny?" he asked me.

"So, you're an officer *and* a gentleman?"

"I do okay with all that lovey-dovey crap on occasion."

"Of course. My bad. I should have never doubted you, Billy."

"It's okay, Jules," said Jessica. "We're doing the legal ceremony at city hall tomorrow morning."

"Well then, by all means Billy, please proceed."

As Jessica and Brett looked deeply into one another's eyes and read their heartwarming wedding vows, I looked around and could only think about one thing. Marrying Leo. The thought of finding my prince charming made me feel giddy like a little schoolgirl.

I never told my bridal bestie, Scarlet, that I, too, had envisioned my dream wedding dress from an early age. The dress belonged to the golden-hued, fairy-dusted ballerina bride. As luck would have it, I had captured the image on the last page of my old design journal.

I envisioned the same shimmering cream organza and floral embroidered organza overlay for my ball gown. The skirt would have so many layers of crinoline that it could practicality stand up on its own. And the hand-beaded, iridescent sequins and pearls on the sweetheart bodice would follow an intricate Parisian all-over flower pattern with just the right amount of beading.

I wasn't paying the slightest bit of attention to the ceremony. Instead, my mind jumped to bridesmaids' dress styles, when Billy asked, "Jessica, are you ready for your sister's send off?"

I watched curiously as Jessica pulled out a small black plastic bag with a pink ribbon attached at the top. She and Brett walked hand-in-hand over to a tranquil spot by the small lake. Brett held the bag while Jessica untied the bow. He placed his arm around Jessica's waist as she slowly turned the bag over, releasing the ashes and allowing the wind to carry Sammy Jo's remains across the water as birds flew escort overhead. I would have jumped out of a plane ten more times just to share in this beautiful moment again. Between experiencing the love of a new wife and sister, and taking my leap of faith (something I would have never done a year ago), I would remember this day for the rest of my life.

Moments later, I felt a powerful gush of wind and heard the chopper overhead. I looked up and saw the rescue basket clipped to a long cable attached to a winch on the helicopter and wondered if, instead, I could learn how to live in the wilderness.

I'll skip the details of the helicopter hoist operation. Just reverse the skydiving fall, but make it more nerve-wracking because we were going up to a tiny, hovering aircraft, not down to terra firma. But I made it, with some kind soul grabbing me out of the basket and safely lifting me into my seat. All the way back to the airport, my heart continued to pound like a jackhammer on Michigan Avenue, which is where I wish I were instead of on my first—and last— extreme wedding adventure.

When I was walking across the tarmac, leaving behind this whole misadventure, Captain Hound Dog headed over to join me and extended his hand. My entire hand and wrist disappeared in his grasp.

"Nicely done, Fancy-Pants," he said, giving me a paralyzing handshake.

I was barely able to eke out the words, "Thank you."

"Hey, before you go, can you write down the name of your shop? I'd like to refer all my future brides so you can make them custom jumpsuits for their big newly-wed jump."

Since designing bridal onesies wasn't my thing, I was about to give him the name of my biggest competitor and see if Lulu's Couture would go the extra 10,000 miles for their brides like I had today.

Then I decided, what's an extra jumpsuit here and there, as long as these thrill-seeking brides were fine leaving me safely back at Belle's Bridal? Because, even after all that happened today, I was still willing to jump through hoops for my brides; I just wasn't willing to jump through an airplane hatch door.

As I headed toward the exit, I heard Captain Hound Dog shout after me, "I'll admit, I had you pegged all wrong. You're not so fancy after all. You've got guts. From now on, your new nickname is Cargo-Pants."

At the exit of the Longmont Aviation Airport, Leo was standing outside a black Jeep Wrangler while the three kids were watching a movie in the back seat of the car.

I ran over to Leo and took him in my arms. I didn't know I was capable of smiling so wide. And the smile he returned was just as genuine.

I couldn't stop staring in his eyes. He was the most caring, kindhearted, honorable man I'd ever met. I didn't care about my pink velour track suit anymore because Leo's warm heart was all that I needed.

"I love you, Leo."

"I love you, Jules."

It felt so good to finally say the heavenly words out loud. I only wished that I had yelled them from the top of Long Peak Mountain when I had the chance. No matter, at this very second, I was on cloud nine and was not planning on getting off anytime soon.

ACKNOWLEGMENTS

A s a successful fashion designer who grew up working at Mira Couture, named after my stylish mother, I have had countless memorable experiences working in the fashion industry. My intention in writing this book was to celebrate my family's incredible 45 years in the custom clothing business. Over the years, we've been delighted to work with celebrities such as Cindy Crawford, Vanna White, Renée Fleming, Mrs. Wayne Newton, Yolanda ("Lonnie") Ali, wife of Muhammad AlI, and our rare male client, basketball legend, Michael Jordan and his former wife, Juanita Jordan. Chicago being a political kind of town, we've created dresses and fashions for a whole host of local and national figures and their families, such as South Carolina Governor Nikki Haley; Senior Advisor to the President, Valerie Jarrett; Nora Conroy, daughter of former Mayor Richard M. Daley; and public affairs specialist, Jayne Thompson, wife of former Illinois Governor James R. Thompson. Other important clients include Illinois Supreme Court Justice Anne Burke and wife of Alderman Edward Burke; Susan Buffett, the late wife of investor Warren Buffett; Inese Driehaus, wife of philanthropist Richard Driehaus; Sun-Times columnist Sherren Leigh, founder of TCW Magazine; and Sun-Times columnist, Michael Sneed, among others.

For every celebrity who came into the shop, we've been

blessed to work with thousands of extraordinary women: mothers, businesspeople, doctors, teachers, artists, and writers who coursed through the store on a daily basis. Though fictional, Brides Unveiled was inspired by my unforgettable time designing apparel for these fashionable women. After the flourishing business sold in 2014 to the remarkably talented designer, Julie Mersine, I wanted my time at Mira Couture to be remembered as more than just a store full of magical bridal gowns and feather-light tulle veils. It was where little girls' dreams came true, including my own. It was where I grew up and where I raised my son. This wonderland was my home; the seamstresses were my family. Thank you to all who have touched my life in countless ways. I am indebted to the fantastic staff at Mira Couture, the wonderful clients, and most of all, my amazing family. I offer the greatest thanks to my loving husband, Lou for having infinite patience and supporting me throughout the process. My heartfelt thanks go out to our children and my parents, Bogdan and Mira Horoszowski, for being my daily source of inspiration. I'm incredibly grateful to Meg Murphy in helping me through the earlier draft of the book, and the thoughtful Lynda McDaniel, for her guidance and wisdom. I'm truly appreciative to Brittiany Koren whose knowledge and insight was invaluable in publishing the novel. Many thanks to Eddie Vincent for the lovely cover design, and the team at Written Dreams, including Devin McGuire, Patti Fiala, and Denise Kirchmayer. I also want to thank Amy Allen at CS Brides Chicago and Chris Schmidt at The InterContinental Magnificent Mile, who partnered with me for the spectacular book launch. I am particularly thankful to Gretchen Bonaduce, Stacy Jo Haney, and Trisha McDonnell, three fabulous women who started out as clients and whom, today, I feel honored to call my dearest friends. One of the many joys of being a mother is giving my son, Alec a better understanding of the world we live in while encouraging him to live life with love, grace, and gratitude. Meanwhile, I owe an endless amount of gratitude to Alec for encouraging me to write my story and for setting my dream in motion.

ABOUT THE AUTHOR

Yvette Klobuchar has designed beautiful custom clothing for nationally recognized political figures, professional sports icons, Fortune 100 CEO's, and hard-working moms. Her designs have been featured in *Harper's Bazar, In Style, Town and Country, Chicago Magazine,* and *Modern Luxury.* Yvette has appeared on Oprah, The Learning Channel, FOX, ABC, NBC, and WGN. She worked as a fashion model for fifteen years and held the title of The International Queen of Poland 1991 and Mrs. Illinois America 2001. A graduate of Lake Forest College, she splits her time between living in North Barrington and Chicago with her husband and son. She also has two grown stepdaughters. ***Brides Unveiled*** is her debut novel. Visit her website at www.yvetteklobuchar. com.

CPSIA information can be obtained
at www.ICGtesting.com
Printed in the USA
LVOW01*0514251115
463885LV00002B/2/P